IMAGO

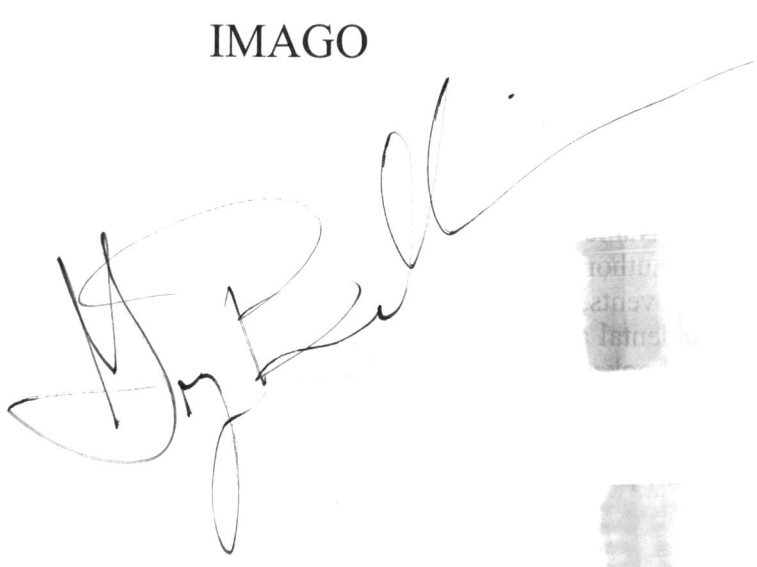

Greg Belliveau

Credits
Cover Design: David Sladek
Editor: Sherry Derr-Wille

What they are saying about *IMAGO*

IMAGO is Cormac McCarthy meets C.S. Lewis in this search for human identity in a dystopian world. Belliveau's masterful prose blurs the edges between genre and literature while taking the reader on patrol through a landscape of rubble and despair. —*Derek Wade, author Murder in Marin County*

Greg Belliveau's story puts him in the company of China Miéville, or the Kazuo Ishiguro of *The Unconsoled,* of films such as *The Matrix* and *Dark City.* Beyond that, there are tantalizing echoes everywhere of *The Divine Comedy.* Readers, hang on tight, Greg Belliveau will take you on one hell of a wild ride. —David Long, author of *The Falling Boy* and *The Inhabited World*

"*IMAGO,* by Gregory Belliveau, is a wild, futuristic ride where Christopher Dante must assess friend or foe, life or death and fight or flight at every exciting twist and turn. The joy of Belliveau's writing is that he creates highly complicated and mystical worlds and populates them with strong, relatable characters. You will rejoice in their triumphs and cry in their defeats. "IMAGO" is a multi-layered, gripping adventure that will entertain and challenge your sense of what is real and what is imagination." —Ty DeMartino *Playwright/Screenwriter*

"[A] surreal and propulsive ride." —Jason Allen, author of *The East End*

"Belliveau drops the protagonist, Christopher Dante, and the reader into a world where being watched and monitored is not only the status quo, but it's also an accepted part of life. When Dante shares a vision with his uncle, his life is uprooted and sent spiraling out of control. Belliveau's prose is as fast paced as the action itself, and you can't help but get sucked into Dante's world."
—Kase Johnstun, Author of *Beyond the Grip of Craniosynostosis* (2015 Gold Quill Winner, League of Utah Writers) and Host of the *LITerally* Podcast.

Dedication

To Patricia, Kaitlin, and Meghan

Part One

Christopher

Chapter One

I see the room and hear the voice. It is the same every time. The room is white, white cushioned chaise lounge before wall-to-wall glass, and behind the glass...a deep blue horizon-less expanse of water. The voice booms out. The voice? Well, I wake to the voice, like an alarm, and it too is the same, same words in the same order, *Sing to me, oh muse.* The image of the white room, the white chaise lounge and the deep blue water behind the wall-to-wall glass...vanishes. It's a code, this voice, a complex equation, something other than words but words all the same. I have stopped trying to make sense of this, stopped trying to be surprised or afraid or panicked or even intellectually inquisitive.

Every day I can remember, since the first time I ever woke up, Pow! The vision of the white room and the blue water followed by the voice, it's once again morning. I am once again shoved back into *the world of men, time and things.* That's not original. It's a phrase I discovered sprayed across a crumbling brick wall in the middle of Cogstin.

I was pulling copper in the evening with my uncle Hal, working as a scrapper, ripping out pipes and tearing up old wooden planks in the abandoned parts of the city when I stumbled on it. It was multi-colored and beautiful. At the end of the last letter of the last word like a wondrous punctuation mark: a butterfly. The image triggered something deep, but of course that feeling was soon Reduced Down, that sense of astonishment, of wonder, was disassembled, deconstructed into its component parts: physical, molecular, binary levels, distilled into meaninglessness 1-0-1-0-1-1-0, etc...a habit formed, molded from an early age, like breathing or walking. I can still see the symbol of the butterfly, the magenta outlined wings. I say nothing to Hal, just open the imaginary chest of things I don't understand and place it inside.

I work for my uncle Hal, my legal custodian, at times my shadow, keeping watch, keeping me under control, a barrier between me and Agent Smiley of the NRM Bureau of Corrections who waits for me to break parole, the wrong place at the wrong time, sitting sober with the drunken Hal and Max or perhaps leaving a piece of metal art carelessly lying about. Agent Smiley is not his real name. I have no idea what that is. His smile is so large, and he's about as creepy as a human can be...so Hal and I make fun of Agent Smiley. Hal says, "Listen, Stretch, you know how it is. They're look'n for a reason is all. Bloom where you're planted. What choice do you have? Show me a man's choices, and I'll show you a man's future." Hal's an alcoholic with a good heart. "You're a fine scrapper, boy. Embrace your life, don't run from it."

I have known Hal since I can remember. I actually thought he was my dad at one time, but he explained I was orphaned, abandoned on his door step. The mythology of this event, much like most of Hal's stories have an underpinning of fable, of telling the tale too many times so it becomes something altogether different than probably what actually happened. He's not my father, but the only father I know. Hal is all I have, and he is enough.

I asked him about the voices one time. His large brow crinkled, puffy eyes squinting as if he was trying to see through into my head. He trundled his lips with his sausage-like fingers and said, "What voices?"

I stared up at him, a man mountain, hands on his hips, overall bib pulled taut across his enormous stomach like a canvas tarp pulling back the moon, work gloves dangling from his back pocket, fingers splayed out like a rooster's cockscomb. "Can I have some more eggs?" I said. He seemed relieved with the deflection, still his face soured like when he missed some good copper or being awakened after falling asleep on the job site after an all night bender. He never asked about it again.

My job is temporary, working for Hal at U-Salvage, and that's not just wishful thinking on my part. I know that letter is coming. I know my life will finally begin, time served, literally. The NRM can't keep me under observation forever. It's just how it is. Every male child is monitored until the powers that be verify you are not some sort of miscreant. I've been waiting longer than others.

"Just bad luck," Hal says. "Sometimes the big guy has to show the little guy who is boss."

I grew up with the inspections. I grew up with the salvage yard. This, like Hal, is all I know. "The NRM checks everyone," Hal says. "It's just the way of things. But there will come a time," Hal says and smiles. He pats me on the shoulder. "The letter will come, and when it does... You'll pack your bags and say adios to me, to Max, and to this Universal Salvage Company forever."

He grabs me by both shoulders and puts his nose nearly touching mine. "The past is the past, Stretch. The future means new beginnings. Change is good."

Well, change may be good, but Cogstin will never change, it's beyond changing, more like a ghost city, a dead city, a city of ashes. Yes, I discovered that phrase too, sprayed across a cement archway under an overpass: *City Of Ash, Awake!*

Today and the rest of the foreseeable future is about inventory. Hal is under a lot of pressure to make sure all his ducks are in order, and all his ducks are actually ducks. He and Max have been selling scrap on the side. That has raised some eyebrows somewhere above. Hal is beside me, as we walk around the large metal-sided out-building which holds the dump truck, the backhoe, the metal cutting torches and skid steer, all the tools to scrap in Cogstin. The sun is just coming up over the horizon, a red hue above the walls to the yard. I hear yapping and yelping in the distance.

Hal grumbles, "Time for another hunting trip with Max."

He stops, grabs the straps to his overalls, forearms resting on his enormous gut. He is three hundred pounds of sheer pride, legs apart, a slight smile on his face as he surveys the vast racks of stacked corrugated sheeting, coiled wire, layers of reclaimed bricks, lumber, everything that can be taken, everything pulled and popped and sheered from the abandoned city of Cogstin. I must say the cool breeze, the red hue and the vast expanse of metal walls, does have an effect.

"Inventory, boy. Today is all about inventory. Keep those nosey Neds out of our business. You know the drill."

I nod my head. "What's there is there, and what's not there that should be...is still there."

"Good lad," Hal says and slaps my back. "Max and I will work on the dump truck in a bit." I watch him wobble to the storage building, and understand full well that "work on the dump truck with Max" means drink vodka and talk about old times until both are napping.

I use the lift to move slowly up and down the rows, the hydraulic whine as the metal platform raises high into the air, then slowly down in fits and halts. I count the scraps we have, check the numbers they have, make sure they match, and make a note of what we need to scrap next time in Cogstin. I do this until lunch. After lunch, I do it again. It is monotonous and lacking in any mental acuity whatsoever. I find myself distracted by the red plains beyond the scrap yard walls.

These are the Great Sand Flats that sweep as far as the eye can see. I lift myself just above the wall, stop for a moment to listen for Hal and Max, the radio, all is calm. I turn to view north, the dead city of Cogstin rising up into the hazy cloudy horizon. I turn to the south and rest my arms on the four-by-four beam framing the metal wall. They are red, the flats, red sand blowing and drifting, gathering in great clouds, settling upon everything exposed. Far beyond them are the mineral mines, of which I have only heard about. I think how dry, vapid and lonely is such a place, so similar to the ruined world of Cogstin, and immediately I think of the white room and the white chaise lounge with the great blue water beyond the glass. My head aches and my stomach aches with the resonance, and I feel an inexpressible sadness. My talkie buzzes. It chirps again. It's Hal. "Stop lolly gagging out there, boy. Time for some steaks."

When I make it to the house, Max has already made drinks and Hal is standing over the sizzling meat with a set of tongs.

"So, we even out today, Stretch?"

I take my drink and sit next to Max who has to lift his large nose in the air to sip from the martini glass. He wipes his thin caterpillar mustache in satisfaction. We talk about the inventory. About Max's garage and what cars he is currently working on. We eat and drink and laugh. All the while I see the great sand flats juxtaposed to the white room and the blue water. After dinner, the sun nearly completely down, a cool and comfortable breeze ruffling the large umbrella, Hal leaning back with contentment.

Right then, I suddenly ask, "Have I ever been in a white room with ceiling to wall glass?"

Hal is motionless like he's asleep, but I know he is not. Max chortles, "I don't know, have you?"

"I was just curious," I say.

"Not unless you have one hidden in the salvage yard," says Max.

He toasts the air and laughs. Hal is sitting up now and staring at me like he's going to draw me. "That's an odd question, Stretch."

"It's just, well...have I?"

"Anyone for another one?" Max says and stands up.

Hal blinks several times, like something is in his eyes.

"You want to come with me to make the drinks, Hal?" says Max nudging him.

"No, I'm fine. Go ahead. A round for all of us," but his voice is a whisper, like he's somewhere else.

Max walks into the house. "A white room," Hal says, mumbling. "A white room."

"Have I been there?" I say. I am leaning forward now, intense. "Have you seen it?"

Max comes hurrying over with new glasses filled to spilling. "Sorry for the wait, gents. Here we go."

He looks at me, then Hal. He puts the glasses down and kicks Hal's boot. Hal comes back from where he went, smiles broadly at the liquor and toasts Max and me.

I sit back in my chair frustrated. I watch them laugh and talk about the same things they have laughed and talked about since I can remember. Max brings up the drudgery of inventory. Hal pauses, toasts the air and tells the story of how he and Max switched the rack numbers on the NRM U SALVAGE Director just as he was about to scan the barcodes...and... "You should have seen his face, boy." rumbles Hal, slapping his thigh. I think in my head simultaneously as he says, "Ducks to Dimes, did we get a talking to after that, eh Max?" Max toasts the air and gulps his drink. I'm not sure why this bothers me so badly on this particular night, but I walk out of the kitchen and head to the little shack behind the metal out-building in the scrap yard.

Chapter Two

Space, confined, self-imposed, ordered space comforts me. Yet...while the small shack with its large wooden bench, wooden shelves, wooden drawers filled with pliers and metal snips, screw drivers, cold chisels, hammers for various uses, coils of wire and straps for binding, multi-various rivet guns placed on multiple wooden shelving with cans of paint and corrosives lining the wall...and yet, while all this surrounds me, this space is a space for subversion..

I close the door behind me, turn on the dim light and settle at my work bench. I open the drawer and pull out the small wrapped object. Careful, so careful, with a gentle motion I pull back the cloth folds to reveal the metal flower, the thin leaves of tin bent and folded delicately in a cone around the wire stem. I have meticulously placed polished glass in each petal, filed, smoothed and rubbed so it flushes perfectly to the velum of metal, delicate, dangerous, a heretical rebellion of glass and steel. As I stare at the beauty, allowing the specific moment to enthrall me, I smile at the ease of rebellion. Like a switch turned off, click, I surpass the instilled framework to 'Reduce Down' to never allow the awe or terror or wonder to penetrate the interior of the mind. It's easy, really, to analyze, resist while one peels the layers back. First, the organic and inorganic/sub categories of minerals, primary elements/molecules to atoms to simple binary codes—a barcode, something scanned as a simple black and white label. This is my secret. Surrounded by this world of salvage, of disassembly, of deconstruction—this constructed object, this flower-wonder has become reclamation. In this secret act, I know I have undermined the very foundations of the society in which I live, breathe and have my being.

Like an addict, I know this is wrong. I know this is harmful, this choice to view the flower, the flipping off the switch, and like an addict I tell myself that this will be the last time, that I will tell someone about the flower, tell Hal how I am feeling, what I have been doing for all these years. I will tell him I am indeed worthy of probation, a felon of the highest order. In that recollection, that faux confession in my mind, I feel the weight of my treachery lift, a completed act, all the guilt and shame and terror...gone at that moment. Yes, this time I'll do it. I'll find a time tomorrow, probably at Max's, pull Hal aside and confess.

This time, I know, like the hundreds of times prior—this time will be just like all the rest. My secret. My space, for me alone. I know in that moment I have crossed some line.

I hear a noise outside, a finger of wind lifting and shuddering the aluminum of the roof. I quickly place the flower back into the cloth wrapping, to the back of the drawer. I feel the longing once again. I see the white room and the wall-to-wall glass before me. I hear in the wind a song, filling me, mournful, a calling, and I want to weep for in it contains the sadness of all living things.

The next morning, we are at it early. Pages and pages of scanning barcodes and double checking the inventory sheets. The sun is now gray through the gray clouds. There is no hope of it appearing, not after the Event. Four hundred years ago, and a thought strikes me hard: that day, that moment, that exact second the last person saw the last full rays of sun blowing down upon the ground like an ancient god, the heat, warmth and brightness...a thing to be worshipped. Now...gray clouds, gray sky, gray horizon with shades of gray finally turning to the blackness of night which then cycle back to gray. There are times, I have seen it, when the city of Cogstin, the epicenter of the Event, recycles the clouds to deep black, a cyclone of heat, vortices rising, lifting, expanding over the skyline, sucking up the moisture from the lake, dumping it back upon the city, a gray slick mud of ash and grime. Hal and I have suffered several of these storms when scrapping in the city. I have never seen the Great Lake, however, but to hear the stories of such immense bodies of fresh water fills me with a sort of longing, a hope for something else, something out there yet to be discovered.

My talkie crackles as if on cue. "You work'n or sleep'n out there, boy?"

The voice is slurred, a humph and guff-awe. He and Max must be drinking their vodka and watching the scanners again. Every item relayed to the master inventory list, digital, immediate, damning to me, for I have moved only a row in the last two hours. I look at the endless, towering structures filled with the disemboweled and ruined Cogstin and sigh. I lift my hand scanner and begin to register the bundles of bound and sorted metal flashing.

I get back to business, my mind concentrating on the scanning, checking and flipping through the thick book of inventory, flipping back. Within an hour, my mind is wondering off again toward the secret metal flower, its latent power snuffed out by the cloth wrapping and the closed wooden drawer. Soon the talkie crackles and pulls me back to the land of living and I finish the day without incident.

Toward the end of the third week of scanning and combing through the aisles, we are all a little stir crazy. There is not a whole lot to do at the Salvage yard, and so every third Friday, Max, Hal and I head to Max's tavern/garage to drink beer as well as talk to the locals. Tonight, the monitors are filled with cycled warnings about Cogstin's weather pattern and increased activity and sightings of IMAGO. I see the magenta butterfly symbol flash upon the screen, followed by the small scrolling text with updates as well as the ever familiar call to action if any citizen should see any suspicious activity: call the NRM hotline... Hal comes over and slides me a beer. He is jovial and slightly buzzed from his 'hard day of inventory' with Max. He leans in close to me, his man-mountain frame hunching forward consuming the table.

"Okay, Stretch. Let's have it."

I look up from my daydreaming, grab the beer and take a sip. "What are you talking about?"

"This." Hal waves his hand about then points to me. "This moping and distraction. All of it, boy. Why, you are...well...Just acting weird." He sips from his rocks glass, face flushed. His splotched red, large jowls sagging and jiggling. It's soon apparent he is not really concerned about what I have to say but more what he's been wanting to say to me. "You know, Stretch. Everyone your age...well, maybe not everyone, but anyway...everyone around your age feels the way you're feeling. Why the NRM is taking longer to finish their observations...who knows. You know this thing ain't no science. You know how it is, boy, the waiting." He clears his throat and mimics the sartorial voice of the announcer we all have known since childhood. "Never Again. Remember, you can never trust DNA, but you can always trust the NRM." He gently touches my shoulder, and I know he is sincere. "Listen boy, they'll clear you soon enough. They always do, and this whole business of probation, this whole hassle of checking in and wondering...all of it will be gone. You ain't no terrorist. Everyone knows that." He slaps me on the back. "You sure as hell ain't much of a Salvage Inventory Specialist either." He gulps his drink.

"Hal?" I say meekly.

He raises his glass and shakes it at Max who smiles, his thin caterpillar mustache arching up.

"Hal, I need to talk to you." I lean in close. The noise of the other conversations, the low rumble of laughs and protests as they throw darts and shuffle about, the same old men, the same worker bees, the scrappers from U-Salvage, males and females, weather worn and tired—all of this drowns out my words. "I have these thoughts sometimes. I know it's stupid but..."

"Yes, yes, yes," Hal says as he waves his hand back and forth. "I know. The white room and the walls of glass."

"That, but also..."

"I've been thinking about what you said the other day."

He is leaning in now, the crowd less noisy. Someone laughs near the bar. "I remember something about that."

"You do?" My heart begins to race, hands sweaty. "You've seen it?"

"Well, no, but it's made me think about something. I think I..."

Suddenly, Max slaps Hal on the back and sets a new drink in front of him, the lemon wedge angled precariously on the glass lip. "What are you conspirators up to, heh?" He pulls up a chair, and Hal is suddenly flustered.

"Noth'n, Max," Hal says. "This one here is nervous about the waiting is all."

Max looks at Hal inquisitively, then at me. He is smiling, that caterpillar not quite lifted on one side, so that it comes across as a smirk more than a smile. "Waiting for what? The letter? Why the nerves?" He leans, eyes wide like he's Agent Smiley or something... "You hiding something, Christopher Dante?" His face is next to mine and I can smell the bourbon on his breath. We stare into each other's eyes. I see Hal nervous and hesitant. Max smiles, a broad, deep, jovial smile, creases at his eyes, caterpillar sweeping up. "Ahhhhhh." He pulls away and grabs both of my shoulders. "It's normal, Christopher. We've all felt it. It's part of growing up. You know. That moment right before adulthood. Right before you're shoved out of the nest. Ain't that right, Hal? Right before you gotta fly...boom—kicked right out on your own."

Hal lifts his drink in a toast. "Here's to fly'n."

"Cheers," Max says bumping the glass with his fist. He waves at the bartender who has taken his spot and orders another round for everyone. He begins to talk about the dump truck, his new solution to why it won't start. Hal does not make eye contact with me, and I see him drifting off into his alcoholic haze.

Max drives us home and Hal has been mumbling in the back seat. He mentions the white room, the glass. He laughs to himself, then snores. Max shakes his head. "He's really snookered. I better help you get him to bed." We pull into the driveway, and Max hurries to the car door. He's leaning over Hal, tapping him on his enormous jowls. "Hey, no crazy talk, buddy." He shakes his head a bit. "You hear me? No crazy talk." He looks at me. "Let's get him up." Hal wakes, looks about. We hoist him out of the back seat and lift him from both sides. The whole way to the house: "You're so good to me. I love you both." He is slurring and stumbling. He stops, stares at me as if seeing me for the first time tonight. "Stretch? Well, when did you get here?" He concentrates on my face. "I need to tell you something. I remembered something." He taps his head, then blinks several times.

"Come on, big guy," Max says and shakes him a bit. "Let's get you into bed. You're in no shape to be standing, let alone having a conversation. Here we go."

We stumble and hoist Hal through the front door and directly to bed, fully clothed, shoes stabbing into the darkness. He lays like a dead man, save for his enormous belly rising and lowering rhythmically. I untie his shoes, pull them off and set them on the floor. I walk Max to the door.

"You better leave him be," Max says with a chuckle. "One of you needs to be ready to work tomorrow." Max turns to leave then...turns back. "Hal mention anything crazy lately? You know, anything out of the ordinary?"

I immediately think of our conversation, the white room, the glass, Hal's interest. "No," I say. "I know he's under a lot of pressure...inventory and all."

Max stares at me, the caterpillar a straight line above his lips. "I'm sure that's it." He turns around and walks to the car. I watch his headlights disappear into the night. I go to Hal's room hoping to talk, but Hal is snoring.

The next morning, we are back to inventory again, and I can tell something is bothering Hal. He is distracted, almost sad, morose. I ask him what is wrong, and he tells me that we need to talk. "After Max leaves. Later tonight, Stretch. There's something I remembered. Something I need to work through."

~ * ~

I take inventory all that day in the hot sun, up and down the racks, counting the stacks of lumber, the blocks, the coils of wire, fudging the numbers where needed. Around five o'clock, my radio chirps. It chirps again. It is Max. Something has happened to Hal. *Come quick*! I slam the carriage down to the ground, jump the cage and dash to the out-building where they've been working on the truck.

Chapter Three

Hal's legs are limp, feet fallen sideways, left and right, his enormous body hidden under the dump truck. He looks like he could roll out any time and say, "howdy, Stretch," but it is obvious as I move closer, the jack has jack-knifed out and the weight of the truck has now crushed Hal where he lay.

Max hurries to me. "I told him to use blocks. Does he listen? Does he ever listen?"

Max is slender, arms and legs and nose like a bird, fingers black from grease, face streaked, breath stale and pungent with liquor.

I call out to Hal. No response. I try to peer under the truck, but there is no space. That truck has been resting on blocks for months on end. "Get the other jack!" I scream. "There! Over there! Pump the jack," I say, feeling Hal's ankle for a pulse. I try again and again. It is weak but there. Max and I heave and pump. The plate finally reaches the metal, hisses and lifts, slowly and steadily, the great weight from the crushed Hal. The rollers underneath the dolly have collapsed, and we end up pulling and ripping his shirt, slowly dragging him from the truck. The disk brake unit has slashed into his right side, and I see that his head is severely wounded, the bridge of his nose smashed flat, his eyes hollow.

"Hal? Hal?" I scream and move to his head. There is blood trickling from his ears. "Call someone. Call them now!" Max fumbles for the phone. I pull off my coat and plug up the gash in his side. Hal's face is pale, almost gray.

I hear the ambulance and think, *how could they get here so fast?* Two men race into the barn, clear us away, and pull Hal onto a gurney, inserting an IV, checking for a pulse, a plastic mask over his nose and mouth. Agent Smiley greets me by the ambulance.

He must be close to seven feet tall, large shoes, long arms, a sprawling sun hat on his pale, bald head. A useless gesture in the gray world of Cogstin. It is late afternoon and he still wears his sunglasses, horned-rimmed black things. He does not speak, just shifts his chin toward Hal on the gurney, back to me, to Max, back to Hal, to me. When he hands his identification to Max, I feel a sense of panic. His fingers are long, longer than human fingers, and whether it was the trick of the gray light, absence of light, play of shadow—whatever the mechanics, the illusion was the same, the dark shadow against the dull metal: fingers, spindly branches, ending in sharp points, thumb and forefinger daintily holding the edge of the leather wallet. This is a redundant gesture, for we all know the characters in this reoccurring scene. There is an awkward pause. I notice there is a shadow from the warehouse and now one from the Agent. I hear a sudden intake of breath and think it is from Max, but it is from the tall figure. Quite suddenly, the agent smiles broad, so broad a mouth should not smile that broad, a glint of teeth behind his lips. He steps from the light, this agent...Agent Smiley...stands before us in the thickening shadows, exhales...

"Christopher Dante," he says, almost a wheeze, a bag of air suddenly squeezed in order to make a sound, like one playing a bag pipe. "Once again...trouble...surrounds you." Agent Smiley's speech pattern is as strange as his figure, like he is getting the hang of it as he speaks, something once forgotten pulled from a shelf and fumbled with. The pauses are in the wrong places, the syllables pitched too high or too low with too much emphasis in awkward patches.

"I want to go with him," I say.

Agent Smiley pushes me back. "No." My chest throbs where his palm has touched me. "I need to go with him. What if he's..."

"You have caused enough trouble...for...a day." Agent Smiley says. He looks at my bloodied hands.

"This is from..."

Agent Smiley nods his head at Max. Max hurries after the dying Hal, and a paramedic closes the doors behind them. He turns to me. "We...will investigate...the incident." He follows the paramedic into the front seat of the ambulance and drives off, the lights on top flashing red and disappearing into the red dust from the Great Sand Flats swirling and clouding in the evening haze.

~ * ~

Max comes in later that night. He makes a martini for him and me. We sit on the couch in the living room in silence. I watch him gulp one down, then two. He munches on an olive like a summer day on the porch. He drinks another. I have as many, but don't feel a thing. Maybe it's the adrenaline. Max is slurring and not very forthcoming with his information. "He's fine. Everything is fine."

"How can it be fine? His head was a crushed melon. I needed a mop for all the blood."

"To modern medicine," he toasts the air.

"Did he say anything? Did he wake up?"

"Sure."

"Which one?"

"Which what?"

"What did he say?"

"Oh, I have no idea. They wouldn't let me in to see him." Max is nodding now, the drink tipping and spilling into his lap. I catch the drink and cover Max with a blanket.

Around midnight, I can't sleep; worried sick over Hal. I walk the perimeter of the salvage yard, the outside of the corrugated metal walls, my flashlight dangling uselessly to my side. Hal has been there for me. Hal kept me in line. I recalled his calming voice, his gentle nudge when I would despair of my parole, my past, the darkness inside that so desperately desires to escape. Once Hal stared me right in the face, his hands firmly on my shoulders. "There is hope, boy. There is always hope. You must choose it, cling to it. What is the sense without it? Snowflakes, Stretch. Snowflakes. Nobody the same. That means purpose." He was so earnest in this. Now he is gone, somewhere in a hospital bleeding out.

I hear a movement, a rustling of bushes, something quick scurrying, and flash the light toward some shrubs, call out, threaten. Nothing. When I walk over to the shrubs, I see a small pattern of prints, but it is hard to make them out because of the blowing sand and the darkness of the night. They look like paws. I see footprints as well, heavy boots. It's probably an illusion, a collection of paw prints. Hal calls them yappers. What they are is unclear. Max and Hal hunt them on occasion. I imagine a rodent or a dog. That is when I hear it, distinctive human whispers. This was a decoy. They are inside the compound. I run as fast as I can and make it to the entrance, flashing my light this way and that. The stacks look gargantuan, shadowed and ominous. The alleyways are masked in grey shadows, and for some reason I think of Agent Smiley. Gooseflesh pops on my arms and the back of my neck. I shout some braggadocios nonsense, my legs like noodles. I hear the whispers again, carried in the wind, and with them the sound of spray cans, hissing, the rattling ball bearing. I flash my light to the right, then dash off to the end caps, back against a stack of coiled wires.

The scrap yard is organized, thanks to me, in rows of like materials. The coiled copper wire near the coiled coaxial cable, next to the coiled ropes and vinyl siding. The plates of glass are next to the plates of steel next to the plates...well not plates but blocks of cement. I rush to the cement blocks and hear the voices again. They whisper, more like hiss, to one another, and I grab a metal post and creep toward them. Near the center of the salvage yard is my little shack. It is a place to escape, from Hal, from the prohibitive world that surrounds me. Two aisles down. Then one. I turn the flashlight toward the ground, take a deep breath, then with quick steps rush through the doorway. A scramble, a rustling, and finally...quiet. I look around at the shadowed room: cabinets, shelving, my metal working tools laid out neatly like a surgeon's operating table. I can sense someone is there. In fact, I know someone is there. I see an empty spray can on the floor. I walk around the room, talk out loud, reason with the intruder, flash here and there with the light. It is then I see it...the butterfly, the same one I saw in Cogstin, the symbol of hate, the symbol of IMAGO. A sort of terror seizes me, and I dash back to the house, locking the door behind me. Max is nowhere to be found.

I sit on the couch with the lights on. I sit and nod with sleep, Hal's shotgun next to me.

Chapter Four

The light of day has cleared the cobwebs of fear, placed everything back in order, the warm sun comforting and stark in the hazy mid-morning sky. I take the shotgun and carefully walk out to the salvage yard. The shack door is ajar and I push it open with the barrel, turn on the light. The paint can is gone from the floor, but there on the table is the symbol of the butterfly, the beautiful magenta lines trailing off the wings, and next to those are small objects made from scrap metal. They are lined up in a row, intricate, complex animal shapes: a crouching lion, a howling wolf, an eagle with outstretched wings. They are beautiful, awe inspiring, finely sculpted pieces. Most of all, they are illegal. If Hal caught me with this...if Agent Smiley caught me with this...breaking the most crucial law of the NRM. I hear a car pull up in the driveway, and I shove the figures, surprisingly heavy, into a drawer, then pull a large canvas tarp over the butterfly. When I lock the door behind me and turn around, Hal and Max are heading into the house.

I recall the huge nearly deceased Hal lying on the floor, his face caved in, his side an enormous open wound. "How are you feeling?" I say seeing him with a bandage loosely tied about his head and laughing and talking to Max.

"Stretch," he says and stands. "It's great to see you, boy."

"The doctors did wonders," says Max looking at Hal. "Miracle workers. They never cease to amaze. This fat man was pretty messed up."

Hal looks at Max. He sits down and grimaces. "I sure was. Absolute miracle workers."

I'm staring at Hal. I'm placing his wrecked image of last night against the fresh bandaged colossus seated before me. Maybe it's not Hal.

No, it's Hal: the plump fingers, the sagging jowls, the dangling earlobes that should attach but don't. The bandage looks like an afterthought.

"Would you like some coffee, Stretch?" Hal says.

Max is already pouring me a cup and placing it at the empty seat. I sit down, sip from the cup, staring all the time at Hal, like he's a ghost in blue denim overalls.

"What are you gawking at, boy? It's me. I'm all here, every bit of me." Hal pats his stomach. "I could use some breakfast, eh Max?"

Max stands and begins the process of cracking some eggs and making toast, his fingernails marked with black grease, a streak still on his neck from yesterday afternoon.

"How many stitches did they put in your side?" I say.

I think of the milky red opening, the presentment of intestines bulging and drooping from the gaping hole.

"Quite a few," Max says, walking over and patting Hal on his shoulder. "That was something." He turns to me. "Hey, stretch, grab the plates would ya."

We eat in silence, and I am constantly glancing at Hal. I have the uncanny feeling I am in some sort of play, the actors now engaged in the second Act and I, the audience still reeling from Act one. We talk about inventory. We talk about a hope of getting into Cogstin. We talk of the bureaucracy that runs the city, the various stamps of approvals needed, the impossibility this close to our deadline. We talk of the weather and the day ahead—and never about what happened only fourteen hours earlier. I am confused, but happy. I realize at the table how desperately I would have missed Hal had he died and how alone, utterly alone I am in this world.

~ * ~

That day I am completely lost in the inventory. Remarkably, Hal and Max work on the truck. Max underneath it now while Hal sits and sips orange juice and Vodka from a tall glass. All day I take breaks and lock myself in the room with the butterfly sprayed on my work bench. I secretly take out the metal objects that were so neatly placed on the wood, admire the mechanics, the finely meshed body parts and the movement. The wonder and awe of such pieces force my National Reduction Method to trigger. I actively suppress it so the feelings and emotions from the art cover me. Every noise outside, every high-pitched laugh, I hurriedly place them back in the drawer, like a child who has stolen a toy from a drugstore. I grab sand paper from the cabinet, and begin rubbing out the butterfly on the wooden table.

Why would IMAGO be here? What did they want? They are ruthless, some say not human at all. I have heard they have secret powers of mind control, can vanish while you are staring right at them. Hal pounds on the locked door and I nearly go through the roof.

"What's so secretive back here, eh Stretch?" He looks around. "What's the tarp for?" Hal walks over to the covered desk and lifts the edge. "Spill paint?"

"Yeh," I say handing him the inventory papers on the clipboard and stepping between the remaining wing of the butterfly and him.

"Well how's it looking so far?" He pages through several sheets, then taps the paper with his finger. "We're never going to make it, boy. At this pace... Never make it. They'll be auditing us for sure. Looks like a quick dinner for us both and back at it."

That is exactly what happens, and around eight o'clock, the salvage yard cast in shadows by halogen bulbs, I on the lift with flashlight in hand, I see the NRM Bureau of Corrections sedan pull up to the house. It's a spot inspection from Agent Smiley. I see the utterly surreal picture of the huge Hal and the tall skinny Agent walking out toward the locked shack. Agent Smiley is dressed in black, a bowler hat upon his head. By the time I get to them, he is already inside.

"I told'm to come back tomorrow, Stretch. I told him so. There's just too much to do for all this nonsense."

Agent Smiley must stoop slightly so not to hit his head on the exposed joists above. "There has been...terrorist activity reported in your area," he says opening cabinets and moving chairs.

His voice is strained, again, the awkward pauses that make his sentences sound unnatural. "What is this?" I look at the covered table, the neatly placed metal working tools, and I don't remember setting them in the corner like that. Smiley pulls the tarp back to reveal...a blob of paint where there should be the half magenta butterfly wing.

"I got sloppy."

I see his long spindle finger poke at the green and blue, nail chipping into the wood. His jaw is protruded and large, too large for his hairless, pale, egg-shaped head. He sucks in air. "You should be more careful," he wheezes. That is when he steps to the drawers.

"This is harassment," I say, moving to cut him off. "What do you expect to find? Coiled wire? A stolen metal scrap?"

"Step away from the dresser drawers," he wheezes, like it tires him. "There have been terrorists spotted in your area. They are after something, perhaps someone, perhaps infiltrating, recruiting..." He pulls open the top drawer filled with tools.

"Want a screwdriver?" I mock.

"This is quite out of line," Hal says stepping up to Agent Smiley.

He tries to be intimidating, but he's failing miserably. Smiley turns on him, a savage look flashes across his face. We both step back. "Outside," he hisses.

A real dread has filled the small room. Hal and I are outside before you can snap a finger.

This is it, I think. I will be in cuffs within ten minutes, escorted to the black sedan and taken to some prison. Why didn't I just throw the metal animals away? A drawer slams shut. "Get in here now!" roars Agent Smiley.

My stomach is an ice ball, my hands trembling as I walk into the room and see the drawer where I had placed the metal animals. It is pulled out and tipping toward the floor.

"Where are they?" Agent Smiley whispers, wheezes. "Where did you hide them?"

My throat is dry, hoarse. "I don't know what you mean."

I see him ball his fists, then straighten his fingers, pointed daggers on each hand. He stoops down so that his face is inches from mine. I want to cry, to scream in terror, his animal features, his hairless white face and head. *Calm. Stay Calm.* Suddenly, unwillingly, I am back into the white room with the white chaise lounge staring at the deep blue water as far as I can see. It is beautiful. It is forever, and I hear a voice screaming, *Sing, oh muse! Sing!* I blink my eyes, Agent Smiley staring at me, emotionless, a new found courage within me.

"I know you are one of them," he wheezes. "I know you are colluding."

I want to laugh, a great relief surging through me. He didn't find them. He thinks I'm hiding the IMAGO terrorist. HA! He thinks *I'm* a terrorist.

"This is harassment," I say. "I'll report you."

"Enough," Hal says. "We've got most of the night before us, and we'll still not come close to finishing the inventory. There's been a misunderstanding of some sort." Hal escorts Agent Smiley and me from the room. We walk to the house. Agent Smiley is silent as he walks to his car. Finally he speaks, "I know, Christopher Dante." He pokes me with his dagger finger and it hurts. "I know you are one of them." He stoops into his car and drives away.

"I need a drink" Hal says. "You want one, Stretch?"

"What did he mean? I'm one of them. One of who?"

"He's a nutter. The screws that hold the screws are loose inside that man's head. It's nothing."

Hal wanders inside, and I wander back to the shed. The tarp is pulled down, and my metal working tools are lined up neatly where I originally placed them on the workbench. I pull the tarp back, and there is the half magenta butterfly wing staring back at me. I go to the dresser drawer, which is closed now, and pull it open. The metal animals rattle and fall backward. My world feels like one great magician's trick unfolding before my eyes.

I work late into the night, the sun hovering below the horizon, and I can see the dust storm gathering far south over the Great Sand Flats. I pass by the shack without glancing up, place the clipboard of inventory pages on the counter and head up the stairs. Hal is passed out on the couch. I am half tempted to raise his shirt just to see the stitches, but I am sick of magic tricks and illusions. All I want to do is sleep.

Chapter Five

I wake to the smell of bacon. It's early in the morning. It has been a week since Agent Smiley's visit, and we have one last day to finish the inventory and send it to the NRM Universal Salvage headquarters. Hal is cooking downstairs. He is on edge, nervously pacing across the small kitchen, grabbing the milk carton, situating the butter, re-situating the butter, straightening the coffee mug, missing the plate with the eggs, swearing, then bumping into the coffee mug, a splash of brown now on the counter.

"Your head looks good," I say.

"My head?"

"The bandage is off."

"Oh, right, yes right." and then, "We need to get on the road."

"I thought we were working in the yard today; inventory."

Hal turns his back and fidgets more with the pan of eggs. "No inventory today, Stretch. Got an opportunity. Once in a life time."

I stare at Hal, bloated chin and tattered baseball cap, his face a mask of reddened, dry skin from the hard weather, the relentless wind off the river. "Today is the last day, Hal. This is it. You know what will happen if they audit us."

"I know, Stretch. I know. We'll be back in plenty of time to finish. I promise."

I watch him scurry some more, back turned so not to face my stare. "What? You win the lottery or something? What?"

"As a matter of fact, Stretch. We did." He pulls out an official letter from the NRM U-Salvage Headquarters. He unfolds it and hands it to me. "It's a miracle," he says. "I mean, how many times have I submitted my request. Now, just like that, Stretch." He grabs the official letter from my hand and flicks it with his sausage finger. "Just like that," he whispers. He suddenly turns around and hurries over to a wooden table where a map of Cogstin is rolled out. "I've been looking at the maps and..."

"Sector 17."

"Sector 17, Stretch, and no mistake. No one's been there. In the hundred years this has been opened to salvage..." He draws a line with his finger up the Cuyahoga River and stops on Sector 17. "Gold mine."

"Or a bust," I say.

Hal is not listening. He is lost somewhere deep inside his head.

"Exactly." He turns. His face brightens up, a beacon of hope, contagious. "Since we don't know until we get there...we need to get there. Now eat up, boy. Eldorado awaits."

Hal hurries from the room and rummages in the garage. I look out the window at the ominous clouds to the west and south, enormous, the red clay dust from the mineral mines giving them an apocalyptic feel. I gulp down my coffee and help Hal load the skid steer, the dump truck, the shovels, bolt cutters, tarps and check the gauges on the oxy-acetylene cylinders. When I finish, I shove the ham sandwiches and gallon jug of water next to Hal's fifth of vodka hidden under the extra Carhartt bibs. Lastly I step on the platform for the long and brutal day ahead.

Chapter Six

It's not like I hadn't enjoyed a normal childhood. Hal took me places. I had friends. Sure, I was an orphan. Sure, I see a white room and blue water, and hear a voice in my head. Who doesn't have crazy around them? Hal tells me everyone's got issues.

"Learn the rules, keep the rules, break the rules, make new rules," he says with a smile and a wink.

I've seen Hal break a few and make a few of his own in the days working for him in the city. None of that matters now, at least in my head, as we move slowly down the Cuyahoga to the heart of Cogstin.

The river is old. The original settlers mention it in letters, nearly a thousand years ago. It was a world full of mythical animals: horses, cows, pigs, and the river knew them, this same flowing stream of time and space. I listen to its gurgling, rushing over rock and log. I think I can hear its voice, and I wonder what it is trying to say. What changes it has seen? What history captured, witnessed, released. Some say it links the Great Lakes to the Ocean on the opposite side of the continent, but those who know such things are long gone. Those who could tell us, choose not to. I have heard many rumors like this; have heard beyond the sprawling suburbs of Cogstin, beyond the Great Sand Flats that stretch as far as the eye can see from the outskirts of Cogstin. Beyond all of this, there are great woods, mountains that defy the largest of skyscrapers, but I have not seen that. It is really not considered important by the NRM Committee. Turn on any smart phone or tablet or computer screen, Advanced Screen TV, log into the National Reduction Method Network and you will never see those types of things. You will see vapid shows from comedy to cartoons, from how-tos to the latest in NRM technological advancements. You will never hear or see anything about the great woods, the giant mountains or the ocean at the end of the Cuyahoga. They probably don't exist, but who really cares. It's like Hal says, "What good is any of that to us? Has any of that dream'n put copper on your barge or money in your pocket?"

It's Hal who stirs me from my thoughts. He calls out from the consul, "Look sharp now, Stretch."

He takes up the binoculars and scans the scene. "Look sharp," he whispers. He is throttling down, then shutting off the engine all together, and we all but drift silently toward the gate archway.

I feel strange, my head thick and foggy. I understand what comes next, for it has taken many forms these past twenty years. I look at the gate, but it is no longer the gate before me. It is huge and black and terrifying, and I understand something lurks there, something forgotten, waiting in the earth below it. I know this is not real, a dream, something in my head, like the voice and the white room with the blue water. The catwalks and pigeon roosts for the guards are all empty. The floodlights glow in the haze of the early morning, but no one is present. Silence.

"Take the helm, Stretch," Hal says. "I'm going for a walk."

I watch the fat man nimbly leap onto the wooden platform, secure the bow and stern lines, before hobbling past the half-stacked pallets of salvaged planks, and disappear into the Gate Master's office. That's when I hear it, a whistle, like steam releasing from a kettle, something eerie, something beautiful, something that gives me gooseflesh and demands a response from my NRM training, a sudden onslaught of analytics, but it defies them all. It is melodic and low, haunting, and I am struck so deeply, so profoundly my whole body shivers, and I see the haze around the barge, the smoke on the still water of the Cuyahoga rise, thick and sentient, in a slow vortex up from the cold water. It rises up from the dense layer of mist into the form of that wondrous sound, into...a human shape, a woman's shape with long arms pulling at my face, and that sound like the water, the earth and the wind. A sadness, a sudden and deep pathos churning in my chest so I cannot breathe, weight like layers of debris, a collapsing building upon my ribs, that low whistle, shaping into words, into something familiar, louder, louder, louder and finally like a scream: *SING TO ME, OH MUSE.*

I see a great shadow come from the black gate. Hal screams and disappears into a void somewhere beyond...

"Take the helm, Stretch." Hal says to me as my head clears.

I blink into the realm of men and time and things. The mist is gone, the Gate Master is waving us in, Hal waving back, the guards stand at ease in the pigeon roosts and observation towers, a buzz of movement, of stacking bales of copper, aluminum, coils of phone lines on wooden spools, the normalcy of life on the river. I watch Hal leap up nimbly onto the platform and tie the bow and stern line, the Gate Master shaking his hand. The guards are patting Hal on the back, jumping onto the barge for their daily inspection. My knees want to fold in on themselves, but I steady them along with my whole body against the consul, fiddling with the throttle lever, engine off.

I turn, and nearly run into Mr. Tough, a tall, thin rail of guy with ankle-high trousers and mirrored aviators. He loves to adjust his gun and stuff his thumbs under his belt like imitating the television ads. His face is glossy, teeth slightly visible through his closed mouth, like the lips can barely contain them. We call him Mr. Tough, and he has been here as long as I can remember, still I don't know his name. "What are you hiding today?" he says with a sort of smile, but not really a smile, a sneer perhaps.

"Only the usual contraband," I say. My head is still spinning, and my stomach is nauseous. I step away from his shadow and busy myself with securing an already secure tie down.

"You look...strange today." He stares at me, intense, like he is reading my face for something that isn't there. At last he smiles a large toothy grin, animal in nature, a chimpanzee mimicking something unfamiliar, empty. I feel a deep dread, but it vanishes as suddenly as it comes. Hal returns with the correct documentation, the daily seal slapped to the side of the pilot house. Finally, we are traveling down the Cuyahoga, the large gate closing behind us. Soon we are in the city of ashes, alone, the gloom and haze of a new day settling upon the abandoned landscape like fog on the moors.

Chapter Seven

Cogstin, so rumor has it, was a thriving city of nearly nine hundred thousand people. That was before The Event. That is what the government called this unexpected pulse of energy from an unknown origin. The Event took place four hundred years ago and wiped out the city, turned it to ashes. Some say a strategic preventative strike, others, an act of god. Whatever the cause, it ended all life in the city, and changed our world forever. Four hundred years since The Event. Four hundred years...and the past is forgotten, a dream with only a feeling of dread somewhere just out of view. What do you remember from four hundred years ago? The culture? The practices? The religious beliefs? What could you say for certain about the destruction of a city four hundred years in the past? I know what I've been taught. The history books from the NRM Bureau are quite specific. We learn it from the beginning. Using ancient technology known as quantum physics, a scientific team in Cogstin opened an alternate dimensional portal known as IMAGO. The two universes connected. The folks on the other side were not exactly good neighbors. What was opened needed to be closed. To put it plainly...someone closed the door. Boom! No more Cogstin. A once glorious city reduced to rubble and ash. A city of glass and carbon imprints. The one for the many. That is when the NRM Bureau instituted the National Reduction Method which teaches every inhabitant of the continental U.S.—from her first days in elementary school to the last days of high school – 'Reduce Down' all emotional, religious, and potentially dangerous artifacts so we may never be seduced again by IMAGO. Every child born in this world is monitored, checked for IMAGO contamination. Never again. You cannot trust DNA. You can always trust the NRM.

Of course, that is the textbook version. Four hundred years is a very long time, and it hardly has anything to do with me or Hal or scrapping for copper and wood and cement. In fact, the only thing we 'Reduce Down' these days are mountains of concrete: A ruined skyscraper to the bucket of the skid loader to the chute of the pulverizer, to the barge that carries the sand back up the river and to waiting trucks. In the meantime, I wait on a letter from the NRM Correctional Bureau stating I no longer have to spend my days pulling planks and copper and pulverizing ruined skyscrapers into sand. I can leave Cogstin and Hal forever. I can become something more. However, more and more, that seems to be an illusion. More and more it looks like even this sentence I am currently serving with Hal is going to implode. It's possible we are on a wild goose chase and not finishing up the inventory as we were supposed to.

I watch Hal swig from the vodka bottle, place it behind the Carhartt bibs, wipe his mouth and shoot me a massive I-Love-My-Job-and-You-Will-Too smile. He turned amiably around and whistled. I step up to him and slapped him on the back.

"You promise we'll be back before the sun goes down, right?"

"Hmmm? What did you say, Stretch? Yes, yes, yes, of course. Once in a life time shot today, boy. Once in a life time."

The cityscape is draped in fog, a lingering cloud of gray that never really goes away. The sun is obviously ascending, but like looking up through murky water, the light source is indistinguishable from the ambient glow. These ruins that surround our barge, the collapsed buildings, the doorways and windows, glassless and empty eye sockets, are familiar. We hear a diesel skid steer rumbling, hydraulics whining as it scoops up the rubble and dumps it into an unseen rock crusher. We turn the bend to our right, and see the sparks from acetylene torches, the metal workers masked in welding hoods, oblivious to our passing. These sights are familiar, for we pass them every day. It is when we follow the river back to the left again, that we see the second gate. This one has no pigeon roosts with guards. This one has no bustle of workers rolling spindles of copper wire, or stacking bales of compressed metal scraps. This gate is black and thick and made from reflective composite I do not recognize. A single person stands on the dock, legs spread apart. He is clothed in a yellow biohazard suit, a breathing mask upon his face, eyes hidden behind round copper frames and mirrored glass, his thumbs tucked casually under the belt and holster on his hip. We dock.

"Papers," he says through a microphone within the mask.

Hal gives him the papers.

"Highly unusual," he says.

"Our lucky day," Hal replies.

A pause, silence, a long stare. I feel creeped out by this guy.

"Come with me," he says.

He leads Hal and me to a locker room with similar biohazard suits. We put them on. The guard secures them. "Anything punctures the suit," he says, "you have ten minutes." There is a sinister tinge of hopefulness in his voice.

"Ten minutes won't get us too far, hey Stretch?"

"Our lucky day," I say and my voice travels through a mic and into Hal's headset.

We follow Mr. Hopeful in our biohazard suits to the barge. He points to the gauge on our wrists, "If the needle hits red...you have ten minutes."

Again, the awkward tone as though this devastating event would somehow make his day. Hal nods, and we lumber onto the barge. All I can think about is how our barge is filled with jagged, snagging objects. The gate opens slowly inward, and Hal steers us right down the middle.

I turn to see the gate closing behind us, and Mr. Hopeful in his yellow biohazard suit, legs spread apart, thumbs in his belt standing on the pigeon roost far above us.

It truly is the city of ashes. I see layers of it, like a grey powder. It swirls in small dust devils, spinning up, moving slowly, dissipating into gray haze. It's the ruined buildings that truly catch my eyes. They are all the same height, all of them. The result of a sustained and overwhelming force.

As we turn a sharp right with the river, we come face to face with horrifying depictions of skulls, some with horns, some half broken, all in red. Some have eyes that seem to move as we move, others empty, shaded black. They are covering everything. That's when we see a sign made of skulls. *CITY OF BONES.*

After that, a beautiful butterfly with trailing tails from either wing. Of course, this is the symbol of IMAGO, the greatest threat to humankind the world has ever known. I wonder if this is new or a four hundred year old snapshot of a destroyed evil. Hal thinks the latter.

"Maybe this was a bad idea," Hal says.

He is serious, more serious than I have ever seen him. He reaches behind his console and takes out the bottle of vodka, realizes he can't drink it with the suit on...puts it back.

"Hey," I say, "It's our lucky day. What could go wrong?"

Hal steers the boat towards a small dock. It is made of the same composite as the gate, and I can see my image in its reflection. We tie the barge off to the large iron cleats and stand together facing the ruins. It does not take long for Hal to get his head right, size up the situation and analyze the materials that present themselves.

"Good copper here. My god! The pipes are still intact. Look at it. A gold mine." He turns. "Good rock here," he says.

This is a euphemism for the tonnage of concrete to be pulverized and moved up river. "The metal roofing and siding...it's all still here."

We step off the dock and walk down an alley, Hal surveying the material, all of it still there. Four hundred years, and everything is still in place, no decay. A four-hundred-year-old tomb. It's like finding a mummy in a sarcophagus perfectly preserved. Even I feel the thrill of new discovery. This is the greatest find we have ever seen.

Hal looks down at the gauge on his wrist. I look at mine instinctively. There is a small signal of radiation, but the needle is quite some distance from the danger zone. "Let's get to it," Hal says. "You know the drill, Stretch."

We begin our unloading. Hal attaches a chain from the skid steer to the pulverizer and tows it slowly off the barge. I amass the acetylene cylinders, the torches and wheel them over to the small utility vehicle, heaving them into the bed and securing them. It takes us about a half an hour to establish a work area, Hal pointing to places he wishes to demolish, a child discovering hidden Easter eggs.

He tells me to start cutting metal on the west side of the work zone.

I drive the Gator over to perfectly intact metal roofs and siding, and unload the cylinders. The suit makes the welding mask nearly untenable. I persevere and carefully climb upon the metal roof to begin the arduous process of disassembly. That was when I sense it.

It is like a radiating wave, not flowing out but flowing inward with me at the center. It is a wave of fear, of outright terror, a feeling, a recognition perhaps something followed you, tracked you, cornered you, and only too late do you realize your predicament. I turn off the torch and glance around, pulling the welding mask off of my face in a drastic and panicked motion. My breathing is erratic, and my biohazard mask is beginning to fog.

"Hal, are you there?" I say into my mic.

Pause.

"I'm here, Stretch." He follows it with, "Everything okay?"

I look around, the graffiti and ruined buildings now just ruined buildings and graffiti. "Yeh, just checking in," I say.

I look toward Hal, and hear the skid steer humming, the pulverizer groaning and rumbling under the massive loads. The haze around the city seems thick and impenetrable. I put the welding mask back on and cut metal for three hours, the flash of the fire and sparks and blackened metal, neatly stacked piles of aluminum. I get into a groove, my mind wandering and skipping to different images. I think of the metal objects, the vanishing act, their reappearance. I think of the white room and the blue water behind the wall-to-wall glass, how peaceful.

Something moves in the corner of my eye, and I look up. I push the welding mask up, once again feeling that undulating wave of terror move closer and closer. Again, the movement just out of my direct sightline.

NOTHING LIVES IN COGSTIN. This is a fact taught to us from very early on. Cogstin is a dead city, filled with radiation, a tomb, a memorial, a lesson for the living. NOTHING LIVES IN COGSTIN. No dog, cat, cockroach, insect or fungus... Nothing. It is a city of bones and ashes.

A piece of rubble tumbles from the top of a ruined wall. I stare at it, my limbs frozen into place still holding the torch, the blue flame sputtering. I can feel my heart explode inside the biohazard suit, my plastic mask now a sheet of fog. Again, just out of peripheral vision a flit of shadow.

"Hal," I say softly, but he does not respond. "Hal, You there?"

I glance around again, and to my horror realize the silence. No skid steer, no Pulverizer, quiet, my heart beating faster and faster. "Hal? You there?"

I turn the torch off, drop it where it is and scramble down from the metal roof. The space between my last step and the ground much greater than I remember. I fall to my knees. I can feel it now, the presence, something void of good, a malicious mind, something hungry. And it is not long until I am running toward Hal. At first, I do not see him. I see the skid steer abandoned with the shovel high in the air. I see the Pulverizer, conveyor belt empty, motionless. That is when I see Hal, on his back, face mask cracked, the oxygen squeaking out of the small space like air from a rubber inner tube.

Ten minutes. Ten minutes is what Mr. Hopeful said. That was it, then you're dead. I pull Hal up, shake him. His eyes blink open, then close. "Hal, stay with me."

He opens his eyes again, then smiles in a dopey smile.

"You're drunk?"

"I waited for you to come for lunch," he said with a mouthful of cotton or marbles, "but you never came, nope...never came."

"Your mask is cracked."

"Yep, I fell down." He smiles again.

"Hal! Your mask is cracked!"

Hal sits up. "Well, would you look at that." He taps it dumbly.

"We need to get you out of here."

"I'm fine. I'm fine, Stretch," words slurring, eyes droopy. He laughs and points at me.

I follow his finger and see the large slash through my suit. I'm breathing the air just as he is, and it's been way past ten minutes. I breathe again, and again. Hal sits up. I reach up and unclasp the metal clips that seal the helmet to my suit. There is no radiation signal coming from the gauge on my wrist. The air is gray, like the ground, and there is a thick scent of damp earth. I hear no sound, an oppressive weighted feeling like the coming of a storm. I unclip Hal's helmet as well and pull it off, and this seems to revitalize him a bit.

"Just took a nap, Stretch, is all. Was waiting for you to show up for lunch like I said, but... Hey, the air. We can breathe. Don't that beat all," he whispers.

I pull him to his feet, and we walk around like new beings in a new creation. Hal takes off the suit and wads it up. "Don't need that anymore."

I take mine off as well. He pauses, looks down the river, looks back at me. "We should keep them around. We'll wear them out of here. Don't want that bureau fellow to think anything different than what he thinks, if you know what I mean?" Hal taps his head with his sausage finger.

"You okay?" I ask.

"Right as rain," he says and gives a thumbs up.

"The sun will be going down soon," I say. "We still have at least two hours of work ahead of us."

He walks toward the skid steer like everything is normal, pulls himself up and starts the engine. I walk back toward the western quadrant, that feeling of oppression once again returning. I climb back on the roof, put on the welding mask and begin to cut the metal again, every once in a while, glancing up and around to calm my nerves.

An hour passes before I notice the smell. It is a smoky, oily sensation that seems to enter my pores. At first, I think it is the metal and the torch. However, soon the torch is out, and I am standing on the metal roof searching for the origins of the acrid odor. Further to the west I see a trail of charcoal colored smoke in the gray haze. It moves like a snake, the air heavy and still, so that I clear my throat to be sure I have not lost my sense of hearing. It writhes, spinning, and I am not sure if it is a dust devil or my imagination, but I know one thing. I must follow, and I do.

The alleyways are dark from the gloom and the gray ash swirling, but I climb on a broken ledge of concrete and see the black smoke. Two blocks away? Maybe. When I turn the corner, I smell it. It is deep, pungent, almost sweet. My gorge rises and I gag. It is the smell of death, profound decay, the burning of something organic. There is a shadow now from the setting sun and the buildings surrounding me. I move quickly into it, for fear that I am being followed, the same feeling I had hours ago upon the roof. The fear returns, the undulating wave of terror moving in, ever closing, rings about me.

NOTHING LIVES IN COGSTIN! I say this over and over, remember all of the history, the lectures at school. NOTHING LIVES IN COGSTIN. It is a dead city. It is the city of ashes and bones. Four hundred years have passed. The wind suddenly picks up, a whistling from just beyond the intersection of abandoned alleyways. It gets louder. Louder. NOTHING LIVES IN COGSTIN. Louder. It is a voice. Louder. It is a kettle blowing steam. Louder, louder, louder, and suddenly a voice clear, resounding: SING TO ME OH, MUSE! I fall to my knees, the odor so strong now it fills my mind with darkness, oppressive, all consuming. I am kneeling near the origin of the smoke, before a great door. On the doorposts, a splash of red paint, darker than paint, and I cover my face because I know it is not paint. The voice screams in my head, and I cover my ears. "ENTER," it says. "ENTER. SIIIIIIIIIINNNNNNNGGGGGG!" it screams. I slowly rise, and step through the smoke and into the darkness within.

Chapter Eight

It is a dream, I think, what takes place next in the world of men and time and things. I see it only in dreamscape and understand it in the dream logic. At first, I see nothing, then realize I must be in an alley, a dark tunnel. It must be night. It does not matter I have entered through a door of a building. It does not matter I have been breathing the air Mr. Hopeful says will kill me, breathing it for nearly an hour or more.

No, the room has become a dark tunnel. The pungent odor I smelled earlier is aromatic and fresh as something just beginning. I am not afraid. I am an observer. I walk through the tunnel, amazed at the smooth walls that suddenly change into stone, rock walls undulating, curved, and becoming light and shadow. I see this, but it does not strike me as odd. I turn to look at the cave walls only to find pictures of animals, sketches of lions, charcoal sketches at first rudimentary lines, than more mature depictions, subtle shading giving the haunches dimension, the face vivid and realistic.

It is moving now, forming movement from the early sketches, and I think, *of course it is moving*, and I scan the earlier lines touching them with an understanding of a child's epiphany of the inner workings of a clock. I imagine the cave art lion to move and search, seeking, roaming, gracefully running toward...a gazelle.

The gazelle is eating, every once in a while, pulling up from the thin lines of charcoal grass, moving its head back and forth. It senses the lion. I sense the lion too, and suddenly realize I am the gazelle. I should fear the cave art lion. I smell the animal skins and the past decaying carcasses. I understand the lion's appetite is insatiable. It is a blood lust, it is like a god of ancient days wanting sacrifice, demanding flesh and blood. That is when the cave art lion and the gazelle—in dreamscape logic—naturally transform into a cave, just a cave, and on the wall are hundreds of small, red hand prints, the pinky finger curved.

These are signs to me, and I understand them. As I walk further back into the cave, a terror begins to rise from my ankles, to my calves, to my knees and spine, erupting in gooseflesh upon my arms. I am naked, alone, and it is I who touches the cave wall, pressing my berry-stained hand upon it, understanding completely why I do this. I feel a loss within me, a deep, deep loss, a weight, a hole perhaps, something taken from me I cannot replace. I being to groan, then chant. The chanting fills my ears, makes me cry, the loss profound, eternal. The chant becomes a wailing, and I find myself once again placing my red palm upon the cave wall as a symbol for this sorrow.

A voice whispers, *further, further, further*. I keep walking, the ground sloping down, down, down. *Further, further, further,* the voice whispers. It is a song now, a beautiful whispering, important song. Soon I am following it, but I know there is something terrible before me, something that is from the beginning, something that must be worshiped, feared, something demanding too much for my mind.

Finally, there it is, a stone slab, and upon the stone slab are arms and feet and torsos. It is terrible, beautiful, horrifying, and I realize the smell is actually burning flesh. There are small limbs and large limbs, old limbs. I understand them, know them. I do not understand, and I do not know them. My head hurts now. I feel an intense pain in my side, but I cannot move from the stone slab. I realize I am next, I will be put on the slab, and what I think is the back of the cave is only a midway point. Torchlight and groaning is coming from somewhere down the tunnel, coming closer. The pain in my side intensifies. *It is time*, whispers the voice. *It is time*. I hear something terrible approaching and images flash upon my imagination, of Mr. Tough and Mr. Hopeful, lumbering toward me, down the tunnel, lumbering ape-like with fang and claw, closer, closer... Finally they say, *SLEEPER, AWAKE!*

I am thrown back into the world of men and time and things. My wrist alarm is going off, the needle pushed far into the danger zone. I have fallen sideways onto sharp cement blocks. I push myself up and before me is a table where something smolders. I recognize it immediately, turn my head and vomit. The smell of decay and putrefying flesh so overwhelming I fall to my knees. That's the moment I see the book. I pull it to me and stumble out of the small building.

Hal is calling me on the walkie talkie. "We need to go, Stretch. Do you copy?" Without even looking at it, I hide the book between the two tanks, and as I am packing the Gator to go, I hear a low growl, something sinister, something disturbed that was not meant to be disturbed. I hear the crunch of bone, but I am already driving away as fast as I can.

Hal has his biohazard suit on again, the crack taped up from the inside and out. He has repaired my suit and I put it on, the wrist guard meter still pointing in the danger zone.

"I think the winds have shifted," Hal says. "There's a reason nobody comes here, Stretch." He looks at the load of stacked corrugated sheets, and pats it with his hands. He looks behind me, then back to the setting sun. "Not bad at all." He punches me lightly on the shoulder. "Hey, you okay?"

"Yeh," I say, still shaken from the vision. We load the Gator and the tanks onto the barge. I slip the book from the tanks and wrap it in my coat, untie the bow and stern lines. We are heading back down the river toward the black gate.

The journey to the black gate is slow, the barge, weighted down with gravel and steel scraps, strains against the current of the river. The gray of the day mixes with the light from the setting sun in an explosion of orange, and just like that it is night on the river. Hal turns on the halogen lights and we make our way to the black gate. I don't see Mr. Hopeful. I don't see anyone, but the gate swings outward as we approach, and we pass through it. The dock is empty. Hal steps off the barge to find someone, and again I feel a shiver run up my back. Someone is watching us, but I can see nothing in the dim light of the docks.

Hal returns. "I guess we don't check in here," He says. "We don't need these any longer."

He and I pull off the biohazard suits and toss them in a pile on the wooden planks. We are off. I look back toward the gate, just as we make the left bend in the river, and see a shadow under the light, standing next to the mound of yellow suits, a figure, tall, elbows out, thumbs tucked into the belt. I tell Hal, but by the time he turns the figure is gone.

We check out at the main docks, the bustle of river life humming as the workers finalize their tasks for the night. Hal unloads the barge, rolling the truck and the gravel, the copper, the sheet metal onto the dock. Mr. Tough is there asking Hal questions, asking about the paperwork again, how there was a mistake, that he had actually gone to Sector 17 illegally, but this time they would allow it. How did he get the proper signatures? And he would have to inspect the barge for contraband or illegal smuggling. Hal raises the letter, flips it with his fingers. "You sent it to me," Hal says. "I didn't request it."

Mr. Tough looks at the letter again then hands it back to Hal. "Highly irregular," he says. "We will inspect the barge."

Mr. Tough calls to his crew through a mic clipped to his shoulder, and in seconds five other figures looking a lot like Mr. Tough appear from hidden doors. They are moving rapidly toward the barge, and I have an overwhelming sense of anxiety. The book! It is still stuffed between the acetylene tanks. "Hal," I whisper, "The vodka bottles." Hal looks at me and then at the barge. He hurries to the men to block them from entering. If Mr. Tough finds the vodka bottles, Hal could be banned from the river for up to a year. I hear him arguing with Mr. Tough, how there must be an inspection order, that if there is no inspection order, there is no inspection. I hurry, unnoticed, to the barge and enter the cockpit, out the other side and over to the book covered in my jacket. I take the jacket and my lunch pail, stuff the vodka bottle into the secret hold under the planks in the pilot house, and walk out the door with a wink to Hal. Mr. Tough points to the official inspection document again, says that everything is in order, moves Hal out of the way, and leads his men onto the deck of the barge. The inspection takes an hour. By the time we are paid for the scrap and gravel, drive home to the house near the river, Hal and I are exhausted.

It isn't until after dinner that I even think about the inventory. Hal is already asleep on the couch, sonorous snores coming from the living room. I walk down the hall to my room. I reach under the bed and pull out the strange book, open it. They are the pictures from my dream, lions on cave walls, red handprints with the curled pinky finger, a gazelle eating grass, all rendered in charcoal. I page through the multi-colored drawings, pictures I have only heard about in whispers, illegal pictures, forgotten for over four hundred years, and something deep within makes my mouth go dry. I have seen these pictures before, these words filling the pages, familiar, known. I flip rapidly through it, and a single paper falls from the binding and onto the floor. I pick it up and read.

FIND US.

Chapter Nine

I have never really believed that rooted in the complex is the simple. This is what we are taught from an early age, the very essence of the Reduction Method. What appears to be so powerfully wrought with all the nuances and patterned complexities are really merely basic elements combined, and those basic elements can be Reduced to binary codes. I have never really believed such things. A most rudimentary object such as a fly in all its simplicity is still beyond the human imagination—it is a mystery. What it sees, what it thinks...if it thinks, and if it does not...what drives it? What commands it to breed, to seek food, to exist? If not, a sentient being, then a being governed by time and genetics which in itself is making it part of a universal, sentient force of some kind?

Don't get me started on the human machine. I pick up metal and cut it into pieces, watching my hands and fingers move deftly, each digit bending in instant clarification with what my will, my imagination sees. A piece of sheet metal into petals of a flower, imitating the natural world of time and space, but giving it new meaning in that it is not organic but an imitation of the organic. It has become an opposition to the organic with a history before it. First it was organic metal, forged in a factory, sheeted and screwed to a building in the heart of Cogstin—a city of constructed progress. That city was nuked and turned to ash and rubble by the very hands that created it. It was this I pulled from the destruction, cut into thin strips, subtly reshaping it into a representative object of life, of beauty, perhaps even remembrance with depth and meaning because of its context to the world of men and time and things. Mystery, not simple.

These thoughts leave me when I realize evening has come, the sun sinking below the salvage warehouse. I see Hal with a hurried pace and worried look, round the corner of the steel structure, bulk painted in shadow and light. I place my flower next to the eagle, the howling wolf, and the lion. I cover them up with the heavy cloth tarp, turn and again take up the acetylene torch, flip down my welder's mask and begin to cut the sheet metal. Hal taps me on my shoulder. I fake surprise.

"We've got company, Stretch."

I keep cutting the metal into strips. He taps me again, pulls on my shoulder. "Hey, Stretch. Something's up. We've got company. It looks like he's got a bug up his—you know what." I put the gear down and start walking with Hal toward the office. Before we can take five steps, we are met by Agent Smiley. His suit gives an appearance of one single piece of clothing. He stands in the shadows of the metal building, face obscured in the dimming light.

"Christopher Dante," he says.

Gooseflesh is up and down my arms, the back of my neck.

"Accounted for and present," I say, but there is no smile on Agent Smiley's face.

"You were in Cogstin, Sector 17, yesterday?"

It takes me a moment to understand his strange cadence. "Yes. Sector 17."

"Did you witness something?"

Hal turns to me, eyes wide with wonder.

"No," I say.

Hal hunches his shoulders, eyes narrowing on me as if I know something he wants left alone.

"You were in Sector 17 yesterday," continues Agent Smiley in his staccato tone, "and you witnessed something. Correction. You removed something."

Now Hal is pissed at me, his hands on his hips. "I knew this would happen, Stretch. I knew I shouldn't have taken you. Did you take something?"

"No, I did not take anything. You saw me board the barge. Did I take anything with me?"

Hal ponders this. Agent Smiley's chin moves from Hal back to me, to Hal, to me. "I'm sorry, but if Christopher says he didn't take anything.

He didn't take anything. That's that."

Nobody moves. Agent Smiley stands tall like a tower. Again, maybe it is the trick of the fading light or maybe the angle of the metal siding, but his shadow seems to grow bigger, wider, taller, arms outstretched, a flash of movement—then nothing—a mere shadow.

"So," Hal says, "Unless you have papers or something, or know something we obviously don't...we need to get back to work."

Agent Smiley does not move, just turns his chin to me, back to Hal, back to me.

"We found something," Agent Smiley says. "We found something in Sector 17." He reaches into his coat and pulls out a folder. It is thick and large and doesn't seem to make sense that it came from his inside coat pocket. He opens it up and hands me a picture. It is the graffiti from the walls: a huge butterfly and next to it the word *IMAGO*. He pulls out another picture and hands it to me. It is gruesome; dark, severed legs, arms, torsos strewn about a large table. Hal pulls it from my hands, gasps and hands both pictures back to Agent Smiley.

"I think we've had enough of this harassment," Hal remonstrates. "Now if you do not mind, I think we are done here."

Hal looks big, bigger than I remember. His hands are balling into fists, then relaxing.

Agent Smiley does not move. At last he turns and strides away without looking around.

"The nerve of those people. Always threatening the little guy. Who do they think they are?" Hal walks to the front lot to see that the agent has gone.

I go back to my small metal shop, but I sit there staring at the dirt. I think of those legs, arms and torsos on the table. The ugliness, and a tremendous sadness weighs me down. I think of the butterfly graffiti on the stone archways, the small building, the blood on the doorposts, the strange dream I had in Sector 17. Still, there is something else about the pictures that bother me. I think I recognize who was there, but the more I try to consider it, the faster it flutters away, scattering into fragments only to reemerge on the borders of memory.

Later that night, our phones are buzzing with text alerts, the television scrolling the emergency message at the bottom of our programs—that night Hal and I sit dumbfounded at the significance we are only now comprehending. The notorious terrorist organization IMAGO has captured helpless citizens, tortured them, cutting them up and leaving them in the city of Cogstin as a warning. Hal and I look at each other, and Hal quite suddenly, breaks down into sobs. "That could have been us. Oh my God. That could have been us."

Chapter Ten

The next afternoon I sit at my work station behind the salvage garage and fiddle with a wafer-like piece of aluminum, punching holes through the middle, staring through them at the gray, monochromatic sky, the eternity of night and cold beyond that. I imagine the earth spinning, alone, void of life, a forgotten rock in the blackness of space and I alone on the prison planet. Hal's eye stares back at me.

"I see you're hard at work as always."

"You remember Orange?" I ask, moving the aluminum to the side of Hal's enormous head, and once again stare at the gray sky.

"Of course, I remember Orange."

"The cat."

"Oh, right. Orange the cat."

"Buried back there somewhere, if I recall."

Hal looks at me, pulls the piece of metal from my hands. "What made you think of him?"

"*Her*. Orange was a...*she*."

"Tough to remember being that her name was Orange."

"Do you remember her?"

Hal scratches his head, glances toward the back lot, the endless rows of scrapped and crushed cars and parts and refrigerators and washing machines and metal posts inventoried and cataloged and digitalized. "I can't say I do remember her, Stretch."

"I do, like it was yesterday. She wasn't even orange, but a rust colored calico with black and white. She used to lay on your lap near the welding station when you fell asleep." I look up at Hal. "You don't remember?"

"No, Stretch, I don't. There were probably hundreds of cats passing through here. If I had a nickel..."

"You fed her from the table. I can see it." I point at my head, between my eyes. "Right here. Vivid as a movie. Orange making that annoying sound, a chirp, a whine, something. You called it cat speak and claimed to know what she said."

"Cat speak? Hmmm. That's catchy."

I pull the aluminum from Hal, who has begun bending and ruining it unconsciously, and place it on the table. I notice the letter in his hand. "I remember finding her stiff and dead. I must have been five...maybe six years old. I remember the flies gathered on her open eyes."

"Good god. That's not a pleasant thought," Hal says.

This feeling is driving me now, something deep and weighty, a voice, a shout, an eruption of something trapped. "I didn't get it," I say in a whisper. "I didn't understand that she was actually dead, not coming back. Do you remember?"

Hal shakes his head and shrugs his shoulders.

"You took a shoe box and we wrapped Orange in a towel. You dug a hole out there." I point past the coils of copper wire stacked five high and as far as I can see.

"What's wrong with you, Stretch? You need to remember your school lessons. Reduce It Down. Like you've been taught. This ain't healthy. You know what the NRM Board of Health says about such thinking. Dangerous, Stretch. Not good for you."

I do try to Reduce It Down, but the process is useless. A storm of emotion overwhelms me...it's a cat! Just a cat! A mean one at that...but nothing stops it. I am awash in pain and loss, a sorrow so profound that I must turn my head from Hal.

"I almost forgot the reason I came out here, Stretch," Hal says. He is awkward, out of his element, removed from my blatant show of emotion. "I got another letter from the NRM Bureau. Says here I've been granted rights to go back to sector 17. Can you fathom that, boy? What the heck is go'n on? First, they tell me to go. When I get there, they tell me it was a mistake. Now they tell me to go again. Maybe this is another mix up? I sure as heck don't want that agent back here. Creepy guy."

I wipe my eyes, acting as if I am stretching from boredom then take the letter. It is the exact same as the last one, same wording, nothing new...like it was the first letter and not a follow up. "Seems legitimate to me."

"I don't want to go back there," Hal says. "All that terrorism stuff going on. No thank you." Hal points at me. He is animated now. "Did you see the latest threat alert? Did you? It's all over the news. Something bad is happening."

I look up at Hal. His large jowls are shaking, the enormous T shirt stretched to popping over his stomach. He is panicking. I don't remember Hal ever panicking. "Let's not go," I say. "Let's just tear up the letter and act like we never got it."

"If we don't go," Hal says, "that's all she wrote. Never again."

"But the terrorists."

Hal looks at me, then the letter, then me again. "That's serious, and this could be a mix up. Don't want another mix up," he whispers. "Not with that agent from the NRM Corrections Bureau." He pauses for a moment. "Well, time and money are the only things keeping us from working...since we got neither...I got no excuse—and neither do you." He winks and walks back to the warehouse to continue his inventory list.

That afternoon I work in the stack yard, driving the forklift, moving pallets of crushed and banded metal from one side of the yard to the other, to make room for the new deliveries. My phone buzzes and chirps with the latest terrorist updates, how IMAGO has been spotted in Cogstin, and how the NRM was countering. With all that fear and alarm, I keep thinking about Orange's death. How could Hal not remember? We sobbed like babies at the mock funeral. Hal took out his pipe afterward, tried lighting it with matches, but the wind was so strong, nearly blowing the fedora from his head, he just clenching the unlit pipe stem in his mouth and patting me on the back. I close my eyes, the power of that moment once again consuming me... Hal was dressed in a suit back then. Hal in a suit! What a memory. Hal clean shaven and dressed to the nines. A pipe and matches. No one uses matches today...an artifact in our history books. Perhaps I was mistaken. My phone buzzes again. Another NRM alert warning of terrorist attacks near Cogstin.

Hal and I turn on the TV. The NRM Entertainment Channel scrolls the latest terrorist updates across the bottom of the screen. We wait. After forty-five minutes of waiting, a talking head comes on to explain the threat has been eliminated, and regularly scheduled programing will now resume.

"Well," Hal says rubbing his thighs. "That's something, ain't it." He looks at me, then the TV. "I guess I'll make a scrap run to Max's place. He's got some discarded copper." He slaps his thighs. "Okay then."

Hal won't be home tonight, and I'm wondering what has sparked this sudden turn of events. Max may or may not have copper scraps to give to Hal, but that is mostly a happy afterthought. Hal is headed to Max's garage, and a bender is usually to follow. Max will call by midday tomorrow asking me to pick up the inebriated Hal. It's been several months since Hal's last one.

I turn off the TV and listen as the flatbed truck pulls out of our driveway. I am alone, and the pensive mood inside me, the hen that has pecked at my inner shell all day has finally broken free. I pull the shades down, lock the doors and lay the strange book I found in sector 17, the book of cave paintings and pages of text, on the kitchen table. Turning to the lions, gazelles, trees and grasslands, the hand prints, I page through them, hypnotized by the majesty and beauty. I know subconsciously I am participating in an illegal act, to view something corrupting and emotionally charged. My first reaction to such ancient and powerful images is to Reduce Down: break down the lines on the cave wall into charcoal or berry reductions mixed with water or spit or sweat, go further even to the very elements that create such charcoal, the molecules of carbon... This time I stop myself, push the method aside and allow the emotions to flood over me like water.

I hear the voice resonate in my head; louder, louder, louder: *SING, OH MUSE! SING*! I am in a dream state now, inside my imagination. The lions, the gazelles, the grass and the trees are real and moving. I a spectator to it all. *SING!* Soon, the random images become a pattern, and they make sense to me, a message, a story. I see a thin shadow, an ancient man with staff or spear crouched before a fire. Another arrives, another, many shadows, tall and thin, squatting down before the cave art fire. Before them appears, or was there all the time, another, with skins draped about his head and shoulders, his arms lifted high in prayer or story or chant. The lions move and hunt, they too crouching, watching, ready to spring. To my horror they are hunting the men. Soon they surround the fire, the charcoal grass hiding their presence. I want to shout, try to shout, but the men around the fire cannot hear me. A lion, an enormous male with mane, tooth and claw leaps into the air.

I am helpless. I raise my hands in protest, palms blocking the lion. To my amazement: the lion is held in suspended animation, harmless, a three-dimensional display. *Sing to me, oh muse! Sing!* I step up to the image, the charcoal lines of carbon mixed with sweat or blood or spittle, see the shadows and shades that create the illusion of the real, marvel at the image captured, the image of a hundred-thousand-year-old imaginative act. I rotate my hands and the lion rotates in all its intricate-lined wonder. I leave the lion and step to the storyteller, his arms raised, turn to the men crouched listening, unsuspecting, content, maybe tired from the day's hunt. I turn again to the lion, observing at my leisure and the magnificence of this moment, the wonder of it all, observe the lion's fangs, great pegs of solidified bone, sharp and menacing, notice the taloned paws spread wide for tearing flesh—I observe it all and decide: This should not be. To my astonishment, my thoughts translate into action. There are no more fangs and claws that tear. This makes me laugh, and for the first time I notice the crouched men are chuckling too. The storyteller is drawing a toothless lion without claws, coldly captured on the stone wall with charcoal lines and shadow.

I spin the lion, stop the spinning, and pronounce upon the lion a mane of sunflowers and it is so. Now the toothless, clawless lion explodes with color, hardened stalks of brilliant yellow petals with large black centers filled with seeds, interwoven and thickly set about the great beast's neck. His tail, the wiry tuft of hair now sprouts the same, a sunflower blossom on a horny stalk of green. I laugh. The crouched men laugh. The storyteller, now in full glory, throws his hands about and draws the flowered tail. As for the lion's hide, there is no longer the tanned and burred-infested hide, patched with scars and wounds and disease, but red handprints, handprint after handprint, and it is I who now have the red paint and am making the prints, and now it is the storyteller filling his flower-lion with hand prints, and I notice the small curled pinky finger in the print, over and over and over, a slight separation from the others, a slight turn at the first knuckle past the nail. I am laughing. The storyteller and the crouched men are laughing, the lion spinning, turning, swooping, dancing, now up on two legs like a circus animal, now jumping, a glorious ballet of color and irony and power and joy, and the terror of that day, the day when one of them was killed—that sadness and terror and humiliation of death, for the moment, has vanished in the dim light of the fire.

Suddenly, just as quickly, I am sitting in the white room with the white chaise lounge, staring at the great blue water beyond. I understand the book and the room are connected, but I cannot understand how. I know the words I have read on the page are mine. I also know they are not words, equations really, lines and lines and lines of parenthetical numeric phrases, words, symbols, a code, an encrypted message just for my eyes alone. Because of the room and the book, like Hal's injuries and the incident in Sector 17—I am displaced and cannot anchor to anything. Flash. I am staring at the open book of cave art in my Uncle Hal's house at night. It is late, and the house is quiet and dark, cold and oppressive. I am exhausted, bone weary from the event. I close the book and fall into my bed with my clothes still on and sleep where I fall, my imagination a dark void of empty space.

Chapter Eleven

I work all day, and there is still no sign of Hal, no call from Max. I notice the texts scrolling across my phone, my tablet, my television screen, always the same:

TERRORIST ALERT—HIGH. BE ON THE LOOK OUT FOR SUSPICIOUS BEHAVIOR. IMAGO SPOTTED IN COGSTIN.

I feel lethargic and numb all that day, as if I had taken part in some bacchanalia revelry the night before. I put down the tin snips and pliers that are useless in my hands. I walk away from my metal artwork and cut through sheets of aluminum until the sun goes down. The sparks and mundanity of it all soothe me. Even after I put away the acetylene torch and wheel the tanks back into storage, chain up the sliding metal door—even after a full afternoon of filling space, there is still no Hal. Max always calls. I figure by the time I go to bed that night, Hal will stumble through the door. He does not. I call Max's place, but no one picks up the phone.

It is after fits and starts that I finally fall asleep. My dreams are filled with shadows and oppressive feelings, something restricting my chest, a suffocating presence, a terror in the room, lurking.

I wake in sweat and panic, rapid breathing, sitting upright, my blankets wrapped tightly around my legs. That's when I hear voices outside my door. It takes me a few minutes to unwind the sheet, gather my thoughts, that I am now in the land of the living, terra firma, feet resting on the cold wooden floor boards. I walk to the door, open it and say, "Well, this is late even for..." but I do not finish, for there is no-one there—at least in the hallway.

I stand in the darkness and listen. Yes, someone is speaking, whispering, or is it weeping? The sound is unfamiliar. I step into the living

51

room, expecting to see someone crying, but instead it is empty, dark, just as I left it. The sound is coming from the kitchen, perhaps. The house is small. I would know if someone was there or not.

I creep to the kitchen door which is closed, place my ear against the thin board. Still the sound is a whisper, muffled. Someone obviously afraid. I open the door, but the kitchen is empty as well. That's when I notice the outside door is open, a brisk November wind blowing papers about. The yard is dark, but I see that the storage building door is open, and there is a faint light coming from inside. The voices are louder now, and I can distinctly tell that one of them is Hal's.

I grab my coat and hurry across the darkened yard. There is a deep, deep feeling of dread overtaking me, a terror pushing me back from the storage building, a nearly physical presence warning me to stop, go no further if you value your life! My breath is short, panicky, and as I place my back to the metal siding, I know that whatever is within is something terrifying, animal, a stain of evil I have never experienced—and Hal is facing it.

I want to run away, but I fight that urge, and peer around the corner. The building is cloaked in shadow, so it is hard to determine what is out of place and what is supposed to be there. The acetylene tanks, the tines from the forklift, a tarp pulled over fifty-gallon drums of gas. The voices are louder now, and I can understand several words.

"I didn't know," Hal says, pleading, crying, chanting. "I'm sorry. I didn't know."

I move into the shadows and head toward the dimly lit corner. The dump truck gives me cover, and I stoop down next to the front tire, searching for my next strategic location.

"Silence!" a voice hisses, and just the sound nearly forces me to the ground.

There is an oppression, such a great weight I can barely move, and it is a sheer act of will to even lift my head. Hal whines again, his voice muffled. I move slowly, eternally slowly, step by step by step, the oppressive weight increasing like some invisible hand placing stones upon my back. I am finally to the edge and peer around the corner. An enormous towering human-like shadow, a darkness overlaid into the air, a void of space rather than a present material thing, but there none the less—this stands before a whimpering Hal. He is nearly prostrate on the ground.

"I am sorry. Forgive me. I am sorry. I didn't know. Please." Next to the eight-foot-tall shadow man is a giant sack, twisted and tied. I realize it is not empty, for something is struggling, growling, whimpering, struggling again. The sack is larger than Hal, a bulk, something captured.

"You were warned, forty-eight!" the shadow man hisses. "There will be no next time." The voice is low, yet familiar, forced, discordant cadence, and I immediately think of Agent Smiley. Suddenly, a snake-like movement, a strike, Agent Smiley lifts the giant burlap sack into the air, like a bundle of feathers. The creature within struggles violently, but Agent Smiley does not waver, nor does the explosion of desperation seem to move him: a fixed spot in time and space, a substance made of stone. With one swift movement, Agent Smiley pulls the struggling thing toward him, grasps it firmly in his hands and squeezes. A growl, a yelp, a terrible, desperate spasm, then stillness. Agent Smiley drops the sack to the cement floor. "Take care of this...abomination," he hisses. The silhouette of Agent Smiley morphs, his arms spreading out, hands clawed, out and out and out, his lower jaw opening wide, wider, unhinged and gaping, talons for teeth on top and bottom jutting out, the jaw still opening, an abyss of horror and pain and hunger. Agent Smiley suddenly screams or calls or howls. Hal's face is to the ground. "Please. I'm so sorry. Please. Please." It is at that moment I am the most afraid. For the evil, the aura, the presence of the thing is so terrible, I too find myself flat to the floor, face down in fear, an inky darkness filling my mind and chest. When I can look up, it is only Hal remaining, and the giant burlap sack next to him on the floor.

It takes several minutes to pass. Hal slowly lifting his head, searching for the all clear. Soon the once terrified Hal gathers himself, takes several deep breaths and stands to his feet. The atmosphere has changed. Hal is now humphing, talking to himself, pulling the vodka bottle from the storage bin nearby, ferociously gulping, gesticulating again in anger.

"Come here—Tell me! Who do they think they are?" Followed by "Damn scary, that's who." Another swig from the bottle. He ponders the sack, the enormous lump of whatever hides behind the burlap. He drinks again then kicks the side of the bag in protest once again. He contemplates the bag again, grabs the twisted top and pulls. It might as well be a thousand pounds. He can do nothing with it. Hal drinks from the bottle and tosses it on the ground, rubs the side of his hips, looks toward the house, back to the sack.

Hal walks toward me, as I step around the side of the dump truck to counter his movement. He stops at the sliding metal door and peers out at the house. I peer out at the house, the kitchen door wide open. Hal scratches his head, then mutters something, turning toward the sack, back to the door, to the sack, pauses, scratches his forehead again, hurries to the back of the building, mounts the loader with the backhoe and rumbles it to life. With great effort Hal heaves and pushes, pounds and leverages the great sacked thing into the bucket of the loader.

"Tell me what to do," he mocks. "Come here and threaten me. Here! If the other time wasn't enough! What did I do?"

He mounts the loader again, backs it out the sliding metal door, and drives the sack down a dirt aisle, the headlights blasting into the pitch-black night. I run a little way behind completely lost in the unfolding scene.

Soon I hear the engine slow, and it takes me a good five minutes to catch up to the tractor. By the time I get to the place where he has stopped, Hal is already seated on the swivel chair and digging a hole with the backhoe. The arm juts out, then pulls back, the bucket full of dirt. He does this many times, and I wonder about the sack...what it could be, the significance of what I have seen. Soon the hole is deep and wide. Hal turns the tractor around and pushes the giant burlap sack and the thing inside into the open grave. He kills the engine and sits there. He pulls a bottle from a small cooler stashed in the glassed-in cab. His phone rings. It takes him a moment to find it. It drops. He curses and searches for it, then answers.

"Yeh." Silence. "Well, fine thing, Max! Why the hell didn't you say something?" He pauses. "Sure, sure, sure. The next time that thing shows up, I'll be sure NOT to tell you either. What were you thinking? No. No. I said...NO. I've got it taken care of. Yes. What? No, of course not. He's asleep in the house. I'm hanging up now." Hal does so.

He sits silently in the seat of the loader. I hear him swigging from the bottle. The phone rings again. He picks it up but does not answer. Hal places the phone in his pocket, starts the loader, and pushes the mound of fresh dirt into the hole. He turns toward the house, and in the highest gear possible, he drives it back to the storage building. I run after the tractor, for fear Hal will realize I'm gone, but that is the least of my worries. Hal turns off the tractor, the phone ringing again, and I realize it hasn't stopped ringing since it first started. He jumps down and heads toward the house, just as several men grab him and beat him to the ground. *Run!* a voice in my head screams! *Find me! Run for your life!* Instead, I squat in the shadows and watch as they pull Hal, who is struggling and screaming, "I took care of it. I'm telling you. I took care of it. Please!" he cries. "Please. I don't want to go back to Cogstin. Please! Please! I didn't know! Please!" He is sobbing now. "Please not back to Sector 17. Please no." They shove him into their large SUV and drive away, NRM Terrorist Bureau painted on the side.

It isn't long until I have the loader backed to the hole and am digging up the fresh dirt slowly, methodically, trying not to ruin the thing below. The hole is deep now, and I flash the light into it. There is the burlap bag. The bucket has torn the bag, and something is splayed out below, the dirt covering all but a small portion. My throat is dry, my skin clammy. I don't understand anything I see. I don't understand the schizophrenic person who has buried the thing in the sack, the terror that was Agent Smiley and what I witnessed in the storage building. My head is clouded and filled with fear.

I stare at the bottom of the hole, at that thing in the sack killed by Agent Smiley. I see it as clear as the sun, even in the darkness of the night: Sunflowers, like a discarded bouquet partially hidden in dirt, but it is not a bouquet. It is the sunflower lion I created in my imagination, and I know this because just below on its front shoulder—small, red handprints, and all with the pinky fingers separated and curled slightly inward at the first joint. I quickly fire up the loader and fill in the hole, the thing from the sack under ten feet of earth, gone forever.

Soon I am in the house, taking the book of Cave Art, packing it along with clothes, a knife, a flashlight, filling my backpack with everything I know to survive the coming November days. I grab my zippo, fill it with fluid, stuff it into my pocket, go to the kitchen and take the second letter from the NRM Committee which gives Hal permission to enter Cogstin, and I head to the storage building. I am crying now as I fill the motorcycle with gas. I secure the pack, start the engine and pull the bike to the doorway. I know where I must go to find answers, to find Hal: to the city of Cogstin, Sector 17. I pull the note from my pocket, the note from the book of Cave Art: *FIND ME*. I don't know why, but I know they are all somehow connected: the book, the note, the visions in my head, the thing now buried in the salvage yard, all of it. I race toward the Cuyahoga River, the dawn just breaking the horizon.

Chapter Twelve

I feel the coolness from the river, a mist in the air as the sun moves above the gray horizon, and I pull up to the first gate, park my bike and head to the docks to see the harbor master. Mr. Tough is behind the desk, and when he sees me, he secures his thumbs in his belt. "Papers," he says, and his face is stern, mirrored aviators when no aviators are needed. He moves his lips awkwardly, and whether he wants to speak or trying to hold something back, I don't wait.

"I need information," I say.

He stares at me, and I see my anxious face in the mirrored aviators. "I'm looking for my Uncle: Hal Dante."

This registers, or perhaps it's a gas bubble, but Mr. Tough moves his lips again and says, "Dante."

"He was supposed to go to Sector 17," I say changing my tactics, "and...well, I sort of had too good of a time last night...if you know what I mean...and promised to meet him a little later."

Mr. Tough just stares at me. "Papers."

I hand him the letter from NRM, and he looks at me, then looks at the letter...back at me. "Yes, he came through here at five twenty-three this morning."

"Yeh, so, like I said, I'm supposed to meet him at sector 17."

"Highly irregular."

I'm starting to panic. My insides are jelly. Whoever took Hal is about to take me. *Easy. Think. Calm down and think.* "Why don't you scan the barcode. I'm telling you, this is a letter of special permission, and if I were you...well...I wouldn't want to be you when the NRM arrives."

Mr. Tough looks at the letter again, then at me. He scans the letter...and I am half waiting for several more Mr. Toughs to come through hidden doors and capture me. Instead Mr. Tough hands the letter to me. "You have permission to enter Cogstin."

"Of course, I do," I say, but my voice is hoarse, and it takes all I can do not to run away.

I gather my backpack, just as Mr. Tough grabs me tightly by the arm. "You have been assigned Boat 23, slip 7." He pulls me in the direction of the docks, releases me and walks away. I take the jon boat with an outboard motor, and soon I am heading up the misty, winding river toward the second gate.

Again, the cityscape is draped in fog. I wonder if it ever sees the light of the sun, if it ever has been filled with life, color, anything but ashes, dilapidated and crumbling ruins, and the reek of the dying and dead. As before with Hal, I turn the bend to my right, and see the sparks from acetylene torches, the metal workers masked in welding hoods. As I take the next bend, I come to the second gate. It is blacker and thicker and even more sinister than when I first saw it with Hal. There is the yellow-suited man with his legs spread apart, and the round copper frames of mirrored glass. He is holding an assault rifle with a banana clip. There is no one else around.

I think of turning the boat around, but I don't. I think of the warning texts and scrolling messages over the TV and tablets and phones the last several days. The jon boat pulls up to the dock, and Yellow Suit steps over and points the gun right at me.

"Step from the boat, Mr. Dante," Yellow Suit says through a mic.

"I need to tie up the bowline," I say, and I reach for my backpack, then turn.

"Leave everything in the boat. This is your final warning."

I raise my hands, and realize with astonishment the bowline has been tied already. I wobble and reel, walking unsteadily over the seats and onto the dock.

"Papers," Yellow Suit says. The copper rimmed lens on his yellow mask are goggle-like, like a deep-sea diver's helmet.

I hand him the paper. "They said the same thing at the first gate, and if you..."

That is all I can say because he has knocked me to the ground with the butt of his gun, the pain a white-hot heat upon my head. I know I am gashed and bleeding, my vision blurred as I blink rapidly and raise to all fours. He lifts me to my feet like I am as light as air, the grip around my bicep—a vice, and he tosses me forward so I collapse on the dock again, scraping my knee and bruising it.

"Hey!" I scream. "What are you doing? I'm here to see..."

My voice is cut off by a sweeping kick from Yellow Suit so hard the air is out of my lungs. I lay huddled in a fetal position, mouth opening and closing like a fish tossed onto dry land.

"Get up," Yellow Suit says in his mic'd voice, calm. "Get up."

He kicks me again in the back of my legs, spinning me like a top. I open my eyes and see Hal's barge tied to the inner dock and feel the fear overwhelming me. I try to stifle it, catch my breath and stand. Yellow Suit pushes me with the barrel of the gun, poke, poke, poke, and we walk together toward a darkened doorway. I know if I go through that space, I will never come out. Yellow Suit pokes me again, and this time, I sweep my right arm back, turn my body and tackle him. The yellow suit a thick, slick rubber. He struggles under my weight, and I punch as hard as I can right into his mask. Punch, punch, punch. I hear the glass break, the hiss of escaping gas, but on my next swing, I am caught from behind and thrown back toward the black doorway. My arm is bloody, sleeve torn and shredded. It is Agent Smiley who heaves me to my feet and tosses me into the opening—no emotion on his pale face, his tall frame stooping as he drags me through the threshold, down stone steps, my knees banging and bashing as I struggle to keep up with the terrible force pulling me. His grasp is merciless and iron-like. I think perhaps my shoulder is pierced through with talons so long they jut from my chest and back. I finally give up trying to step with his enormous, inhuman strides, down, down, down, down, and my head fogs from the pain and the terror. All I can hear are tormented screams and howls. I do not know if it is from me or helpless souls in hundreds of cells to my right and left. There is no light, no direction, just empty space. Agent Smiley tosses me into the stone cell so hard I am knocked unconscious from the blow and fall face first to the cold floor, a fleeting thought circling through the darkness: please, please, please, do not wake up.

I do wake up, slowly, synapses not quite sparking properly from the severe beating, circuits thawing, registering the damage throughout my body and the seriousness of my predicament. Someone is whimpering then howling in the cell next to me, a clinking of chains, as if he is suspended in midair.

"Help me," the voice says. "Oh, God, please help me. I don't want to die. Please." The voice loses its strength and fades to sobbing and jingling, the struggle for life fading.

My cell is pitch black, so black I cannot see my hands before me, nor my broken body. I feel them to make sure I'm actually in the world of men and time and things. It is cold, and I am shivering. My pants are soaked with my emptied bladder. I hear a noise to my left and move quickly to the opposite side until my back is against a stone wall, damp and cold.

"Who's there? Who are you? I've got...a knife. You come closer, and I'll kill you."

I sweep my hand out this way and that, but hits only empty air. Again, I hear the noise.

"Stay back! I warn you." That's when I remember the Zippo in my pocket. Is it still there? I grab it, pull it out, but my fingers are numb and swollen, so it falls to the floor. I crawl about and feel a hard-cylindrical object, recognize the iron shackles with wrist and ankles still attached and recoil in disgust.

I pull back in horror, reach out again, sweeping across the floor, and find it, flip it open, chip, chip, chip. Flash! The cell explodes in light, so bright it takes a moment for my eyes to adjust. The rat's stream across the floor, under the mounds of bones, rustling them, so many that the human carcasses seem to move on their own, and they disappear into the small hole in the corner. The rotted corpses are dried and weathered, their bodies preserved for decades in the earthen tomb, all broken and torn asunder in the same manner, a predator's gluttonous act of violence. The lighter becomes too hot to hold and I close the lid, hopping the metal case from one hand to the next.

I flip the lid again and spark the flame to life, investigating the walls, the stone door with bars, as the howling and pleading across the hallway begins again. The desperate struggle against the chains, now in anger, now remorse, then silence. Every time the light flashes, the rats disappear into the hole, reemerging when the flame goes out. I am panicked now, and my hands shake. I pull my legs up to my chest and huddle against the wall. An hour passes, perhaps a day, a week, a year. I am lost, my mind dark, and I fade into a restless sleep, shivering and alone.

Through my subconscious I hear the growl, the thudding, and in my imagination, I see the same vision I saw in Sector 17: the tunnel, the lumbering animals, tooth and claw as they race toward me. Unfortunately, this is not a dream. I hear the screams and pleas from the people trapped around me, as the doors are flung open, growls, howls, cracking, sputtering gasps as something gorges and tears. I pull the corpses across my body and hide, cover my ears and sob. I clamp my lips tight as I hear the sniffs, taloned feet or hands on stone. In my mind's eye I see Agent Smiley, a black void hovering over Hal in the storage building, his jaws opening wider, wider, wider still. They are outside my door now, grunting. I hear them pull on the steel bars, pull and shake the door in such violence the door may rip from the hinges.

Suddenly, from somewhere far away, beyond men and time and things, somewhere lost inside me or perhaps beyond the universe—I hear a whisper, subtle, slow, steady, increasing in force, a sound, a voice, a song, like a warm breeze in a sepulcher. I am crying now, and I cannot stop. The animals outside are pulling on the door, smashing into it with their shoulders, silt falling from the stones above.

The song is still there, louder now, a force, louder and louder. The animals outside howl then roar, clawing at the stone door, smashing more violently into it. The growls are groans, then whimpers, as the song transforms into a roaring thunderous waterfall of sound, power and violence. It is a deeply felt, piercing presence that fills the cell with resonance so that the stones above shake, the side walls shake, the door on its hinges shuddering. Still the song increases in pitch and intensity. It is no longer a song but a weapon that bursts the ear drums and penetrates steel, a beam, a shattering force that blows the stone door into fragments.

I scream against the violence, for fear it is Agent Smiley, taloned and fanged. There is only light in the doorway, then a shadow, walking closer, closer. I scream into the sound. A hand pulls away the corpses, the bones breaking as they move; another and another until I am lifted, propped from both sides and dragged out of the cell. The door next to mine is open, and I see...Hal chained and hanging naked from the ceiling. "Help me!" he says. "Help me," and he jangles the steel in frustration.

"Go! Go!" screams a voice. "They'll be back with force!"

They carry me down the hallway. Up and up and up and up until the gray of day and the warmth of the sun covers my face and limbs. I open my eyes, but can see very little. "Hal! Hal!" I cry. "You need to go back!"

"Shut him up!" Someone hisses from my side. My world goes black once again, as the hood is pulled over my face. To my horror, just before the darkness, I see a figure spraying an enormous butterfly over the door of the entrance to the cells. I have fallen from hell into the very jaws of the devil. IMAGO has taken me prisoner.

Part Two

IMAGO

Chapter Thirteen

The city of ashes, Cogstin, is not a metaphor. It is reality. Ashes sweep across the surface of the streets, settle on abandoned cars, collecting on rubble from ruined buildings. It is in the air, small jagged particulates that slice and splinter the lungs. There are places filled with smoke, literal ashes of ancient remains, spontaneously combusting from the radioactive hotspots deposited four hundred years earlier. The clouds are seeded with ashes, which swell, leak acid and ash upon the emaciated city, which evaporates in superheated clouds of gas, and the cycle continues all over again. Cogstin is a weather pattern, a self-contained eco-system of death and decay...

Or...at least that was what the NRM taught us since we could walk. So, my fear of where I am; the fear of who I am with; the terror of what will happen to me—these are real and present. Either it is from internal panic or the external environment, but whatever the case, I am gasping for breath under the canvas hood. We stop. A powerful hand shoves me to the ground. The hood comes off, and for the first time I can see my kidnappers.

They could not be farther from each other in form. Both have a ruthless quality about them, and both have large machetes strapped to their sides. I imagine the hacked limbs and torsos on the ancient table from sector 17. I understand it was they who acted out that heinous scene. Both wear leather masks—copper-rimmed goggles like Mr. Yellow's suit. They are cloaked in large military overcoats, knee length, split and tailed in the back. The fatter one has a collar up, the other, tall and thin, has it pressed down. They are huddled together near a fallen block wall, animated about something. The tall one pokes his finger into the chest of the fat one, and they seem to almost go to blows. Instead, both turn and face me. The fat one turns back to the tall lanky one and begins the waving all over again followed by the poking.

The smoke and ash cloud around us is so thick I soon bury my head between my legs. The tall thin man removes his backpack and carries it to me. He rummages through it, pulling out something floppy and discolored. He faces me, and I kick for my life. *I will not go down easily! You will not hack me into pieces. Not here!* I think. But it is useless to struggle, because the thin man is so strong.

I am pushed violently against the wall. A knife is to my throat before I can even react. I squint through the stinging, biting ash and wind to see a masked-face nose to nose with me. I feel his acrid breath against my lips. In one quick motion, he pulls something over my head. I too now wear a face mask with copper-rimmed glass. My breath calms, my eyes blink open. I can see clear and bright through the dark ash, the lens modified to collect and filter the light, the place about my mouth now filtering the saturated air. I hear my kidnappers breathing through the mic'd earpieces.

"Let's move, pal," says the fat one. "We've still got a long way to go."

We set off, the fat one leading, the thin one behind, and we scurry intentionally across the exposed streets and creep with senses heightened through the abandoned and wrecked buildings, halting at the doorways, scurrying again across another street, into another building, again and again and again. After an hour of this, we come to the cement and iron-railed banks of the Cuyahoga River. North of us is a bridge, heavily guarded. I realize now we are actually in Sector 17. I see the familiar buildings where Hal salvaged the corrugated metal, pulverized old masonry, trucked it to the barge.

"Stay down," the fat one says. I watch him lithely hop the stone wall and reappear several blocks ahead. I think: *how did he get there so fast?*

"Let's go," says the thin one and shoves me hard in the back. We creep under dilapidated roofs, squeeze through holes in walls, sidle against door jams, and finally squat down only thirty yards from the bridge guards. They are dressed in black body armor, helmets with face mirrored shields.

In their hands they carry assault rifles strapped around their necks. Five of them in all stand like cemented pillars.

That's when I see the fat terrorist with his military coat, splayed out. He carries a knife in one hand and something else in the other, his knapsack now on only one shoulder, unzipped. Slowly he creeps to the edge of a metal wall, crouches low, then quickly starts to wave his hand about. I see he is not waving...he is spray painting graffiti! One bottle after another. It is beautiful and bright, and shadowed, a figure, nearly three dimensional and standing upright with his hands raised in surrender. I realize I am unable to distinguish the fat man from the drawn image until the original steps back. The fat man whistles loudly, and leaps on the wall with no effort, jumps on the other side just as several guards come around the corner, both seeing the surrendering figure and drawing their guns in alarm. I watch as the fat terrorist emerges on the bridge, and with several strokes from his machete, the guards fall headless, a white liquid spurting from the cavity. He moves silent and quick, too quick for girth, and surprises the guards near the picture, cutting their legs, then stabbing them ruthlessly in the neck, again the white liquid pools where they lie.

I want to scream, but my breath is caught in my throat. They had lives before today. They had children, perhaps, waiting for them tonight, wives, a lover. Now they are no more. A great sadness comes over me, and I refuse to move.

"I said let's go," says the thin one sternly. He shoves me hard. I do not get up. "There will be others soon. Let's go!"

"You'll have to kill me," I say defiantly, staring up into the brown mask and the copper-rimmed goggles of the terrorist.

The thin man stands there with his hands on his hips. He looks over to the fat terrorist and shrugs, then points to me. The fat terrorist shrugs. "I don't have time for this," says the thin terrorist and he grabs me by the back of my coat and hoists me up as if I was a toddler of three years old. He throws me over his shoulder like a sack of wheat. He carries me kicking and screaming across the street, down the bridge and into the gloom, sirens and more guards only now arriving behind us. I can hear them shouting: "You! Near the wall! Don't move. Keep your hands where we can see them." ...then a burst of gunfire.

The night is long and now we are running faster between buildings, hiding longer in the shadows, the sounds of guards closer and closer. It is soon obvious to all we cannot outrun them. The thin terrorist throws his pack down and hurries into the darkness. He grabs metal sheeting and wooden spindles empty of wire, throws them into a pile and disappears again into an adjacent building.

I look around at the high walls, the two openings. We are trapped. The fat terrorist unclips his pack, and when the thin man returns, this time with a shopping cart filled with materials of all sorts: wires, metal hinges, a pot lid, empty paint cans and bundles of cloth—when he returns, they set to their work. They do not speak, one anticipating the other's movements. The thin man pulling material and bending, draping, securing this and that. The fat one spraying with his paint, sweeping his arms back and forth, stuffing one can in the sack, then pulling out another—efficient, quick.

"Get in," says the thin man and pushes me into a hole in the constructed thing. "Huddle up toward the back. Now! Do as I say!"

I obey and pull my knees up to my chest, just as the fat terrorist squeezes through the opening, shortly followed by the other. I hear the dogs whining and growling as they sense our presence. The fat man raises his index finger to his mask where his mouth should be.

"They're close," says a guard. "There's only two ways out of here." I can hear the body armor as it moves against itself. The guard closest to us tapping the butt of his rifle with his fingers. A platoon of men with dogs enters the walled space. "You smell something, Caesar?" says the leader to his dog.

I feel the sweat beading on my face, rolling down my brow, stinging my eyes, making them blink. For some reason I think of the book of cave art, the gazelle, head bent eating the charcoal strands of grass. It hears the dog and jerks its head up, the scent of death in the air...and then...bounds away!

"What was that?" Says a guard.

"They're on the run!"

"Release the dogs! Caesar, Go! The perimeter is secured! Stay sharp!"

The dogs howl and bark, and the noise disappears far into the distance. The fat man raises his hand palm out motioning me to stay put. Two guards stand only inches from us, their shadows stark against the cloth.

"Did you hear that?" says one guard. "Shine your light over here."

Suddenly a full beam of light casts upon us, and I know it is just a matter of crawling out at gunpoint. The thin terrorist raises his arm slowly, thumb tucked under the fingers, palm down, ever so slowly, vertically, thumb and fingers moving now as though he was rubbing something away.

"A snake," hisses a guard. "It's a snake!"

The thin terrorist reaches for a paint can, silently lifts it and shakes it two times.

"Scan for biofeedback."

"Where?"

"There it is!" The flashlight beam swings wildly. "It's over there."

"Where?"

"Nothing here," says one.

He quickly leaves the enclosed area, the other following behind.

We are in complete darkness. We wait, and wait, and wait, and then the thin terrorist rolls out of the enclosure. The fat man is next to him as I crawl out.

"The camp is only a mile from here," says the fat man. "What the hell were the dogs chasing? That's some good fortune."

"No such thing as good fortune," says the thin terrorist. "Let's go."

They suit back up, and while the fat man ties his boot, I glance over at the constructed thing we crawled out of. I cannot find it. All I see is a mound of trash: abandoned roller skates, a shoe with its toe blown out, an abandoned freezer, the door nearly torn from its hinges, a toilet without a lid, a downed power line ending in a puddle of water, overturned paint cans, a porn magazine, moldy and torn. I realize that I was looking at the container, a stage prop for live theater.

We hurry out of the enclosure and across the streets, following the guards who are pursuing something else, somewhere else. The thin man suddenly stoops to the ground, his fingers pressing into the mud. "They're fresh."

"Can't be," says the fat terrorist. "They've been extinct for hundreds of years."

"Not this one," says the thin man.

He stands, looks right at me, then back into the distance where the tracks disappear from view.

We turn from here and head in the opposite direction. When we arrive to the camp, there is a small fire and a small figure dressed in the same large overcoat and discolored mask with copper-rimmed goggles.

"It's all I could do not to kill him," says the thin terrorist.

He hands this other man my pack that contains the book.

"Not until he's tested," says the figure by the fire. The voice is raspy, hidden behind static. "If he fails that. Well, that will be the easiest of our problems to solve." The figure stands. "Quick thinking in the enclosure. Good work."

"The snake was in the moment."

"Oh, a snake this time, Stutz?"

"The porn mag was stupid, Caravaggio," says Stutz, the thin terrorist, to the fat one. "Stupid ruins everything we've worked for."

"Hey," Caravaggio argues, "it all worked out. It was dark. No one saw it."

"This is not the first time," says Stutz.

The tone in the camp suddenly turns sour. The leader raises his hand. "Enough. Better judgment next time." Caravaggio lowers his head. "Just having some fun."

"Fun is something we cannot afford." He continued, "I've secured the perimeter," says the leader. "We need to make an early start tomorrow. The sooner the test, the sooner we'll know."

They sit me down near the fire, give me some dried meat and a tin cup of clean water. It is tasty and satisfying. I feel the weight of the day settling upon me like a heavy blanket. I stare into the flames and drift off to sleep. The three huddle together discussing something, the shadows from the light hide their faces. My last thought is of the cave wall, the hunters around the fire and the mad storyteller chanting and drawing the terror of the prison and the Black Gate away.

Chapter Fourteen

When I awake, I find myself completely naked, laying on my side and bound to a metal table, leather manacles squeezing my ankles together, my wrists pulled forward so my biceps straddle my chin, a wide leather strap across my waist. My breathing is staccato, panting, my mouth stuffed with a cotton cloth. I can hear voices behind me.

"His genitals are intact."

"This is not surprising. Remember twenty-five?"

"How can I forget."

"His heart rate has spiked."

I feel a breath next to my ear. A black fear, thick like fog, a deep dread has settled upon me, and I am unable to control anything.

"Calm down," the voice whispers in my ear.

It is familiar, and I recognize it as the leader of IMAGO from last night. "Either you calm your heart rate and steady your breath, or you will die. Neither of these outcomes concern us."

I am angry now, the fear subsiding to a flight response. I struggle, but can barely move.

"Did I not win the bet," says another voice. "I told you. Did I not call this one? Time for the quick goodbye."

"Not yet," says the leader. With an authority: "I said, not yet."

I pant and wheeze, grit my teeth and explode once again against the bindings.

"Hold him down, damnit!"

A hand presses on my cheek. It is the leader's voice. "If you move again, it will be your last." He holds a blade next to my right eye. "Do you understand?"

I nod. I concentrate on my breath. In and out. In and out. In and out. I feel a cold, wet cloth at the base of my spine, but do not flinch, the blade the size of an airplane's wing to my eye. Breathe in and out, in and out, in and out—and then a stabbing pain into my spinal cord so deep, so intense, so white hot my whole body shudders. I scream as loud as I can through the wadded cotton cloth in my mouth.

"How long? He's blacking out."

"Almost...through..."

This is the last I hear, for I disappear into darkness. I dream of conversations, muffled, intense. Someone is angry, resistant. I feel tugging and tearing, pricks like electrical current making my forehead explode, my eyes bulge, something slender and dexterous, penetrating my skull plate, piercing the soft sponge of my frontal lobe and into flesh beyond. I think the pain cannot get worse, but it does, a new sensation of heat and light. I realize I am not in control of my body now. This dream body extruding and releasing as it sees fit. All of this like a vague memory, swarming like a cloud of insects about my unconscious self, a separate moment. I cease to care, floating now in a pool of black.

When I awake, it is dark outside, and my body pulses and stabs from various, concrete locations: my temples, my left forearm, my left side, my groin. There are tears in my eyes that leak into the stubble on my cheeks and chin. I feel the soft pressure of a tissue against my skin. My head, hands and feet are still tied down, but I am now in a surgical gown lying on my back on a comfortable mattress.

"The tests are nearly complete" says the leader.

I now understand that it is not a man, but a woman. She steps into my sightline, and sits down next to the IV drips and monitors near the front of the bed.

"What did you do to me?" I whisper, and my voice sounds faded and weak.

"Only what was necessary," she says.

She has short cropped hair, a densely woven cotton scarf around her neck, with the familiar NRM checkered military pattern, faded grey, a leather coat hiding the rest of her body. Her face is gaunt, pointy cheekbones, eyes sunken from malnutrition and hard living, black rings like bruises blending into the nearly permanent goggle impressions.

"What do you want?" I say.

She smiles slightly, a true reflection like a surfacing fish that disappears somewhere back into the depths. "Only the truth."

"Are you going to kill me, like you did all those others?"

She is silent for a moment. She stands. "Perhaps. That is not up to me."

She steps up to the IV drip and hooks up a bag with a blue solution in it and walks out of the room, closing the door behind her. Within several minutes, I am groggy, uncertain, and calm, numb, drifting back into the pool of darkness.

Once again, I awake, eyelids opening into the intense light then closing, then opening. I am no longer in my room, but on an operating table, in a half-sitting position, arms secure, legs secure. Around my shaved head is a metal halo with many wires streaming from the crown. I can feel the pressure where it is screwed into my scalp. I close my eyes again, for it is too much trouble to leave them open...my will to fight is gone.

"I need you awake, Mr. Dante," says a voice near my ear.

There is no sympathy or kindness. It is flat, cold and matter of fact. "Increase the Adderall." A minute passes, and I am hyper aware of my surroundings, my senses exploding.

"What can you smell, Mr. Dante?" Says the voice. "Lilacs, perhaps. Cinnamon?"

As he speaks the words, I smell them, subtle hints of burnt wood with cherry overtones, lavender, rose, the green grass with dew...all of it.

"What are you feeling?" says the voice in my left ear, still matter of fact, even stern. "Coldness on your toes, as if you have stepped on ice? Now sand, the water warm...and now...hotter...hotter...red hot coals?"

I cringe, then breathe in short pants as the searing pain burns my flesh.

"We are ready," says the voice, and he steps into the light to adjust something on the metal halo.

I see his wrinkled face, gaunt, silver stubbled cheeks with thin lips for a mouth. His glasses are perched on his bald head, a ring of matching silver hair on the sides. He wears a white lab coat with food stains, blood stains, grime at the cuffs and neckline. My senses are so heightened I can tell he is worried about something, I see and understand the minute facial features: the subtle line at the corner of his mouth, the small pulse of blood in the raised temple vein, the slight tightening of his right jaw muscle.

There are others in the room. Stutz sits at a computer terminal, his thin back moving ever so slightly as he types and adjusts various monitors.

The leader is standing next to the doctor, and Caravaggio is sitting in the corner, his large body hunched forward with his elbows resting on his knees.

"Prepare the sensor," says the doctor

"Ready."

"Insert it in the docking station."

I feel pressure as something attaches to the left side of the metal halo.

Something pierces the side of my head. I hear it hiss, a piston releasing, and a shiver convulses my entire body. There is no pain, just pressure, a sense of violation, my eyes wide.

"Attach blue sensors." Another hiss, and I feel a great push on my forehead, like someone testing the pressure of a soccer ball.

"Blue sensors attached."

"Attach red Sensors," says the doctor.

Again, a hiss and pressure on the left side of my head.

"Red sensors attached."

"Caravaggio!" yells the leader. "Sponges, damnit! You know what that will do to the contact points."

Caravaggio is now pressing cotton gauze to my head, tossing the red-soaked material into a pail, applying another and another and another. Everyone stops what they are doing, and gathers around my head. I feel the release of pressure and hear a sucking sound, like a boot pulled from the mud.

"You hit the artery," says the leader.

"Press here," says the doctor. "Harder! Okay...now release. Again. Keep pressing. Good."

The sense of panic evaporates. I can tell whatever they did to my head has worked. The pressure returns, and all return to their appointed places: the keyboard and monitors, the IV drip bag near me.

"Ready," says the leader.

"Begin frontal scan one," says the doctor.

That is when I feel the pain. Unlike cutting, slicing or lopping off appendages...which I would imagine the worst pain possible...this is something internal, personal, violating...that kind of pain. At first, I can hear them talking, but the sound muffles and disappears as though my head has been plunged under water. I am sitting in the white room with the white chaise lounge staring through the wall-to-wall glass at the great blue water beyond me.

I feel a slight prick in the core of my brain, a prick that expands, like tiny undulating ripples in a pond. I realize it is not ripples. It's more like doors opening, one after the other, forgotten doors, doors closed for long periods of time, locked doors, heavily fortified, and opened with a simple click. I am no longer focusing on the pain, although the pain is still present, even intense at times... I am more interested in the doors, one after the other—opening, contents purged, then the next and next, and I see in my imagination a vast infinitely layered space filled with floor after floor after floor and all with millions of doors, row after row after row, and each opening one at a time, the content extracted. I ponder the number of floors and doors, the opening, the extracting, and I realize I know every door, every floor...but how is this possible? No one can have this many memories. No one can remember so many opened doors. Just as this realization settles upon me, I notice an expanding distance between me and the floors and doors, like the sky on a starry night—it gets further and further away, and then I am in the white room again, sitting on the chaise lounge staring at the glass before me and the deep blue has surrounded me. I am submerged, and the glass begins to crack. At first, they are small, hairline things, then a spiderweb of cracks filling my vision, some seeping water, others bowing from the pressure. An explosion of water and shards of glass, and I am now a deep-sea diver seeing the surface and stroking hard, but knowing I have not the air to survive the depth.

Buzzing. Beeping. Alarms. These ring about me, but I am concentrating on the small patch of light and the thin lip of water. I know I must be constant: stroke after stroke; one—two; one—two; one—two. Still the alarms, the buzzing, the beeping. Now they are layered with voices, screams, some commanding, some helpless.

"I don't understand," says a voice.

"We're beyond terabytes now!"

"What's the capacity?"

"Reaching one thousand and twenty-four petabytes," the voice says without emotion.

"We don't have the capacity."

"But you said!"

"I know what I said, Damn it!"

"He is resisting the probe."

"How? How can he do that?"

"I don't know. Quiet please. Let me think."

The plane of light expands before me, but I know it is too little, too late, the darkness below reaching up to my ankles like great hands to pull me down. Stroke after stroke. One—two; one—two; one—two. A hundred feet. Fifty feet. It might as well be a thousand, the surface a heavy lid pressing me down. I know I will die. That is when I hear the voice, the familiar voice: *Sing to me, Oh Muse! Sing!*

I remember the lion from the cave lying motionless in the pit. I did that! I can do that!

Do That!

I imagine a rope, and it is there. I pull it hard, but I cannot make the distance. I imagine fins, and my hands and feet are fish-like in their engineering and beauty, still I cannot reach the surface. *Sing!* The fear and doubt, panic...there is...laughter! It is simple, wonderful—so, so simple. *Imagine yourself above the water!* I do and I am there, back in the white room, sitting on the white chaise lounge, staring at the great blue of the horizon. I am exhausted, all the energy in every molecule of my being exhausted. My eyes begin to close.

"Vitals are flat lining, Doctor!"

"Clear!"

"Nothing!"

"Clear!" The doctor says.

"Nothing!"

"Adrenaline! Now!" the doctor screams.

I feel a great spike enter my chest, a rush of power and energy and breath surge through my lungs, my limbs. I break into the world of men and time and things. I am laughing, a joyous robust mirth that shakes my body like electrical pulses shooting from finger to toes, making me roar and laugh. Stutz and the Leader are screaming and holding my head. Caravaggio holds my legs, and the Doctor fumbles. He inserts the needle into my IV. All I can do is laugh like a lunatic because I don't understand what is happening to me, don't understand the lion in the pit, don't understand Hal under the truck, or IMAGO, or the tests or what I just did in my mind.

That night when I awaken, I see a hooded figure cast in shadow sitting in the corner. I don't know if it is a nightmare come to life or a sentinel set to guard me. Just before I fall back into an opioid sleep, I hear soft music, a song of sorts, coming from the figure. Soon I am back into the darkness of my eternal mind.

Chapter Fifteen

SING TO ME, OH MUSE! Screams a voice in my head, and I wake up. I lay in the bed, my body throbbing. Each pulse of pain from my side, my neck, the biceps of each arm, my chest, follows closely with my probing fingers lightly touching, exploring, identifying more stitches, more lumped and swollen flesh. I feel a lot like a shredded and discarded rag doll sewn carelessly back together. The halo is gone from my head, replaced with small holes and a feeling like I have been skewered with white hot needles. I notice the catheter snaking to one of many bags on the metal post next to me. I'm exhausted, in pain, and drift off into uneasy sleep. I wake—time has been abandoned—and see the same figure of my nightmares, hooded, cloaked in the shadow of the room, that same soft music. I think it is a different tongue... I fall back into a dreamless sleep.

When I awake, the fat terrorist, Caravaggio, is sitting in the dimly lit corner. He has a Cheshire grin on his face. His beard is auburn, wild, like uncut grass, his mustache pronounced and huge sweeping out at the corners of his lips. He wears a brown leather skull cap on his head. The seat looks like a child's play thing, his body large and expansive, not fat like Hal, but big...big hands, forearms, a barrel chest. I wonder how he sat down on the chair.

"Some way to wake up, eh pal?" Caravaggio says. "Out of the dream and... Pow! Wires, tubes and metal crowns. From where I'm sitting—whew. You're one fine mess." He scratches his cheek, burying his thumb and forefinger into the beard, probing, pulling something out, observing it, rubbing it into oblivion. "Tough place," he says, almost to himself. "Thousands of decisions, and everyone a potential trap."

"Where am I? What do you want from me?" I say, trying to leverage myself, but the pain and effort is too great, and I sink back down into the bed.

Caravaggio is there, propping my pillow, adjusting my IV's. I close my eyes for a second to manage the pain, turn my head to address him, but he is sitting in the corner of the room again, his smile gone, eyes serious, chin in hand, body awkwardly hunched forward.

"That's an interesting question," he ponders. "What do *I* want?" He continues to stare at me. "Now the easier question to answer is *where* are you? That I can answer pretty clearly." He sits back and expands his arms wide. "Why, you are in a room with tubes and wires hanging off of you like some damn Frankenstein experiment. The room is located in a secluded facility somewhere in Cogstin, all hidden so *they* can't find you." He looks satisfied with himself.

I breathe deeply, the pain wracking my body, and slowly breathe out.

"There is no other way, I'm afraid," Caravaggio says. "They need all of it or the tests don't work. It's just the way it is."

"What did you take from me?"

"Well, sort of...a bit of everything, really: Spinal fluid, blood, heart tissue, and liver, kidney, and lung biopsies...bone marrow for skeletal structural analysis..." He hunches forward again and taps his chin, then smacks the armrest with a thud; triumphant. "Brain cells! Damnit if I don't always forget that one. Yeh, that's pretty much it."

"Why?" I ask.

He scratches his beard again. "Now that's more complicated, I'm afraid. Let's just say if the tests come out positive...then they don't kill you."

I'm almost too tired to respond, but I do anyway. "And?"

"Yours were...inconclusive. Yeh, that's probably the more accurate way to say it." He stands up. "Hey, pal, listen. It's not as bad as all that. Why the tears? It's not like they'll come in here while you're asleep and garrote you...well, that has happened...but, hey, hey hey, calm down...you'll pull those tubes right out of you."

He is by my bed now and the power of his hand upon my chest is so great I cannot move. He puts his finger to his lips and looks toward the door. "Pal, listen. I'm your friend in all of this. I'm the one..."

Just then the door opens and in steps the tall, thin, harsh terrorist named Stutz. He looks pissed.

"What are you doing in here?" he says to Caravaggio.

Caravaggio winks at me, his hand still upon my chest, and turns toward Stutz. "I heard him cry out. He's all up in arms. I just thought I'd...you know... See if I could help."

"You know the rules. Protocol One: Authorized personnel only during the analysis phase."

Caravaggio turns sympathetically to me. "Does he look like a Protocol One to you?" He winks again at me, lifts his hand, then turns back to Stutz. "Okay, okay, okay. I'm leaving." With that, he walks out the door.

Stutz looks around the room warily, steps to my bed and analyzes the monitor, adjusts the IV drip and switches my catheter bag.

"What did he want?" Stutz says coldly.

I don't like this man, his demeanor, his tone. I don't like his craggy and worn features, his beak nose or large ears. He probably *did* garrote someone while they were sleeping. "Nothing," I say in a whisper. "I was screaming and he came in."

"Why were you screaming?" Stutz says, like he's coldly observing a microscope slide.

"Because half of me is gone. Why do you think?"

"Nonsense," Stutz says. "You're being dramatic."

"What do you want from me?"

Stutz purses his lips, adjusts the IV drip and picks up the full excrement bag. He turns and walks out the door, closing and locking it behind him.

~ * ~

Later that evening...I assume it is evening though time has stopped for me in here. I begin to recall the subsequent events that led me to this place. They are fuzzy at best, I can't help wonder if the drugs and the operations were not meant to do just that. I remember the salvage yard and the backhoe, remember Hal being taken away. I am not sure why and what I was doing out in the yard. I remember some sort of flowers...sunflowers, and I know that fact is significant, the edges that define the memories all but faded. I remember an urgency to pursue Hal. I remember Agent Smiley at the Black Gate and Hal in chains below. I calm my breathing, trying to keep the heart rate monitor from going off and sending Stutz back in...who maybe this time will silence me forever. What tests? What did they want? What did *inconclusive* mean? The heart rate monitor beeps, and I calm my breathing: in and out; in and out; in and out...until the alarm stops. I need to get out of here. Cogstin, as hostile and unwelcoming as it is, would be a welcome relief from the threat of violence, experiments, and terrorists.

It is Caravaggio who brings me food. Potato soup, some hardened bread. He places it on a tray near me, the typical hospital type with swinging arm. The soup is like gruel with small floating white chunks, but I'm famished and scoop it into my mouth, slurping and dribbling, sopping up the broth with the bread.

"Well, Pal," Caravaggio whispers, "They're keeping me at arm's length, but have you thought more about the plan?"

I look up from the food.

"The plan," he hisses, then puts his fingers to his lips.

"What plan?" I ask.

Caravaggio looks frustrated. He sits down in the small chair with a humph and crosses his arms. "All this time I'm thinking about the plan. I'm thinking how to implement it, how to execute it, the end game, the middle game, all the games." He stands up and points. "Now I find out you're not even thinking about it...doesn't come to your...head...." he pokes his forehead. "Apparently you like laying here and being served or thinking in solitude or whatever you seem to be doing while I'm strategizing and working out what Hal said...It's like juggling chainsaws and..."

"You know Hal?" I push the tray away from me and sit up the best I can. "You've talked to him?"

Caravaggio stares at me, intense, deep creases above his brows, one hand stroking the wild, wiry beard. "Of course, I know him. Why wouldn't I know him? You know him. I know him. Let's have a party about knowing

Hal." He looks angry now.

"Hal knows I'm here?" I say, understanding that Caravaggio is getting more and more agitated and crazier, and more inarticulate as this conversation goes on. "So, when do we meet him?"

Caravaggio stops gesticulating and pacing and strokes his beard again. "That's the plan. To meet him." He hurries over to me and pokes my chest. "Now you're on point, pal." Those pokes are like stones falling on me. I grunt. "Sorry," he says pulling away. "Never remember that. Sorry, pal." He stops, stands up, turns to the door, then back to me. "I'll be in touch." He smiles a big Cheshire cat grin again, winks and hurries out of the room. Five minutes later Stutz comes in with a tray of potato soup. I act like I'm asleep, stir when he enters and look at him.

He is dressed in his typical military trench coat. His goggles are around his neck, dirt rings around his eyes, and his narrow, craggy face like leather from too much in the sun. His hair is straw, silver streaked and black.

"Who brought you soup?" he questions. He looks around.

"I don't know. I was asleep."

Stutz blinks, face of stone, eyes small and black. "You eat soup in your sleep?"

"What do you want?" I say, my tone severe, annoyed.

"I want to bring you soup, but someone already has. You have eaten it, and now you are lying to me."

"I told you..."

"Yes...we have established: you were asleep." Stutz has not moved. "Who brought you soup?"

"I'm tired," I say and half close my eyes.

Stutz pivots, walks to the door, then calmly places the tray of soup and bread onto the chair. He is beside me before I can blink; one calloused hand on my cheek, the other under my throat. I feel the steel blade cutting, like a razor near my esophagus. The heart rate monitor is beeping rapidly. "There is a pit beyond the compound. The bodies are mounded and rotting, and the crows and carrion birds feast. You will be taken to that mound, your head laying on your thighs. I will count to three: Who gave you the soup? Two...."

"Caravaggio," I wheeze. "Caravaggio!" The heart rate monitor is chirping louder and louder. Another alarm goes off. "What did he say to you?"

"Nothing! He sat in the chair and said nothing." I say, and believe with all my heart the knife will glide across my throat. I wonder what death will feel like. I think of the pit, the crows pecking and tearing. Surprisingly, there is no slicing. Stutz pulls away. He stands, calmly, and he walks toward the door.

"You may eat that second helping, if you're still hungry," he says without turning around. He locks the door behind him.

Chapter Sixteen

Another night passes, perhaps days, weeks. I have been forgotten by the world. The dream I have is wonderful, terrible and unlike anything I have ever experienced. I am running in a field of sunflowers, their black and yellow heads following me like they do the sun. I exit the field and turn, hands raised like a conductor of an orchestra, the stalks obey, stiff, straight, black seed faces with yellow borders toward me. I wave my hands, and the endless field sings so joyously, something like singing, but not singing, a hymn to Nature, to everything living...to me! I understand, now, completely, a geographical pinpoint of longitude and latitude—I understand that this is the city of Cogstin before The Event. This is me, some form of me that I have never known. I am happy. I am in awe...I understand I am from the outside. That is when I hear it.

It is the thunder of a waterfall, a tornado, a landslide of sound so powerful the earth beneath me shifts, but it is not the earth shifting. I understand it in the dream logic. It is something else, something from here, born in the world of men and time and things, born from fire and pain, a terrible power, an ink-black darkness, sweeping across the distant field, slicing and hacking, pounding and sweeping the sunflower stalks down, burning them to ash. I know I cannot stop it. I know that the power of the song cannot stop it. I see the endless field, a once glorious hymn, now a burning holocaust of smoke and ash. A desert, a plain of forgetting and sorrow. Now I am alone in the world.

I blink awake to the same figure sitting in the corner. The figure is humming softly, and when she sees me stir, she pulls back the hood. It is only now that I recognize her as being the terrorist leader.

"Who are you?" She asks. Her voice is quiet, calm.

"You tell me."

"Tests can be...inconclusive."

"I'm sure my body would disagree."

She stares at me, scanning my reactions, like some wary animal. Finally she speaks again, "Do you hear The Voice?"

Of course, I hear The Voice, I want to say. *I've heard it from the beginning. I hear it every day, all day long. The Voice! The Voice! The damn voice and the white room and the blue water beyond the glass!* Instead, I say, "Now you think I'm crazy. Is that what your tests concluded?"

"Would it distress you to find that you are not?" she says.

"Not what?"

"Sane. Sanity and reality are rarely ever more than an illusion." She stares at me again. Several minutes of silence. "Tell me about your past. Can you recall your childhood?"

I think back, and whether it was caused by the halo and testing or the panic of the moment, I think back and see Hal, bowler hat, pipe in mouth, wind blowing his trench coat and tie. I see him again with a full beard, large bushy thing dark and sculpted. He is standing by a horse and an ancient buggy. He is laughing, eyes a squint of flesh. I feel like leaping from the bed and running, but there is nowhere to go.

"Your childhood, Mr. Dante."

"I can't recall."

"No matter," she says, "Tell me about the book," She is a shadowed stone in the corner.

Now we're getting to it, I think. *What does she know about the book of Cave Art? What could she possibly care about it? Did she put it there? Was this a trap?* "I have no idea what you're talking about," I say.

"The formulas. The text. Is it familiar? Do you understand its purpose? What happens when you read the equations? What do they mean to you?"

I saw the past! I saw the ancients! I stopped a lion in midair and changed him into a flower! "Again, I have no idea what you're talking about," I say. I fake like my arm itches and scratch the fake itch to distract from the pointed question.

"I don't believe you," she says.

"You just kidnapped and tortured me..."

"Rescue."

"What?"

"We rescued you. We did not kidnap you."

I laugh out loud for effect. I stop because it hurts my body and head too much.

"Few leave the prison cells below the Black Gate."

I think of Agent Smiley, of him dragging me deep below the earth, throwing me into the cold, dark cell. I think of the monsters coming for me, the sounds of crunching bone and tearing flesh; the screams. That horror is so real, so present, I want to weep, I want to say thank you, but I don't. "You left my Uncle Hal. You just left him. He was chained up and those...those things were coming."

She stares at me again, that wary animal stare, or more like some computer scanning my facial features and body movements...whatever it is, the silence gives the room a sense of dread.

"Sometimes the many must die so the few can live."

"You killed Hal. You killed all those civilians on TV, all those soldiers. I saw you do it. You cut them down like they were...like they were...."

"Yes," she says unapologetically. No explanation, no sympathy.

"So, those lives for your damn...what...crusade against NRM?"

"Not lives."

"So, they are not lives now? What, you are the scales of justice now?"

"A scale might not be the right metaphor, Mr. Dante."

I grow silent and turn my head. "What do you want from me?"

"That's not the right question."

"I'm tired."

"What did you see that day in Cogstin with your Uncle, that day in Sector 17?"

I think back to that day, the low buzzing noise that turned into a song. I remembered the smell of the burning flesh, the doorway to the dilapidated building, paint or blood swept over the door posts. I remember going in and seeing the altar, the acrid smoke irritating my eyes as well as the strange vision of Agent Smiley and another lumbering toward me down a tunnel...the fear in the room. "I don't know what you mean," I say.

"The altar," she says. "What did you see on the altar?"

My face flushes white, and I feel a coldness sweep over my body. My stomach is nauseous and bile rises in my throat.

"What do you see there, Mr. Dante? You did recognize those limbs, the heads."

My head is light, and I can feel my heart rate race, the alarm beeping louder and louder in my ear. I fight against a will so powerful, so suffocating, it is all I can do to stay conscious. "I don't know what you're talking about."

"There! On the altar! What do you see?" Her voice is authoritative, stern.

I remember falling back, panicked and pulling myself from the small building, feeling the sense something terrible was feasting on the contents of the altar. My head feels light and I lay back as if falling into a pit, helpless.

Stutz opens the door and quickly enters the room. The leader raises her hands to him as if to say, *I didn't touch anything*.

"We're through for the day," she says to him.

"I told you this would not work." Stutz says as he turns off the alarm and adjusts the gauges on the monitor.

"Prepare the *Confrontation Station*," she says and stands up. "It's a shame. I really thought this would go differently."

Stutz and the leader walk out of the room, locking the door behind them.

~ * ~

An hour later, Caravaggio enters the room. He is panicked, sweat on his fleshy brow. "You've screwed the pooch, pal." He is animated, arms waving about, eyes shifting to the door, to me, to the door again. "We need to get out of here before your mind is Jell-O." He makes a crazy person's face, "like a zombie or something. I thought for sure she would break you," he says. "I thought for sure, but you didn't break. Good for you!" He pats me on the chest, the power evident again in his hands. "But this next bit is a real mind noodle. Nobody makes it past that. Jell-O brains. We got to get you out of here." He turns to the door to leave, then turns back. "Don't let'm trick you. Remember, it's all a trick, an illusion, like...like a magic show. Don't believe any of it." He pauses, knocks on his head with his knuckle. "Oh, right. Act normal. Whatever you do...act normal. I was never here." He places his fingers to his lips and hurries out of the room. Another several days pass, and I do not see anyone save Stutz who brings me my meals and acts annoyed at the task. After dropping off the soup and bread—just like that, like talking about the weather—he says, "You're free to leave."

Chapter Seventeen

Well, after everything else, it was not unexpected: Stutz is being less than forthright. He tells me I am free to leave, but he means the room. So, I eat, grab a coat from the rack, and for the first time since my kidnapping, I walk through the door and into the corrugated metal hallway. My wounds have healed nicely, and though the stitches are present, they itch rather than hurt. My head throbs whenever I move it rapidly, but my mind is clear. My senses explode as I exit the hallway and step outside. I see before me an enormous, pitch black body of water, gray foam rolling onto the black pebbled and sandy shore. It is a horizon-less lake of what could be oil or ink. I can barely take it in. The breeze is stiff and cold on my face, but after so long inside, I feel a sense of space, a sense of freedom as false as that may be. The leader, her short black hair matted by the wind, stands on a ledge reading from a book, the dim light of dusk lingering across the horizon.

"Aren't you afraid I'll escape?" I say.

She looks up, then back at her book. Her goggles are on her forehead and her leather coat is spattered with dust from the city. I notice she has no weapon like the others. "My name is Beatrice," She says. She points to the water: "Eels the size of boats out there." She points behind her without looking: "Undetectable walls surrounding our perimeter. There is a way out. If you look for it, Stutz or Caravaggio would cut you in half before you even find it." She pauses for a moment before continuing, "Do you believe in gods, Mr. Dante?" she says, now looking at her book. I recognize the cover. It is the book from sector 17.

"*A* god?" I say, still trying to look for the perimeter walls. "I guess I've never considered more than one, but *many* is just as good as one the way I see it."

"Sing to me, oh Muse..."

My heart races. I stare at her in disbelief. It is the song in my head! She continues with her eyes closed, face toward the water so it is hard to hear in the stiff breeze.

"...of the man full of sorrows
who wanders the Plains of Ashes
To bring us the Light of Life.

"You should know these words. You wrote them." Beatrice says, suddenly standing up. "They are old, Mr. Dante, from just after The Event. They are...a way out. Do you recognize them?" She opens the book to a page exploding with color and cave art.

I act like it is nothing, like someone asked the time of day, but my insides are jelly, and all I want her to do is continue. I see the goggle lines around her eyes, worn deep, dark with grime. I think of what Caravaggio warned me. Is this some sort of trick? An illusion? I see no words on the page...only the lion and the hand prints, the gazelle grazing. It's a trap.

"I don't understand." I say, but I want that book back, want to see page by page.

"Oh, there is more. Much, much more." She leafs through the pages, and with every turn a new image, powerful, beautiful. "You would not be interested in such things that obviously don't concern you. You have never read a real story or heard a true song or observed a real painting. The NRM Bureau has made sure of that. What do you think is the purpose for your prolonged observations? They are designed to catch the anomalies. You know what I mean, don't you? I can see it in your face. You have witnessed those things designed to make you weep or howl with rage. Something beyond yourself that astounds or makes you shudder, question everything, even your very existence...you have, haven't you, Mr. Dante?" She closes the book with a snap. "We have seen the flower."

My head is spinning, and I don't know if it's from all the poking and prodding, the black lake rolling foam upon the shore or the accusations concerning this book...a book I understand, have seen, the cave art, the cryptic sentences beneath them.

She steps in front of my view of the lake, close, intense.

"What is this?" she says to me and holds the book up.

"I found it in Sector 17."

"I know. We put it there."

Beatrice sits on the decayed stone break wall. She begins to leaf through the book again, running her fingers over the images as if over lines of text, back and forth, left to right until the end of the page. At last, frustrated, taps the page. The cave pictures are exploding before my eyes.

"What?" I sit down next to her. "What do you mean *you put it there?*"

"For you to find," she says. Her voice is somewhere else. "So, you could remember."

"I don't know what you're talking about."

"I think you do."

"I've never seen that book before Sector 17."

I know this is a lie. Like the myriad doors that opened before, a vast store of secret knowledge closed off then revealed, I know this book. I know that I wrote it. I cannot interpret the images. They are enigmatic, abstract. I watch the pictures, the sketches, the coded language, as she flips through the pages like a child who has constructed a primitive story board around the edges. I cannot connect to the sense of familiarity.

"I'm sorry," Beatrice closes the book and stares at the black expanse of water.

Her voice is filled with a sadness I have not heard, the sternness, the roughness suddenly evaporated—brief like a shimmer. "There will come a time when you must choose, when you face the teeth of this world. A moment when...all hope is lost. In that moment, you will be forced to choose what you believe to be true: either there is a chance for good, that there is light in this world no matter how dark it appears for the moment...like the night sky with a myriad of stars, tiny sparks of hope. Or that the world is chaos and darkness and there is in the end...only pain and suffering." She turns and faces me, nearly nose to nose. "Yes, there will come a time, Christopher Dante, when you are faced with this choice... When the time is right, that choice will change your world forever."

Unexpectedly, someone grabs me from behind, hard. When I look at her face it too is hard, emotionless. It is she who pulls the hood over my head and binds the strap around my neck. I am bound with ropes and placed on a wagon of wooden slats. I hear the engine start up, and we lurch forward as the clutch releases, the tires hit the pocked and pitted ground, and my body rolls into the sides. We stop. I hear a gate grind open, then close, and we drive into the hot, dust strewn world of Cogstin. I can barely breathe now, my hood caked with soot around my mouth. *This is the test*, I think. *This is what Caravaggio told me about.* A sense of panic seizes me, and I struggle, trying to slide off the back end, only to smash into a wooden gate holding me in. We drive for five, ten minutes, then the jeep stops. I hear the gate drop. Someone grabs my head and shoulders and pulls me out of the back. Someone else grabs my ankles, and I am swinging free then fall hard onto the sand.

"I hate this place," Caravaggio says.

"Push him in and let's go," says Stutz.

Caravaggio leans into my ear and whispers, "Be strong, pal. I'll come for you." With that he unbuckles the strap around my neck and pulls off the hood.

"Untie me," I say.

"Here." He shoves a flashlight in my bound hands. "You'll need this." After a moment, he continues "Remember," he says, face unmoved. He pushes me hard so that my body leaves the ground, rolls down, down, down, down, down until I smell the rotten flesh, and I am lost, alone in the shadows of night as it comes upon Cogstin.

Chapter Eighteen

I smell them before I see them. It is the smell of rusted metal and molded cloth, of burnt plastic. The light of day has faded, now the world is only what my flashlight illuminates, and I realize I have rolled into a pit surrounded by pieces of body parts in various stages of decomposition. It is a holocaust of bodies dumped by IMAGO. It is no use shouting, for there is nobody to help me. I scoot to the sandstone wall and wait for Caravaggio to come and rescue me. Time passes, and he does not come. *This is all part of the 'magic trick', surely.* I peer up at the darkened sky, the pit is vast, and the bodies lay upon one another like discarded lumber. The vision makes my head spin, my imagination a gray swirl. *It's a magic trick. That's all.* I see them still, but I don't want to see them, and soon they are walled off like so many other memories, blocked.

I flash the light upon the steep walls of stone. The wind whips the grains of sand into biting, stinging bees, and I crouch with my back to the precipitous wall. What are these lying about? At first, I think them organic, recognize the infamous clothing of an NRM guard. Have I not seen with my own eyes the ruthless violence IMAGO terrorists have used against these people? Did I not watch them hack down many in cold blood as we fled the gate district? The clothes are rotted and torn. There is a pool of white goo, more viscous than water, like milk or white oil. It has pooled where his waist should be. My hand is saturated with the lubricant, and I turn. I lose my balance and roll onto a head, wires streaming from the neck, and empty eye socket, skin pulled back revealing a metal jaw now bent and dented hanging in an absurd U shape. I recognize them, and one by one I crouch over a face, scanning with the beam of light. Over and over and over and over, hundreds of pieces, mechanicals. There before me in the dimming

93

light is Mr. Tough, and next to his torso and head is an armless Mr. Yellow Suit. There are hundreds of them, splayed out, stacked, hunched up, arched backward, rotted, rusted and moldy. Why are they here? What does this mean? Is this the magic trick Caravaggio speaks of? I crawl and shimmy over and through them, recognizing the various figures from the hundreds of trips to Cogstin. That is when I see the entrance to the cave. It is small, a chiseled stone entranceway, two-man wide and six feet high. There is no way out but through the door, and I hurry toward it. Soon I am running as hard as I can, the flashlight a strobe light from the pumping of my arms.

The tunnel turns left, then straight, then right. I hurry down it. If I can just get to an opening, I am free. I come to a branch. The smell is overwhelming, something old and decomposed, the smell of ancient earth. I run straight and come to yet another branch. I pass another branch and another, and they too smell of death and dying. Something has gathered behind. I stop and look back, a moment of courage, and to my horror I see someone who looks like Max, but not max, like Hal, but not Hal, and the figures pull back into the darkness. *It is a magic trick! This is not real!* Fear takes hold once again and I run. The stone walls scraping my arms, my head tilted forward and scraping the ceiling, the tunnel smaller and smaller. *SING TO ME, OH MUSE...SING!* The voice is so loud that it nearly topples me to the ground, hurting my ears, a sound like nails on the blackboard. *SING! SING! SING!* I know that voice. It is familiar, Beatrice's voice. I run further down the stone tunnel when it hits me sideways. It's Beatrice, she has always been in my head! It has been her voice all along! I stop running and turn to face the terror of the tooth and claw. *Sing!*

It is Caravaggio who pulls me to the side. "Hey, pal! What are you doing? I told you to wait for me." He is angry, panicked. "Hey! Hey, listen to me!" He shakes me hard and pulls me from my reverie. "You listen'n to me, pal? Hey!" He puts his face to my ear and yells. "We need to go! It might already be too late!" Soon we are heading down one of the splits in the tunnel, Caravaggio pulling me hard, his huge body dwarfing my own and filling the tunnel. I can hear voices behind us. "You're screwing up the plan!" Caravaggio says. "Why you trying to screw up the plan? Now Run!"

We hurry down a tunnel to our right, and I feel the ground sloping up, and then we are out into the Cogstin night. "There!" Caravaggio says.

"Run to that light! I'll hold them off the best I can."

I turn to thank him, but he is not there. "Run!" I hear his voice scream. "Don't screw up the plan!" I see Stutz and Beatrice sidestepping Caravaggio and rushing toward me.

I run across the dirt plain. The ground beneath me is uneven and seems to be falling away. The small light grows into halogen beams from a truck. I hcar thc motor rumbling. I scc a largc mass in thc hcadlight. I scc Hal. He is standing with someone else. I run toward them, the ground shifting under me. I hear voices behind and turn to see a clash of lightening, the space between us and the tunnel widening. I see in the flashes, the hordes of groaning, dragging, limping things rushing from the tunnel like roaches from a pipe. Caravaggio is swiping at them, knocking them back, an ancient god at war, throwing them down, the lightening ripping across the plain. I see the leader of IMAGO open her arms wide, she is huge and otherworldly, Stutz at her side. The thunder turns to a low hum then higher and higher and higher. It's a shattering song that penetrates flesh, bone and stone. I fall to my knees, covering my ears. I look back at Beatrice as she grabs me from behind, strong hands pulling at my shirt, then my pant leg. I kick in protest, violently. I feel her stab me, a rush of something, poison...? into my ankle and calf muscle. *Don't believe it. It's just a magic trick. It's just a trick. Like a magic show...* I turn back but she and Stutz are running away. I run as fast as I can toward the headlights before me. I tumble over a wall. I feel arms lifting me up, and I see Hal! He is huge and fat and, in his overalls, pulling me up and dragging me to the truck. I blink, but do not understand, for there is Hal, again, in the truck, behind the wheel, beckoning the other Hal to hurry. I am tossed into the back of the truck where I see Hal grab Hal's hand, pull him up, and they both pull me into the covered bed. I shake my head which is thick and foggy.

"Hurry!" the first Hal says to the driving Hal, and he pounds on the metal wall. The truck groans and lurches forward. We are speeding away from the scene. I can see only darkness, and as I turn around, Hal pulls me into the group while another Hal holds me to the floor and another Hal wipes an alcohol swab onto my neck and injects me. I see all the Hals hovering over me. I feel my legs and arms go numb, feel my body move to the corner of the truck where I watch the flashing lights far off in the distance.

We come to a stop, and I see a Hal jump limberly from the truck bed and speak to someone out of view. I can feel my arms and legs, but I can't move them. Another Hal, dressed in the same outfit, overalls, a T-shirt underneath, pulls me up with little effort and I have trouble concentrating on them all. I think the drug has made me hallucinate, and I begin to laugh. "Tricky, tricky," I say out loud to the Hals. "Magic." They carry me to the edge of the truck and help me out...and there stands Agent Smiley, tall, dressed in black, a bowler hat on his head. He is pale and lanky, and hairless, the sides of his mouth seem larger than his face. I start to shake my head in protest. "No, no, this is a magic trick." Agent Smiley smiles, wide, wider, wider, and I look away.

"Take him to the holding cell," he says in a cadence that is more a hiss of breath.

I look up and realize they have taken me to the Black Gate. I look over to the small door that leads to the stone stairs that lead to the great prisons below the earth.

"It is a magic trick," I cry out. "It is an illusion. Smoke and mirrors." I want so desperately to hear The Voice in my head, but it is silent. I can't even remember what it says. They drag me to the small door and it opens automatically, and it is Caravaggio who stands there. "I'm sorry, pal. They promised me things okay?" He steps aside. "They promised me I could go home. I miss home, pal. What would you do to go home?"

Agent Smiley grabs me ruthlessly by the arm and throws me, like a sack, over his shoulder, his fingers like claws, tearing at my ankles as he holds me tight.

"I'm sorry, pal. I'm so sorry," Caravaggio says.

Agent Smiley stops and faces him. "Prepare the transport," he says in his strange staccato voice. "Make sure they can't follow us."

Agent Smiley enters through the small door and we descend into the eternal night below the Black Gate. I am not headed down the stairs and into the cells. I am placed on a chair in a side cell, built into the stone walls. Agent Smiley shuts the iron door and leaves me alone in the dark.

Chapter Nineteen

It is Hal who visits me first. His overalls are shredded at the knees and in the back, one strap with the clasp torn away.

"Hey, Stretch," he says sheepishly. "You must have a lot of questions by now, and..."

"A lot of questions?" I stand up and feel the pain in my calf muscle. I sit back down, the dim light of the cell casting Hal's face and body in shadow. "How about you start from the beginning. What is going on? Am I in trouble? Am I drugged? I must be drugged." I rub my face with both hands. "I *am* drugged, how can I not be? I see four of you, Hal! Why do I see four of you?" I sit back down with a humph.

"You see four of me *now*?" Hal says alarmed. "There should be no effect from the injections. They specifically told me that. No after effects. They were clear on that point."

"So, I *am* drugged."

"Yes, but not currently. Well, I guess technically you still are currently drugged so you won't put up a fight, but..." Hal raises his hands in protest. "Now, I'm trying the best I can to explain the current situation, Stretch. We're in a real pickle here, boy, and make no mistake about it. A real jam. They want to exact a pound of flesh for it—and that's a fact." Hal pulls a seat out from the corner so the small incandescent light now shines over him. He spins it around and squats down so his large forearms rest on the back. "They're missing something, Stretch, and they think you...I mean we...took it. That day in Cogstin, boy. That day in Sector 17. Do you know what I'm talking about, Stretch?" He chuckles to himself and rubs his hands through his hair. "I hope to god you do, or there will be hell to pay. We give it back, and we all go home...er...whatever it is."

"I was kidnapped," I say.

"Of course, you were, boy. They think you have it too. This IMAGO group. Bad people, Stretch. I'll bet they put you through all types of tests just to see if you were lying. These boys," he points outside, "didn't think you'd make it, not with such ruthless characters, especially the big fat one—he's an evil one. You get trapped alone with him...well...they told me he'd soon as slit your throat. I've been worried sick over it."

My head is spinning. I try to concentrate on Hal's face, but the edges keep shifting on me. "Caravaggio," I say. "He helped me escape. He's not like the others."

Hal rubs his cheek and nods his head. "I don't know, boy. I'd hate to be alone with any of those murdering terrorists." He pauses. "So...?"

I look at him in confusion.

"Did they get it? Did they take it from you? These boys at the NRM Bureau told me how bad this IMAGO is, and you'd sure as shells give up the book, but good god! I thought you were dead! Now, here you are—safe as a nut in a squirrel's nest."

"I never mentioned a book."

"What?" Hal's face flushes, I see perspiration on his forehead. "I didn't say that... Well, what I meant was... Well, I thought it was... It makes sense it was a book. You said as much just a few seconds ago."

"No, I didn't."

"Sure, you did. You're all drugged up now. You don't remember what you said. You said..."

"What's going on, Hal?" I stand up, the pain in my calf excruciating, and I move to the back wall.

Hal looks behind him at the locked door. "I'm gonna be honest with you, boy, I've got a real problem, see..." Whether it is a trick of light or lack of light or the drugs wearing off—I see the coloring and facial features shift. The face is wider than it should be, the defining lines, cheek and chin not quite where they are supposed to be. Hal stares at me long and hard. He pulls out a damp cloth from his pocket and wipes his face. It is no longer Hal before me but Caravaggio, painted and masked to look like Hal. "My problem is this, pal. They promised me my freedom, freedom to go back home, and all I need to do is get the book from you." He is huge now, his full size, and I remember him on the plain swinging and smashing like a Greek god.

"I don't have the book," I whisper, my eyes wide with terror.

Caravaggio stands up. I step back, the pain in my leg so intense that I grimace and lean on the other foot. "I need the book, pal. It's a simple, simple request. You give me the book or tell me where it is. I give the book to them, and I go back home. I know. I know. You're thinking the same thing I'm thinking, right? Why this book? What's the big damn deal with an ancient book of unintelligible geo-thaumaturgical equations, ya know. Exactly!" He smashes his fist into the palm of his other hand. "Makes no damn sense. If it's between that and me going home...well..."

"Where do you live?" I say, because not to say something, anything, would be to bring the wrath of Caravaggio upon me. He is gesticulating again, and pacing, like he's talking to someone in his head.

"Where?" Caravaggio says, stops and points at me accusingly. "Ha ha! You're trying to trick me, pal. I can see that. Where? Not here. Not in this damnable desert. What do they say, 'Better to rule in hell'? Ha ha! How long, pal? How long have I been told that same...?"

The pain in my leg is so intense, so pointed, like something from inside burrowing up, a red-hot boil ready to pop. I reach down to rub it and feel a large bump, skin stretched taut. Something moves under the surface. I fall to the stone floor and push to the corner. Caravaggio is ranting now, deep inside his head, pacing back and forth explaining how it is impossible to stay here any longer, and a promise is a promise. I pull my pant leg up, the same leg where I was pricked during the escape, and I watch in horror as the skin separates, and a beetle emerges from the open wound. Caravaggio stops and looks down. He sees my leg, grabs the hanging light and shines it onto the floor.

"No. No. You tricked me, pal. You tricked me."

He backs away to the door, and I think how strange it is to see such a huge powerful being flinch back because of a beetle. He stares at the floor, at the small beetle between him and me. That is when I hear it. It is subtle, soft, like hair blowing in the wind, then louder. Caravaggio is pounding on the great iron door. "Get me out of here," he screams. He turns back to me, to the beetle, "You tricked me. How did you trick me?"

The sound increases, and I see in my imagination it is actually not an abstract sound but a voice, a voice that is singing, telling a story with a song. It is louder and louder and louder, and it is coming from the small beetle on the stone floor. Caravaggio covers his ears and rushes to the bug. He stomps like a mad man. The beetle moves quick and darts from one place to the next, the song louder and louder. I see another beetle appear, followed by another and another, up from the small drain in the floor, more and more and more and more until there are hundreds, thousands, scurrying. Caravaggio is swiping, stomping, the song gets louder and louder. I see it in my mind; the song is not a story at all but a command, a chant; the same lines over and over:

Come, come, come to me
through pipe and over hill
Up you come and join with me
To do your Master's will.

Caravaggio is pounding furiously now, screaming for the guards. The beetles sweep round and round and round until they create a vortex stacking one upon the other, locking legs to bodies, swirling up and up and up. They are a black shadow now of beetles, shifting as a cloud into the shape of a woman, and I recognize her as Beatrice, the leader of IMAGO. A beetle arm emerges from the swarming mass. It sweeps out and knocks Caravaggio to the floor. He does not move. Two arms shift out from the great cloud of swarming beetles, the form of the IMAGO leader emerging and disappearing within, and they seize the iron bars of the window and tear the great door from its hinges, flinging it into the stone cell.

The song is loud, thundering. I do not know if it is just in my head or surrounding me. The great beetle form shifts to me, Beatrice's head emerging. "You must escape. I cannot help you now. Follow the beetles. You must follow the beetles. You must sing your own song. It is time for your own song! *SING TO ME, OH MUSE! SING!*"

The great beetle cloud collapses to the floor into an enormous pool of black. It moves like running water out the holding cell, gathers in the tunnel as if hesitating, then surges down the hallway. Agent Smiley meets me in the door. Tooth and claw. He is large, his long coat now more like membrane, arms thin and taloned. He towers above me. His mouth is open and gaping, larger than his face, jagged, razor-like teeth fill his mouth, angled and jutting out in odd directions. The beetles swarm about him. He raises his arms in defense. I realize it is not defensive but a commanding gesture that scatters the cloud. Some drop to the floor, lifeless.

I run, the beetles before me. I run until my legs burn, up stone stairs, then plummeting down again. The beetles turn left, I turn left. The beetles turn right, I turn right. But then they lead me to a dead end and scurry into a crack and I am quite alone. The light is dim at best. The beetles and my hope of escape have abandoned me. That is when I hear it, a slow but steady thumping, like a heavy animal with loping gate, bent with a terrible will to find and consume its prey. Once again, I am in the small shack in Sector 17, before the smoldering altar and the haunting sense that something is coming for me. I have no way out this time and there is nowhere to hide.

SING TO ME, OH MUSE! SING!

What does she mean by that? I hear Agent Smiley coming closer. I know if he reaches me, I will die. I think of the lion and the cave art and the men huddled around the fire listening to the mad storyteller and the lion leaping and me capturing it in the air. The book is not before me, and my mind remains blank. I cannot see him, but I can sense him in the vast darkness. Agent Smiley is running at me now, his taloned hands outstretched, an ink black shadow in the tunnels. I crouch near the wall.

SING TO ME, OH MUSE! Screams the voice in my head. *SING! SING!*

I am confused, frustrated, and Agent Smiley is upon me. It is not Agent Smiley at all. It is huge, blacker than the darkest shadows of the tunnel, smelling of decayed earth and ancient bones, it was the smell in Sector 17, the same smell in the tunnels of the compound. I hear his joints creak and crack as he sweeps his arms over me, the razor talons slicing through my shoulders and up my cheeks, deep, flayed furrows, and the blood streaks down my face. Another pass, and I will be no more. This fills me with anger, for why should Agent Smiley have the power to steal my life, my light and in such a dark place? As he comes upon me again, I raise my hand, and for a moment, I sense the fear. I realize it is not a gasp from Agent Smiley...it is a laugh. It is the sound of bloating flesh, the sound of gas and decay escaping from the dead. The sound of mourning, of wailing, of such deep and profound sorrow, hopelessness—all twisted and combined into a single exhalation. Suddenly, it morphs into words.

"You are nothing. Nobody. You will die in a tomb of rock and vanish forever...forgotten. I will feast on your dead flesh." I hear the laugh again.

SING! SING, OH MUSE, SING!

As Agent Smiley swoops down upon me for the final assault, I think of the tiny beetles. The swarm as it breaks against the stone wall, sweeps around, enters the small fissure and vanishes somewhere beyond.

SING TO ME, OH MUSE!

Agent Smiley is tearing at me again, his mouth wide, a chasm of teeth. I hunch over my knees and push against the wall, eyes squeezed closed. I know Agent Smiley is killing me. For some reason I still imagine the beetles streaming, see them in my imagination, swirling upon the floor, scattering, forming. I am with them, hunched over, my back beetle-hard, impenetrable, impervious to spear and claw and tooth, and we scurry, sweeping across the floor, sensing the scent of life. The exit, the gap between wall and ceiling, made by water and time and shifting earth, greater than any power that walks in the world of men and time and things, and like a swarm, a herd, a single living organism made of hundreds of thousands of moving parts, we vanish into it.

Chapter Twenty

I am scurrying. That's how I would explain it. I am scurrying with a swarm of beetles down the darkened tunnels. We move with a single will—driven by a song, and the voice is coming from Beatrice, the terrorist leader of IMAGO. She is part of us, in us, a tether as strong as steel binding us together. I hear something else. It is ancient, terrible, a horrible longing of despair, and it is creeping up from behind. I know it is Agent Smiley.

We stop. I am no longer with the beetles, but am standing alone against the damp stone walls of the tunnel. a small light illuminates my surrounding. It is hidden in a metal, corroded casing above me. The beetles swarm again and take the shape of the IMAGO leader, rising, morphing into human form.

"You must follow us out," she says, her voice made from hundreds of thousands of buzzing wings and scraping feet. "You must follow. It is coming. You cannot withstand another attack."

I sense the dread of Agent Smiley, creeping like damp, decay, a fog of doubt, fear and death. I cannot see anything. I cannot say a word. I am engulfed in something like the stone walls that surround me.

"Where are you?" Says the beetle horde. "You must leave! Flee with us! Flee for your life!" The beetle swarm scatters, forms a new pattern on the stone floor and flows away into the darkness.

"Don't struggle, pal," says a familiar voice.

I do anyway, but am held firm.

"I said, don't struggle. It's useless. Once I've got you, that's it."

I try to speak, but my words are muffled.

"Quiet, I said," says Caravaggio. "One more word, and I'll snap your neck. Like a twig, pal. See my meaning?"

My body goes limp, and I nod my head in agreement. I look around, but do not see him anywhere, just feel him all around me, his enormous body pressing up against the wall. His hand is still around my mouth, so I breathe through my nose in pants.

"I don't want to snap your neck like a twig, pal. You understand? I could if I wanted to. I could do a lot of things. The choices are endless. For example, feel that in the air, that damp and fog, that oily film that will be the worst nightmare you've ever had, surrounding you, penetrating your head. Yeh? Well, I could *choose* to release you right now, pull the curtain away like a magic show, and abracadabra look who's here. You know what it is, pal? You've already met it. It's not very nice, is it, pal?"

I shake my head.

"You wouldn't want to come face to face with it right now and say howdy do?"

I vigorously shake my head again.

"Well, then—Oh look here it is. Better stay calm, pal. Nice and calm. Calm like a farmer's pond."

I feel it first, that decayed earth smell, that hopeless dread that nearly pushes me to the ground and out of Caravaggio's hands. I still cannot see Caravaggio. I can see all of me. I can now see Agent Smiley's deep black shadow casting upon the walls and ceiling of the tunnel. The tiny incandescent bulb fizzles and goes out. Still I can see the shadow within the darkness. Its arms are branched out, long dagger-like points at either ends, moving its head back and forth to smell or sense my presence. And it stops before us.

"Ooooooh," says Caravaggio, whispering in my ear or shouting inside my head, I cannot tell which one. "This *is* exciting. Never really saw that bastard up this close before. He does look vicious. You want me to let you go?"

I want to sob out, to scream, "Oh, God! No! Please! I'll do anything! Anything! Don't let me go!" But I don't. I just shake my head again slightly, for fear Agent Smiley will see my movements and slash me to pieces.

"Good. While we have this moment together, while I have your undivided attention so to speak, pal, let's make a little pact, you and me.

What do you say?"

Agent Smiley is now right in front of us, sniffing, the bones cracking and popping, snapping as though they are rigid things not meant outside a museum. I hear his taloned fingers scraping the walls on either side. We are so close I can now see the leathery membrane that was his coat. The smell is so overpowering I cannot focus my mind, the yellow-white of his face almost translucent. I gag. Caravaggio shakes me ever so slightly.

"Not on your life, pal. One more move and I let you go. No deal. I just let you go." He pauses, "So, we have a deal? A tit for a tat? You scratch my itch. I scratch yours?"

I have no idea what deal. I don't care. I just know if he releases me now, I am dead. I don't want to die. I can sense the beetle horde somewhere far away. I try to imagine them, but Caravaggio grabs me tight, so tight I may break in half. "None of that now, pal. A promise is a promise."

I nod. We watch Agent Smiley move past us, stop, turn around, sniff, turn back and walk slowly away. We stay in our spot for so long I forget I'm captured by Caravaggio, try to move, and am held tight again in his powerful arms. The small light fizzes again, sputters, blinks on. What I thought was the wall itself was actually Caravaggio painted like the wall. He is indistinguishable, a perfect pattern of gray and black stones, mortared and fitted identical to what is behind us. I have a hard time finding his face.

"Thank you," I say.

"You made a deal, pal. A bargain. I plan on you keeping it."

The shape before me moves, and I can see him clearly now, his eyes white and wide, beard a wiry, bushy garden of hair.

"There's two ways out, and I know them both. She'll figure out what happened soon enough, but by then we'll be gone. That thing..." he nods toward Agent Smiley's direction "...will think we're escaping down the river. Instead, we're heading back to the cell block. We're going to walk right out the front door, you and me. Now stay close."

As we hurry up stairs and down stairs, to our left, always to our left and up, as I jog behind the huge man, I notice he is wearing his backpack with the large zippered pocket. We come to the cellblock, and he turns and lifts me up like a sack of wheat. He hurries past armed guards with assault rifles and heavy body armor. They do not even see us. I think of the discarded and abandoned mechanical body parts. They are not real. They are robots, mechanical men or something not human. One senses something, turns about, looks both ways, but stands guard once again. Up the stairs to the first floor, I can see the stairs that lead to the outer door. Caravaggio puts me down, bends over and whispers, "Remember. A deal's a deal." He takes his thumb and scrapes it across his own neck in a death threat.

I nod.

He sweeps up the stairs and the two sentinels guarding the door are motionless, their necks snapped in seconds by something they never saw coming. He waves me on, and I hurry up the steps. We open the door to night. Caravaggio closes the door again, and tells me to stand still. He opens his bag and begins to pull one can of spray paint out after another, spraying my front and back, his front and back. He says, "close your eyes. Keep'm closed." He sprays my face five, six, seven times. "Okay, open."

I watch as he does the same to himself. When he opens his eyes, they are small white orbs in a blending of night. "Now, do exactly as I do. Exactly."

I nod again, and we are out the doors and into the cold night of Cogstin.

I can smell the Cuyahoga River, and the platform is teaming with guards in full body armor and workers in their yellow hazmat suits with the copper-ringed eyes and high black boots. We are in plain sight. We walk, stop, walk, run, stop. Right in front of them all, past several who do not even know we are there. I look at Caravaggio and realize he is the perfect camouflaged backdrop to the wooden boxes and wire spools cast in shadows. Soon we are beyond their sight and out of harm's way. Caravaggio hands me a mask with the filters and mic, and we are racing down an alleyway between two ruined buildings in the heart of Cogstin, a single light, an enormous harvest moon, casting shadows upon the walls.

We stop near an abandoned gas station, the pumps long gone, only the cement pillars and the great portico remaining. We squat under it with our backs to a dilapidated stone wall. Caravaggio shines a light on the severe gash on my cheek. It runs from the bottom of my chin and up into my hairline, just missing my eye.

"You've got a real prize winner here, pal." He rummages through his backpack and pulls out various items: gauze, some scissors, medical tape. He dabs my face. "Stay still. Of course, it will sting. This is fine, no worries, pal. You ever get stitches? Ha! What a question. Of course not. You never asked why, did you? Good god! You work with metal! Physician, heal thyself!"

He shakes his head in anger, annoyance or just plain dumbfounded. Slowly, methodically, he dabs and covers the wound, knowingly, surprisingly gently. When he is finished, he checks the other places where Agent Smiley wounded me and determines nothing can be done. Maybe he doesn't want to do anything else, can't, or all of the above. He sits down and opens a can of peaches. One for me and one for him.

"So, how you feeling after all that?"

"I'm fine."

"How you feeling?"

"What do you mean?"

Caravaggio does not look up from his peaches. "You turned into a damn bug, pal. I was standing right there. A bug! Poof! Who the hell can do that? How do you feel?"

I think about this for the first time, for it was something that just happened, and I decide I don't want to think about it anymore. "Looks like you're in a bit of a pickle," I say. "Agent Smiley and the NRM Bureau can't be happy with you. You double crossed them." I decide that canned peaches sound good right now and after all the excitement I am actually famished, for I have lost count of the days and lack of food.

"Agent Smiley?" Caravaggio looks at me. He points his big finger at me. "I like that. Agent Smiley...the big teeth and all. Hey, pal, that's good. I like that. Got to keep our humor. At least we have that." He claws at his beard playfully. "I never double crossed them. I don't work for them. I don't work for anyone, pal. Besides, you made a deal. Simple, and a deal's a deal." He seems to have found something unwanted in the beard hairs and flicks it away.

"What about your terrorist friends? What about them?" I say. "They can't be happy either."

"Eh," he says annoyed and waves his hand at me. "They don't know what they want. All this waiting and waiting and waiting. I'm tired of this prison planet. I want to go home. Four hundred years is long enough. And now...because of our deal...I can." He stares at me for a long time without saying anything. "Will they be pissed? Yes. Will they kill me if I come back? She might not, but that bastard Stutz would cut me in half before I got out a howdy." He purses his lips and tosses the can against the wall. "What's done is done."

I can tell he's upset and he broods, chin in hands, staring at nothing. We hear a dog yelp and bark in the distance. This is followed by another bark, then another, all from different dogs in different locations.

"Come on," he says. "We can't stay here any longer."

He shoulders his pack and we head out into the night once again, sticking to the shadows from the moon, so round, pale and glorious that it does not seem real but something Caravaggio might paint to deceive me.

Chapter Twenty-one

The dogs are getting louder and more vocal, a scattering from all points. This is irritating Caravaggio to no end, and he keeps moving from one spot to another, always further down the alley. Finally, he stops, and we pull off our masks, able to breathe in the confines of an enclosure. He turns on me.

"So, how is this going to work? You say we have a deal. Everyone says they have a deal, and the deal goes south or someone reneges or dies and the deal's off."

I'm taken off guard. He keeps mentioning this deal that I didn't know I made. If I tell him I don't know, then he'd probably strangle me right then and there. So, I lie. "How do you want it to work?"

He thinks about this, rubs his chin, flaps his arms about and talks to no one. "I have no idea, pal. You just do what you do...I imagine. You just...get me there or something." The dogs begin to howl to one another. They are close, then far, then close. He stops ranting, turns to me and pokes my chest, the thump like someone threw a rock. "Say, pal, you wouldn't be changing your mind...would you?" He is huge and hunched over me, a man-mountain, intense and threatening.

"Where...do you want me to take you?" I whisper.

"Why home, of course. You made the agreement, didn't you? That's the agreement. That's always been the agreement. Get me the hell out of this prison and back to where I belong. I told those rats at the NRM Bureau that. I've been screaming it to Beatrice and Stutz, to Mendel if he cares but nobody seems to be listening to me. H-O-M-E...I want to go..."

Caravaggio cannot continue, for we are overrun on all sides by dogs. Some are fat, some thin with their ribs straining against their flesh, some little, some big. They are barking and growling, more and more of them. We are trapped. Suddenly, I can hear them clearly. They are not barking randomly, but in a cadence where the base tone morphs into a single voice, like the voice in the beetles.

We are behind you, not far. Come to us. You will be safe with us.

Caravaggio sweeps his arms about. "I know you're out there! I can hear it too. He made a promise to me, and he's going to fulfill it, damn you all! I want to go home! I'm tired."

We are behind you, not far. Come to us. You will be safe with us.

He grabs me by the throat with great force, and I dangle in his arms until he allows my feet to rest on the ground. "I'll break him in half!" Caravaggio screams. "You know I will! I'll do it!" At the same time, his mind is filled with anxiety and doubt. "I want to go home. That's all I want. I'm tired, and you know that. I'm tired, Beatrice. It's been too long. He said he'd send me home. I just want to go home." Now he is grabbing me hard again, dragging me about like a forgotten toy. "You call them off! Call them off or I'll snap him in half."

The dogs stop barking and back away into the shadows, their eyes shining in the moonlight. They bark, and it is the voice of the terrorist leader again.

"Caravaggio, you know you can't go home. You know this. The son of Dante cannot get you there. He is unable." There is sadness in her voice now, a longing like Caravaggio. Underneath her words, there is a subliminal layer directed at me: *We are behind you, not far. Come to us. You will be safe with us.* She continues, Caravaggio loosens his grip on me. "Let the boy go," the terrorist leader says. "He cannot do it alone."

"I wanted to go home. They told me I could go home. That's why I did it."

"You know how it must be done. It is all of us from IMAGO. We must all be present."

Caravaggio is angry now, tense, every muscle bulging and veined, ready for the onslaught. He grabs me once again and pulls me close to his lips. "You made a promise to me, pal," he whispers. "We had a deal. Remember. A deal's a deal." He holds me hard with one hand. I hear him opening his bag, then the sound of spray can after spray can going off. He pushes me just as the first wave of dogs rushes at him. He bounds through a broken-down doorway and into another abandoned building. The dogs race after him, howling and barking. I cover my ears and crouch low to avoid them. They fade away into the night, and I realize Caravaggio has escaped, masquerading as a wall, an alley, a doorjamb or the very air of night itself.

It is Stutz, the tall terrorist who finds me. I remember him from my imprisonment, tough like flint, unbreakable and violent.

"Did he hurt you?" he says, pulling out a rag to wipe my face and a bottle of water for me to drink. "Your head," he says, and gently touches the stitches of the wound. "Not bad for a painter. At least some of my lessons did not go to waste."

I pull my head away annoyed.

The leader appears, her face illuminated in the silvery hues of the moonlight. She is hard bit and worn like Stutz. Her short black hair matted and shifting in the night breeze, her form long and lean. She kneels down by Stutz.

"The dogs will never find him. It was a fool's game we played with little room for error."

"I'll scout the perimeter." Stutz stands up and hurries out of the enclosure.

"It was you in my head all these years," I say.

The hardness in her face softens ever so slightly. "How can one know, if they are not sent? How can one awake if they do not call? These are your words." The severity returns. She lifts her head and turns it in the direction of the Black Gate. "Quickly. Our enemy is close behind, and we have no cover in this moonlight."

She puts on her filter mask and hands me mine. Soon we are running through the swirling winds and acrid air, through alleyways and burnt out buildings of Cogstin.

We travel deep into the night, always crouching and waiting, Stutz vanishing, then returning with a scouting report. I wander behind them, the leader always prodding me gently onward. We finally stop somewhere near the Cuyahoga River, near a dilapidated cement overpass. The bridge has long since been destroyed, and only stone columns remain hinting to what once was. This is the widest part of the river, and I know the Leader feels safe here, for I can see the evidence of previous camps.

"This should provide some shelter for a few hours," she says. "You can take off the mask now. There is fresh water in the canteen near the wall."

Stutz goes about building a small fire. The leader unwraps dried meat and breaks it up into a pan. She cuts up some small vegetables and what looks to be several hardened and sprouted potatoes, fills up the pan and places it on the grate of the fire. My head is spinning. I need answers. I don't know what to say or how to say it. It is the leader who sits next to me and hands me a cup of water. I drink, and gulp, suddenly realizing how thirsty, hungry and exhausted I truly am.

"Water," she says. "So simple a thing, seemingly so prevalent, so vital to our very existence, and we don't even think about it. In fact, there was a time in my life when I would go days without a sip." She turns to me. "What is it, young Dante, that distracts us so completely, that we forget to drink water? Without it...we die. And yet, like so many things...what truly matters disappears from our view."

"How can I hear your voice in my head?" I say and stare at the dark western horizon. I can smell the river, hear it as it rolls toward the black lake somewhere north of us.

"Because you asked me to." She sees my absolute confusion. "I want you to," she says. "I've been calling you for a very long time." Her face seems more severe, more worn than I noticed before: crow's feet, blackened rings underneath her eyes. "Now, here you are." She smiles wanly. Her cheekbones are angular, the skin stretched tightly over them. I notice in the light of the fire many thin scars visible that swoop from the edge of her eye and disappear beyond her chin line. I wonder how far they go and where she got them. I think of Hal hanging by chains in the dungeons of the black gate.

"I don't understand any of this. I don't understand who you are...what you are...? What happened back there? How did you...and what was that...thing down there?"

The leader reaches out her hand. It is a gentle touch, and I cannot juxtapose it with the experiments, the horror of the dungeons, any of it. I recoil, then stand up and walk to the edge of the firelight. She joins me, both of us looking out at the river.

"Please, call me Beatrice. That *thing*...as you call it...is not from here. It will kill you if it finds you, and it *will* find you. That's what it does. It's called many names: Gol, Ghoul, Ghūl. It feeds on the dead, the dying. Where we...I...come from...it is what you would call a bird of carrion, a vulture. Here it is the stuff of nightmares."

My head is spinning again, and I feel like the floor has disappeared. "It can't be real. It doesn't make sense."

"Oh, it's real enough."

"If it wanted to kill me, it could have many times before this." I think back to my meetings with Agent Smiley, how he hounded me, surprised me with interrogations.

"It didn't know if *you* were *you*. It needed to be sure. Why disrupt the land of make-believe if you don't have to?" She throws a rock at the river far away, and walks to the fire to eat.

I follow her and take a seat next to Stutz who seems awkward, stiff, perhaps annoyed with me sitting there. He soon stands up and gulps the rest of his soup down. "The time has come," he says sternly. "I will walk the perimeter."

He vanishes into the darkness. Beatrice and I sit in silence, the fire crackling. I hear rustling here and there in the shadows, things moving about. I think of Agent Smiley, hunched over and lumbering toward me in the tunnels of the dungeon under the Black Gate. I lean toward the warmth of the flames.

"What did you mean by *the world of make-believe*?"

Beatrice turns to me, a slight smirk on her face. "What if I told you, you were in a great play, and we are in the final act?"

"I don't understand."

"This," she points about her. "Make believe, story time, a play." She stands up, dumps the remains of the soup onto the fire and grabs me firmly by my wrist. "Come with me. It's time to meet the actors."

Chapter Twenty-two

I follow Beatrice out into the darkness. We walk down a small street, an alleyway really, and she turns into a doorway. It is a large warehouse with conveyor belts and abandoned work stations, but even in the moonlight I can see plates and pots, small pieces of clothing, corners in shadow, but obviously occupied.

"Where are we?" I say.

"It's okay," Beatrice yells. "Turn on the lights. You can show yourselves!"

There is a rustle of movement, shuffling on the floor. I think of the horde chasing me from the stone hallways near the great earthen pit. I step closer to Beatrice. There is a sudden hum as a generator kicks on, a flicker of light above us, the fluorescent bulbs sputtering and humming and buzzing to life all around us. Soon I can see how spacious the warehouse actually is, how high the ceilings, the great windows lined in rows far above us, the glass long gone, now shadowed empty eye sockets of brick.

They come out from every corner; short, tall, fat, thin, all manner of hair, all manner of forms, but one thing consistent throughout: each being is misshaped, malformed, appendages too long, too short, some missing, all missing and being pulled in wagons, some dragging themselves, some with eyes gone, some with no eye sockets at all. It is a horror, something gone terribly wrong, a biological mishap, birth defects on a massive scale. Heads too small for bodies, backs humped and mounded, joints fused and iron stiff, and they all shift and shuffle and timidly approach Beatrice who stands in the middle of the expanse.

"My god," I say. I want to dash out the door, but she holds me tight, a violence in her grip that startles me.

"Look, Christopher Dante. This is the real city of ashes!" Her voice is terse and angry, her fist clenches then relaxes. "Don't turn away. Look at them!"

I stare, terrified of what stands before me. In their grotesqueness and deformity, the abhorrent otherness of humanity, all different, all misshaped and yet... Something...a characteristic here, one there. My mouth grows dry, and I cannot swallow. My head feels light as air, and Beatrice holds me firm. I breathe rapidly trying to concentrate. Yes, they are all different, but many of them many, so many, so, so many have the same distracted, distinct features. A tall thin one comes up and points his absurdly shortened arm at me, fingers like baby carrots. His mouth is pulled sideways by some invisible force, and with great effort moves his lips, and then a sound comes forth. At first, I cannot make out what he says. He repeats it. His oddly shaped eyes widen as I register the word. Again, he says it, and this time it is much clearer, "Helloooo, Stretch."

"What is happening? What kind of trick is this?" I say, backing away. "Caravaggio told me it was a trick, that you'd try to trick me, told me not to believe it." I try to pull away, but Beatrice holds me tight.

Many of them, from various places in the room begin to repeat what the misshaped Hal says, all in different ways, different tones, most unintelligible. As I look at them, I realize that not only do I see Hal's features, but Max's too and even Mr. Tough from the river gate, one even placing his thumb in his belt, the other hand missing, replaced with a flipper-like appendage.

"Look at them, Christopher Dante," Beatrice says, and I see her eyes glassy and emotional. She holds me hard. "These are just a few. There are thousands more scattered throughout the city of Cogstin."

"I don't understand you," I say.

"Thousands," she whispers, looking at me. "I am not from here, Christopher Dante," she says, still in a whisper.

"What are you saying?"

"Open your eyes and see, truly see. Awake, O Sleeper. Awake!"

"They are living..." My mind races back to my escape from IMAGO, the horde, Caravaggio swiping and sweeping them away, and the Hal's, four, five, six Hal's everywhere. I think of the pit filled with mechanical Mr. Toughs and Mr. Yellow Suits, the strewn and wrecked body parts, the white lubricant puddled, slick like oil around them. These are organic. These are deformed...human.

"Remember, Sector 17. Remember the stone table and what was on it?"

I don't want to remember the stone table and Sector 17 and that day seems so long ago, but try as hard as I can, those memories collide with the present. I am there, gasping for breath, the acrid air of that small room, the smoke from the burning flesh upon the table. I can't see. I don't want to see, but I do...I see the body parts as they lay there severed at the joints, torsos, necks. I see so many I cannot count for they overlap one another. They are various ages: an infant leg, a teenager's torso, and the heads...all the heads...and all the same, familiar, in various stages of development. I hear Agent Smiley lumbering, tooth and claw, toward me from somewhere beyond the room. I know the significance of what is to take place, and who is on the table.

"You are not from this world of men and time and things, Christopher Dante," Beatrice says and holds me now with both hands so I must face her. "You have never been from here. You have known this deep down. You have known it all your life. Remember. Remember Sector 17. Who was on the stone table, Christopher Dante?"

I try to pull away, but I cannot. "Look at me. Who was on that table?"

"I don't understand."

"Who was on the table?"

I am breathing hard, and I am filled with emotions now that erupt from within, like millions of doors suddenly flinging open. I know the doors and know the feeling. I try to close them all, but I can't. I sit in the white room on the white chaise lounge staring at the great blue beyond, and I know it is a construct...an imaginative fiction born from terror and horror, from savage pain. I see me sitting writing in a book, and it is not pictures but equations, lines and lines and lines of geo-thaumaturgic and quantum bio-thaumaturgic phrases strung together...and I understand them, know them, they are for me, by me. I see me in the white room with the chaise lounge; writing, planning, earnest, intentional with every word, symbol and parenthetical phrase, for they will be used to save me.

"Who was on the table?"

"Oh, god."

"Who?"

I can't push the image from my mind. I try. I try, but the act is Sisyphus pushing the boulder. I sob and shake my head. She hugs me tight, tight, so tight to block the horror, the pain, rage, guilt, humiliation, and the great darkness that is trying so desperately to overcome me, to pulverize me like fists, but her arms won't let it. The great doors in my mind, the millions of doors burst open, tear from their hinges and blow into ash as my true memories, the millions of experiences pour unabated into my consciousness. I sob and moan. Beatrice holds me, for I understand but do not fully comprehend the great paradox before me: It is I on the stone table. It is my body parts in all its stages of development. It is my facial features on the many heads placed there. My body convulses.

"I don't understand," I sob.

"Welcome back, Christopher Dante," Beatrice whispers in my ear. She holds my head gently, stoking my hair. "You have come back to us." Now she too is sobbing.

Chapter Twenty-three

So, one day you wake up and find out that you are really not who you thought you were. That all those you thought to be a strand in an intricate relational web are not who you thought they were. The terrorist group you've been programed to hate all your life is not who you thought they were...and like an old time commercial, I must intrude here and say, "But wait, there's more." My Uncle raised me...this version of my Uncle, the hard drinking-I'm-going-on-a-three-day-bender-so-call-Max-to-get-me-home...this model, raised this generation of me. Who the hell knows what happened to the generations before this, the four hundred years of generations of my forgotten life? An existential nuclear bomb has gone off, and I am a shadow fixed upon the sand.

Beatrice spends an hour calming me down and explaining in broad sweeps that I have been around in some form or another for a very long time. That my body, the original me, was placed in an NRM Generation Tank where my original cells have been used to clone the imitation, mass produced copies of me. These Generation Tanks have mass produced all those who I have known all my life. The suburbs of Cogstin are make believe, an illusion, a giant theater production put on by the NRM Bureau.

Now, comes the real kicker. Somebody, broke into the NRM complex where they hold the Generation Tanks. They set fire and destroyed the entire complex. They released the originals. Of whom, yours truly, was taken and raised by this last Hal, the alcoholic Hal, all unbeknownst to anyone. Rumors spread to Beatrice and her mercenaries something happened that would change the world, but since they could not be sure it was real...or that I even existed...she began to 'sing' to me, call me awake. She did not know who was the original and who was imitation. She did not know what I looked like or what family I would come from. She had the book I wrote. And this book had the Thaumaturgic equations designed to trigger the original me's psychic break; my awakening. I wrote these to myself, had created a way back. Why? A way back from where? Beatrice will not elaborate.

"All in good time, Christopher," she says.

She knew I would come from Cogstin, because I wrote that city into the book. Her goal, along with Caravaggio and Stutz, was to find me, show me the book and bring me back to my original state with my original memories.

Unfortunately, Hal began to remember, the old model Hal, he remembered the white room and the glass and the water and the book. He was going to tell me about it, and he was murdered. "Agent Smiley, as you call him," Beatrice says, "is not who you think he is. We began to suspect you were the real Christopher Dante, the original, and I believe he did too."

So, with Hal out of the way and replaced by the new Hal, Beatrice had to get us to Sector 17, to show me the altar, to get me the book that would eventually bring my memories back to me. She wrote an official letter from the NRM, and sent it to Hal. She planted the book of thaumaturgy, knowing if I was the original I could use the equations to trigger my return. The next Hal had allowed me to use the book, create the sunflower lion and because of it was tortured in the cells of the Black Gate. Beatrice, Stutz and Caravaggio needed to be sure. "From that point on," Beatrice says, "it was a race to discover if you were the original Christopher Dante, son of Geoffrey and Elizabeth Dante." She looks at me. "You still don't know who you are, do you? Your father was a scientist from Earth. Your mother from our multi-verse called IMAGO, and you are the first born from two separate universes." When Beatrice is through talking, I sit staring at the ground.

A gaunt Hal with a shortened leg, places a steaming cup of coffee before me. I glance up and quickly look away embarrassed, thanking him. He grunts something and stands still. Beatrice smiles at him, reaches out her callused hand and touches his. He smiles, grunts again, and walks away. We are sitting in a closed-in part of the warehouse. It is heated, and partitioned with several seats, a table, a small kitchenette, several bookshelves. A man who looks very much like Max, the Max who owned the auto repair shop, the Max who many nights would drive Hal back home to me after a bender—this other Max sits across from us. One of his eyes is partially closed, the skin of his eyelid sealed too far inward, so that only the pupil is exposed.

"It has been generations," the other Max says. His tiny eye tries to blink, and I notice he is emotional.

Beatrice is staring at me, eyes scanning me like some computer sensor.

Other Max looks at me and smiles. "I thought this would go differently. We..." He points to Beatrice and himself "...thought this would take place at the compound. We were to meet you...Caravaggio," he says with a sigh. "He betrayed us all. Not for all the world, did I think that."

"I should have been more vigilant," Beatrice says. She turns to me. "The only way to psychically call the authentic you, the original you, back is to invoke a paradox. Any other mass-produced imitation would become schizophrenic and eventually destroy itself."

She says this like I am a toaster...not me but the other me's, the thousands of me's over time. The scary thing is, I understand it to be true. I understand and grasp the concept of duplication, lives lived. I must be authentic, for I understand myself to be the original. I say, "So, all the other me's destroyed themselves?"

"You are here now," says other Max. "How is irrelevant." He grabs my forearms and holds them tightly. I notice the digits missing, the digits that never materialized. He whispers:

Sing to me, Oh Muse
Of the man full of sorrows,
Who wanders the Plains of Ashes
To bring us the Light of Life.

I look up, my attention now sharp as a razor.

"These are your words," Beatrice says. "These are words from you while you were...in captivity. They have taken on messianic overtones over the past four hundred years of your absence. Only you know what they truly mean, why you wrote them, their significance."

Beatrice stands up. She is once again a hardened shell. "That's enough for now, Governor. We have so much to do, and the day is coming upon us fast."

Chapter Twenty-four

Several days have passed, and there seems to be a growing tension between Beatrice and Stutz. I see them bickering; low whispers, stern, emphatic gestures, one of them walking away. I find myself lost in a surreal world drifting from a shadow to a shadow and try to hold to what I once thought was solid ground. The events that have transpired have made me wearier of the terrorists, of what they want. I stay to myself, and wander through the buildings, down the connecting tunnels, avoiding the disfigured Hal's and Max's and looking for any way of escape. On one of these walks, Beatrice steps from the darkness and stands near me.

"Hard to believe this was once a thriving metropolis," she says in a flat voice.

I stare at the dust clouds and the ruined buildings just beyond the brick walls. She stares at it in silence. "Have you ever hoped for something for so long, Christopher Dante, that when it finally comes you feel..." She stops and stares at the gray world.

"I have stopped feeling joy," I say. "It only turns to pain."

"I was going to say *terror*. An absolute and final terror, that the thing you expected, the thing you longed for...may be the most terrible thing in the world, and your choices alone have caused it into existence."

"I don't understand."

"Do you believe in the ancients view of prophecy? The myths from our past. There are tales," Beatrice says, "long, forgotten, hundreds, thousands of years old, that certain stories could speak to the future."

I do not speak, for she does not want an answer. I understand that whatever this is has to do with Stutz and their disagreement.

"I have been told, but I have never read it, of the story about Oedipus, the son of Laius and Jacosta, the King and Queen of Thebes. On the day of his birth it was prophesied he would kill his father and marry his mother. Laius and Jacosta pin the boy's feet together and give him to a shepherd to kill him. Thus, end the prophesy forever. The shepherd takes the boy, but chooses not to kill him, but instead gives him to a shepherd from Corinth, a city in a distant land. That shepherd gives the wounded boy to the King and Queen of Corinth who raise him as their own. They call him Oedipus because of the wound in his feet. The boy grows into a man. One day he hears a prophecy that he will kill his father and marry his mother. He believes his Corinthian parents to be his true mother and father. He is so distraught, that he, Oedipus, flees Corinth and journeys to Thebes. On his way, he runs into a caravan. They are disrespectful and harsh with him. He kills the leader and flees into Thebes. At Thebes he has learned the King is dead and a sphinx has ruined the land. Oedipus solves the riddle, kills the sphinx and is crowned King of Thebes. There he marries the Queen of Thebes, the beautiful Jacosta, and..."

I raise my hand. "What is the point?"

"Do you believe, Christopher Dante, that there are stories that tell our future?"

"What? I'm Oedipus?"

"I didn't say that."

"What then?"

"You didn't let me finish," Beatrice says. "It is not the story of the past that is important. It is the story of the present. It is perspective...point of view. That's what matters. When the play begins, Oedipus is King. He is driven by something that he cannot understand or control. A quest to find out who caused the plague upon Thebes. In that pursuit, he destroys everything around him."

"I know who I am," I say in disgust. "I have memories. I have a past. I have lived my life in time and space and now."

"So, Oedipus thought."

"You keep saying this...that I am someone else. That there is more than what I know."

"Do you think this a lie?" Beatrice asks.

"I don't know what to think anymore."

"The world you knew. The world you know. The world around you. Place them one atop the other and see which one consumes the other." She stares at the ruins beyond. "You know the answer."

"What are you saying?"

She looks at me. "Only to be wary, Christopher Dante. You may be fleeing from one prophesy only to find yourself trapped in the very same one." After a pause of consideration, she continues, "sing to me, oh muse, of the man of shadows..."

Suddenly, the veil drops, the hardened shell of her survivalist life falls away, for a moment. I see the pain in her eyes, a deep sorrow for something she is unable to articulate, something long suffering. It is there for a moment, and it is gone, the thick, worn surface of an ocean creature grown accustomed to the teeth of the world. I watch her walk away and disappear around the hallway corner.

That night I dream of Oedipus, a man caught between the destiny he believes he creates and the one creating him.

Chapter Twenty-five

We gather supplies for the final push to the IMAGO compound near the Great Lake, the place where they tested and probed me to determine if I was authentic. Stutz joins us, his filter mask streaked with grime and silt, the copper rings around his eyes making him look like a strange aquatic animal. We move quickly, intentionally through abandoned buildings, at times taking secret tunnels below the city, abandoned subway transit tunnels, up long rusted iron ladders, into the dim sunlight, and all over again. I don't see the compound, even though I am standing before it. Stutz and Caravaggio have camouflaged it so well, that to look at the walls, is to look at a many ruined and abandoned buildings as far as the eye can see. We slip through a secret door, and the place I remember is before me once again.

Stutz and Beatrice are nearly at war now. They do not speak to each other, except in grunts and motions. They have come to an impasse, and Stutz seems to be furious about it. I am increasingly left alone, day after day, wandering the camp, walking to the great black lake, the grey clouds on the horizon, watching the grey foam collect on the gray shoreline. I think of Hal, and wonder if he ever made it out of the Black Gate. I wonder if that was really Hal, maybe just a copy of him. The floor below me once again vanishes, and I feel myself floating in an existential chaos. I watch Stutz and Beatrice prepare and gather supplies. They study maps, and all the while I am left to my own devices.

Several months drift by. One afternoon I receive a summons. Doctor Mendel has asked to see me. The halls to his laboratory are familiar, dark and distant from the main hub of the compound. Every step brings back memories of my capture and testing. Mendel is inside, seated at a table. He has his glasses pushed up on his bald head and is looking through a microscope. "Come in, Mr. Dante," without looking up from the scope. "You are doing nobody any good standing there." Doctor Mendel is a wrinkled prune of a man, sunspots, age spot, liver spot, bruises cover his arms and forehead and neck. His white hair is a ring about his scalp, and his white lab coat is grey and spotted much like his skin.

"Achondroplasia," he says, voice a sort of wheeze from too much cigarette smoke. "Go on, look." He pulls away, and I look at the small blob of cells on the stained slide. "Causes short stature, large head, short limbs...sometimes a trident hand." He laughs. "They can be quite intelligent. That Governor of those slums...he was the first of them." Doctor Mendel pushes me away and stares at the slide again. He makes some notes in a small book. "This one is a real pain in my ass."

"How long have you been trying to cure it?" I ask, poking and turning over various papers. I see a stack of photographs, grotesque humanoid objects that resemble wax works left out in the sun.

Doctor Mendel is silent. He pulls away from the microscope, glasses still on his forehead. "Don't touch those. Years in the making. Cure? I'm not curing anything. I'm trying to make something, not cure it. You can't just mix it together like a martini." He laughs at his own joke. "Here's some ice, some vermouth, some gin, garnish with an olive...voila! There's a human...fresh from the generation tank! The human genome contains approximately three billion base pairs, residing in the twenty-three pairs of chromosomes within the nucleus of every human cell. Each chromosome contains hundreds to thousands of genes, which carry the instructions for making proteins. No, it ain't a martini, Mr. Dante." He is silent again, and pushes himself away, staring at me. "I need blood from you," he says in his smoker voice. "I just remembered. I mean, I used all the samples. Hell, look where that got us."

He scribbles something else in his black book and prepares a syringe. He sits me down on a chair, unfolds my arm, and with a quick fluid movement manacles my wrists to the chair. "You must be absolutely still for this process," he says and ties a rubber strap around my bicep. "We wouldn't want you to escape, now...would we?" I look for some irony or amusement in his face, but there is none. "Make a fist," he says. "That's it, good."

"What do you mean, generation tank?" I ask.

"That's where you came from, supposedly. The evidence is still out, but highly probable. That's all I can say. Highly probable." He taps my vein, then pricks me with the syringe, the plastic tube filling with a deep red liquid. "The data was overwhelming," he says. "still sifting through it. If I can reproduce even a semblance of that gene pool, then the project is a go. Problem is..." He snaps off the plastic tube and places another one on, looking at the full one with gluttonous eyes, and caps it. "The problem being, Mr. Dante, we can't use the mistakes. We need the real deal."

"You are creating them?"

"Who?"

"The Governor. Those...those...humans in the slums."

"Ha! If we were so lucky!" He pulls out a filter less cigarette, taps it on the counter, pops it in his mouth and lights it. The ash glowing read like a demonic eye. He breathes out and talks out the smoke. "That is not the real power...is it Mr. Dante?" He eyes the plastic tube again, snaps that one off and snaps on another, patting my arm gently. "No. The blood can only tell us so much, genetics so much. *Now* that book of yours...well, that's another story. Those equations. That is something. All up in that head of yours." He taps my forehead with an open palm, brutish, mocking.

I can sense the predator emerging.

"How does one get to that?" he says. "We can't just suck it out of you...now can we?" He laughs out more smoke and pushes the used butt into an overfilled ashtray. "One glance...just a single glance mind you, and I understood how powerful that is. It is...beautiful." His eyes grow large, as he moves deep into his own head, the pathways that lead to the book, the equations, translating the untranslatable code. "Quantum Alchemic Thaumaturgy...now that's something. That could change things." He snaps off the plastic tube and pulls the needle from my arm. He spins his chair to the table and busies himself with labels and placing the vials into the appropriate containers. "One look," he whispers. His back straightening and he sits upright. "One look is all." He turns. "An hour. That's it. Just an hour. You'd be here of course, translating it for me. Just an hour, and imagine what we could discover." He stares at me and through me. "The scientific discoveries...just think of it. We could really change things." His hand falls upon my restrained arm.

"I don't have the book."

He wakes from his daydream, shakes his head. "You could get it."

"I don't know where it is."

"You know it all the same." He is getting agitated, his hand trembling. "You could just tell me what you know. Just a little bit."

He quickly wheels the chair away and hurries to a locked drawer, fumbling with the key, opening it with a bang. He pulls out a worn piece of paper and wheels the chair right up to me, thrusting the page out before my eyes. "I got this when they first brought you here. It wasn't easy. Beatrice barely let it out of her sight, but she trusts me, you see...haha! She trusts me. I had only seconds, but I'm smart, you see." He taps his head. He is manic now, breathing heavy and shaking the page before my eyes for emphasis. "Just this. Just this page. You could tell me what it says. You could show me, right?"

I try to move. He shakes the paper and holds it out again. "Just a few lines."

I read what he copied. It is scribbled and nonsensical. I read, but instead of the cave art I see only fragments, an eye of a lion, the legs of the gazelle, images smudged and disjointed, pictures smashed together with no thought or pattern.

"What does it say, Mr. Dante? Tell me. We have all day."

"I don't know."

"Sure, you do." He moves closer. His acrid, smoky breath nauseating. "What does it say?" he asks pointing. "This one, for instance. What does this say? This simple little phrase right here." The paper is now nearly to my nose. I want to laugh, to chide this little, violent man, his grandiose schemes and plans. I want to smash the tiny gears twirling so insignificantly in his head. Instead, I sit there, silent. He shakes the paper.

"How about that one? Oh yes, that one is important. See? It took me quite a moment to write this one down."

I try to wiggle my wrists, but they are bound tight. Mendel is now reading the equations on the paper, turning it, mumbling to himself, saying "That one there. See that one. That is obviously a Quantum number but..."

In frustration, his face reddens, lips puckering. "You know, Mr. Dante. It is a dangerous thing to have such power, such hidden knowledge, a head full of secrets..." He leans close, grabbing my head with both hands, the page crinkling as he presses down. "Bad things can happen in such short time. Bad, bad things. Others should know about these. You see...bad things. Say, maybe an accident to...one of those deformed sycophants of yours...that Governor for example. This is a violent place." He's whispering now, intense. "Violence everywhere..."

Stutz appears in the doorway. He looks wary, cautious, eyes darting to Mendel holding my head, to my hands strapped to the armrests, to the table beyond. "What's going on?" He says.

Mendel unbuckles me. "Work, Mr. Stutz." He is annoyed. "Work, work, work." He walks the piece of paper to the drawer and locks it."

"Well, is he finished here?" Stutz says.

"Yes. Yes. Yes. Of course." Mendel is now back staring through the microscope.

"Let's go," Stutz says to me. "We're headed out for a recon. She wants you with us." He hesitates. "Now!"

"Did you know about all of this?" I say. "Does Beatrice?"

"Let's go," he says, and nearly drags me from the room.

Chapter Twenty-six

We travel out into the city, a day or two from the compound. Stutz bends over tracks, and the two of them whisper, Stutz sweeping his hand across the horizon, before pointing to the east. We make camp that night, but it is Mendel who is on my mind, his grotesque threat, shackling me to the chair, his avarice hands stroking my forearm as he weaves his webs. That is not all. I see clearly the photographs of the 'mistakes', of his terrible mishandling of a human life, the complexity of an angel reduced to a stained drop on a slide. Beatrice tries to pull me from my brooding, but I am silent, pensive, unresponsive to any gesture of communication.

All day we check for signs of the NRM. Again, Stutz finds tracks, but does not seem to be bothered by them. They are animal in nature, single file heading away from the city. The wind and dust clogs our filter masks. We take refuge from the storms in the first floor of an abandoned bank, the great iron door of the vault long since removed, the inside a respite from the storms outside. Stutz does not join us, but stays aloof and watchful.

"Are you aware of what Mendel and Stutz are doing?" I say suddenly. It is awkward, an explosion of emotion.

"Of course," Beatrice says. "Calling you was the long shot, the miracle. We need other alternatives."

"What right do you have to..."

"From your point of view perhaps."

"My point of view? I saw the pictures of the mistakes. I saw them. You are trying to create a generation tank. You are trying to create..."

Beatrice raises her hand. "Enough. You speak from ignorance. A generation tank does not create...anything. Doctor Mendel is a necessity." She stares at me for an uncomfortably long amount of time, gauging something or processing something. I can't decide. Finally she continues, "We all make choices. Those choices are never black and white. Never. You... Well, sometimes you must choose the lesser of evils. Nobody wins, Christopher. We all pay a price...always. I do not wish to speak about this any longer." She pulls the small blanket over her shoulders and turns her back to me. Soon we are both asleep.

That night I dream of those photographs. I scc thcm pastcd on a wall, full scale; the limbs and heads and legs distended and disproportional. I see them groan and cry out, for they become, in dream logic, something captured, helpless. There is no advocate, yet I know I am the advocate; I am the one who must speak. My mouth is eternally shut and I can only watch them moan and sob. Quite unexpectedly, I feel the embers, a slow smoldering fire. I felt it on the table when Mendel poked, pierced and prodded me. I felt it in the cells of the Black Gate. It builds. I felt it when I was manacled to the chair as Mendel points, pokes and shakes his crinkled paper of partial equations. I fixate on this image, Mendel and his damn scrap of scribbled half ass sequences that mean nothing. Impotent thaumaturgical moments that fissile and fade functionless. I see his greedy hands pawing me. I see those damnable glasses propped on his bald scalp like some crown, some illegitimate King ruling over his illegitimate laboratory, his doubt, the great wall separating what is on those pages, those simple, simple phrases one after the other...phrases that to him are the cawing of a crow! Ha! I see his face drop as he realizes he cannot access it, cannot in any way break through the pasteboard to the thing inside...haha! The fire builds inside and builds inside, an inferno. I know others are trying to put out this fire, dousing it with their silly buckets of doubt, fear, envy and hopelessness. This stokes the fire more and more. I see the deformed outcasts cheering the fire, lifting hands, supplicants to this righteous rage, helpless peasants with hope. And then quite suddenly, strikingly, this is no longer about Mendel, never was about Mendel or the misfits.

The groans grow louder, louder still. They are no longer from the outcast misfits, but something familiar, something personal, known. They are no longer groans, but a scream, a sob, a mother torn from her child. I feel it so deeply, a sudden pierce, a spear of sorrow and fear, severing marrow and bone...and I am...helpless, final...I embrace it, this empty abyss of loss, fear, doubt, and soon the sadness is an anger, a rage against the world of men and time and things. I am Oedipus pulled toward an ending I do not want but cannot stop, and this fuels it even more. I reach for the sobbing woman, but she is gone: evaporated, the outcasts: evaporated, Mendel and Stutz and Beatrice: evaporated in the white-hot light of my lunatic rage.

I wake to the night, the wind and the cold. Beatrice and Stutz are nowhere to be seen. I get up from the iron vault floor and find them staring at the horizon.

"Something is wrong," Beatrice says. "We must head back to the compound."

About an hour into our journey, Stutz climbs a tall mound of rubble and peers out over the horizon with his binoculars. When he returns, he is panicked. "Something has happened," he crackles through his mic. "I can see smoke." That is when we run. It is all I can do to keep up with them. I find it alarming that for someone they have spent four hundred years searching for I can be abandoned so quickly. The smoke thickens as we near the compound, a black acrid fog mixing in the already toxic air. A half mile away, we can see small patchworks of flames. When we come to what once was the skillfully camouflaged compound wall, there is only rubble, and Beatrice and Stutz are sprinting as fast as they can into the roaring inferno.

Chapter Twenty-seven

The fire has ravaged the once hidden world. We salvage a few items but everything else is melted and charred into ash; fluttering, blowing carbon remains. All the computer work is lost, all the buildings, food, medical supplies, most of the life support apparatuses, clothing and personal items; burned. Beatrice squats near a smoldering mound that was once doctor Mendel. Scattered around the charred body are blackened electronics, of what used to be the medical lab. The flames from across the way reflect in the thick, copper-rimmed glass on Beatrice's face.

Stutz steps up and squats next to her. He pokes his machete into the ash. "Our data downloads, everything, all our research samples."

Beatrice is silent.

"They will come in force now," Stutz says. "They'll see the smoke..." He stands. "I told you. I told you it was too dangerous!"

Beatrice stares at the smoldering ash. "I'm tired," she crackles in her mic.

Stutz is angry. "Shit!" he screams. He stands up.

"What happened?" I say in my mic. "We can go back to my house. We can go there."

"I told you this would happen!" Stutz yells and kicks the smoldering ash.

"We can go back to that shelter," I say. "The one we just came from. We can go there and make a plan."

Neither Stutz nor Beatrice respond.

"How did they find it? How did they find it after all this time?" Beatrice says, her voice a crackling whisper. "A spy?"

"There was no damn spy and you know this! It was a matter of time," Stutz says. "I told you, but you refused to listen."

"Let's go back to the shelter," I say. "They can help us. We'll hide there."

Beatrice stares at Stutz. "Check the docks for the transit. It may have survived."

"You really want to take that risk?"

"We die either way." She looks at the charred body before her. "He was a good man, like his father before him." She looks up at Stutz. "Gather what you can." She looks at the body again. "We have another task to do. We'll meet you down there."

Stutz is already running into the thick smoke toward the docks.

"You have a way to escape?"

"We're not escaping," Beatrice says. "Not from this. How could we?"

Beatrice stands up and looks at me. I see myself in her copper-rimmed filter mask. "Find something to dig a hole. We need to give him a proper burial. That's the least we can do."

~ * ~

The make-shift trawler has a large mast that Stutz had disguised as part of an abandoned transformer station. When we arrive, Stutz is busy painting the sides of the boat a charcoal and grey swirl. We pull off our filter masks. He hands me a brush and a can of paint, and we proceed to splash it on with reckless abandon. "This is one of the few times I miss that damn painter," Stutz says.

We have very little salvageable supplies, and the trawler has very little stored. We stow away what there is, pull up the lines, and Stutz pushes us out into the current where the Cuyahoga meets the Great Lake. We slowly drift north.

"Where's the motor?" I say.

"No motor."

They have come to the smoke. I can see the flashlights from the NRM soldiers. I now know them to be the mechanical or cloned Mr. Toughs and Mr. Yellow Suits, decked out from head to toe in body armor and carrying assault rifles. We are barely moving, and they will be upon us soon.

"Quiet!" Stutz says and pulls me down.

"Where's the motor?" I whisper.

"No motor," Beatrice says, now joining us as we crouch on the deck.

I stare at the shoreline. I can see several guards nearing the docks. Stutz stands up and yells, "Grab the oars and row!" He takes one. I take one, and we heave the heavy trawler toward open water. A collection of soldiers are now on the dock, and I hear them squawking to one another on their radios. We heave and heave and heave, and very slowly we separate from them. From nowhere, I hear the whine of an outboard motor. We are now a hundred yards from the dock, the lake swells rocking us bow to stern. Beatrice rushes from the cabin at the sound of the motor boat.

"Pull the oars in. Pull them in!"

I watch in horror as the tiny military style boat skips over the waves at an alarming speed, its search light now pinning us onto the water.

"You can't give up," I hiss. "Not like this!"

"Quiet, fool!" says Stutz.

One hundred yards, eighty, seventy, fifty yards...

From the abyss of black water comes something that dwarfs our trawler, an enormous slick, oily skinned snake the size of a whale, humping, arching, razor-toothed mouth gaping wide, and pounding down upon the helpless motored craft, obliterating it. We hear the interrupted gasps and screams as the Hal's and Max's and Mr. Toughs are pulled under or cut in half. We hear the impotent gunshots from the dock. Stutz slowly, steadily slides across the deck, grabs a sheet and pulls it taut, the sail unfurling, bloating with air, and the trawler skimming further out into the darkness of the Great Lake.

"No motor," I say. The saliva has gone from my mouth, and all that comes out is a low moan of despair.

Part Three

Stutz

Chapter Twenty-eight

The Great Lakes—as far as I have known—were vibrant bodies of fresh water. The NRM text books spoke of lakes and oceans as far as one could see, blue, clear, some drinkable, some with salinity, all teeming with life. A sustainable and vital ecosystem where The Nation could harvest a never-ending source of food and aquatic nutritional life. I can remember watching video images of fish processing plants, giant ships on the eternal, horizon-less water, pulling expanses of netting onto the decks, the silver scaled fish flipping and gulping. Net after net after net. I remember asking Hal if he had ever seen these vast expanses of water. He never had. "Has any of that put copper in your pocket or made your life any better, Stretch?" he said. Well, Hal, here's a news flash: There's no giant blue lake teeming with a food source. In fact, it would appear *we* are now the food source.

Beatrice is quite adamant there have been no Great Lakes, as I have been told, for four hundred years, ever since The Event radiated the Lake and all that was in it. For years, no one thought anything about it, but suddenly people, ships, anything on the Lake began to disappear. Researchers from the NRM investigated. They never returned. A NRM navy departed to explore. They never came back. They called it a Vortex Shiver of giant eels. What they learned later was that these were specific types of eels. They grew, bred, grew bigger. First the schools of fish evaporated. Next the larger predatory animals vanished. The once blue waters clouded with eel feces, muck and silt from their bottom-dwelling.

The eels got stronger, bigger, houseboat big, then ship big. They became colossus underwater hunters, killing each other and all things living. They each lay thousands of eggs, are asexual, so there is an endless and self-sustaining ecosystem. Any movement, thumping, thwapping, smacking on the surface of the water calls them. Blood calls them, a micron of blood in a square mile of water. I am now as distressed as Beatrice and Stutz. We have narrowly escaped from the NRM to now float in a lake of certain death.

"Stay down, flat against the deck," Stutz says.

I can hear the leviathans surfacing and submerging around us, a sudden blowing of air like an ancient whale, but Beatrice tells me it is not an exhalation but a sensory inhalation. They are smelling us. They know we are here, but they cannot determine if we are a food source. The trawler is so disguised it looks now like the lake itself, like a piece of debris. More and more arrive, several smaller ones ram into the side of the boat, and this agitates the others. Still more appear. We are in a Vortex Shiver of eels, but the larger ones begin to attack the smaller ones, and this becomes a storm of titans, splashing and feasting, soaring up into the gray sky, thundering down, bits and pieces of flesh splashing a chum onto the surface which incites more and more eels. Our trawler skims away from the storm raging below and above, and soon all we can see is black, rolling water, swells of five to ten feet. Stutz furls the sail and has us drift, so as not to attract the eels.

Beatrice hands me water. "Only a mouthful," she says. Her voice is without emotion.

Stutz sits quietly across from me. The wind is harsh against my face, but the dust and particles are far away, blown clean from the North wind.

"It will be a good twenty-four hours," Beatrice says to Stutz.

Stutz laughs, gulps a tiny bit of water and screws on the cap. "Like we have a choice."

"We need time," she hisses.

"We're out of time. Every minute we do not act, is a chance...maybe our only chance...to get back."

They are hissing and whispering, jerking their hands back and forth as if I do not exist. One thing I know for sure...one thing is absolute: I am the center of the argument.

The day turns into evening, and I can see the gray clouds sweeping across the sky, building in enormous cumulus nimbus far to the north. The shoreline is gone now, and all I see are black walls of water as we drift up one side of a swell and down the other. A sudden shower of black soot pours over us, and I pull my knees up to my chin, and bury my face into my hands to block the acidic liquid particles. Nobody says anything. When it passes, I wipe my eyes and realize my hands are filthy, nails black. My body is wracked with pain, tired, bruised, and cramped. The emotional tsunami has collapsed over me, and I begin to cry.

"I didn't understand the time dimensional anomaly when I entered your universe," Beatrice says, emotionless, like recalling a forgotten memory. "I also did not understand the wormhole collapsed on this side." Beatrice is silent for a moment. Finally, she whispers, "A terrible miscalculation." She smiles wanly, then looks at Stutz. "I was not the only one who made the jump. There were other families. Something else made it through as well. You have already met it. It took you, and many others of us. We are not as we were in IMAGO. We are different, changed. What was once something laborious or perhaps inconsequential has now become...meaningful. National Reduction Method Bureau was created to stop us. It's based on the studies of Isaac Alexander Newton's theories of Reductivity. You have learned about him, I'm sure, but you were never told the real truth, only that it was necessary. It is a systematic behavioral training method in order to eliminate all the emotive power in an imitation so that no psychic recollection may occur. From the beginning, all of us have been systematically hunted down. Anyway, I thought I was the only one of my kind left. I found Stutz and Caravaggio years later. You see, Christopher, we came through the portal and became trapped with no way back. We...and you...are what this universe calls...immortal."

I imagine what it must have been like, alone, hunted, a young girl in a strange world. I look at Beatrice, but I see only me. She understands how I feel, or I should say she once did, in some distant past. I see her as a small vulnerable being, a snail surviving at first hour by hour, then daily, secreting a layer of gel that hardens, then another and another and another for years, decades, centuries, until what was once vulnerable is now impenetrable—both from without...and from within, a trapped, flint-chipped thing.

"You are...immortal?" I ask, my mind beginning to clear, capture, categorize the new world around me.

"*We* you mean," Beatrice has a tinge of spite. "Death in the world of men and time and things is beyond us." She pauses. "Perhaps a Generation Tank *is* preferable to a life of ash, pain and suffering." She purses her thin chapped lips. "*They* wish for immortality, *those* of this world. Spend some time reading their literature. From every generation, every corner of their world, they scream and plead and beg for it. They do not understand the weight and cost of such a choice." She stares right at me. "Are we immortal? If by that you mean we cannot take our own lives in this place, or the NRM cannot kill us, or only by the hand of someone from IMAGO can we die...the Ghūl, one of us—if that is what you call immortal...there you have it. Do we live forever? I have no idea. Four hundred years is an eternity, wouldn't you agree?"

We sleep in restless fits upon the rolling black water. It is Beatrice who wakes me.

"Stay down," Stutz hisses. "It's a Bureau Drone. Do not move or make a sound." Beatrice grabs a blanket and throws it over all three of us. We huddle close together, knees bent under us, arms tucked to our sides. "Calm your breathing," Beatrice whispers.

I can feel it before it appears, a distinct electrical field, like static, making the blanket crackle, strands of hair from my head, on my arms, raising up. I can hear it, a low buzz or whirling sound. It is hovering just above the deck of our trawler. Beatrice begins to hum. What the hell is she doing? I am sure she wishes to die. The song is low, a whisper, and soon it fills my head, swirling in my imagination with pictures. "Sing, oh muse! Sing!" I don't know what she means, and I cannot speak or the thing on the deck will detect us. It is like breathing, like what I have been doing all my life; creating, pulling from abandoned pieces of the forgotten, the buried, shaping, molding what was or used to be into something new...the abandoned moments in my shed...I understand. I think of flight and claw and power and grace and I see it come from the gray sky, huge feathered and ominous, talons outstretched like pieces of steel. The drone dodges, but it is too late. I hear the crack and scrape of steel and composite as the giant raptor collides with the drone. The drone is ready, and we hear the crackle of mic, commands and questions over the speaker. The Eagle separates, screeches and shoots like a rocket back into the gray above.

The drone hovers and hums. I know if the probe scans, we will be revealed. The great eagle thunders down and smashes the unsuspecting drone. They both plunge into the water near the trawler.

"We have only seconds," Beatrice screams. "Unfurl the sail!"

Stutz reaches for the sheet, but it catches on the cleat. He must crawl to the knotted line and fumble with it. The trawler lifts in the swells as the giant eels hump and surface. The eagle is in the water, flapping to free itself from the drone as well as the oncoming threat, while the drone shudders and spins in a frothing, foaming pattern. Stutz unknots the line and pulls the sheet taut, the sail climbs the mast and blows out with the wind. Our trawler is rising up on a swell caused by a titanic eel swooping down upon the great eagle.

"Hold on!" Stutz screams, but his voice is cut short by the thunder of water unleashed upon the deck.

I hear a terrible crack, and see the mast bend and snap, the sail and boom collapsing across the deck and falling into the water. Stutz has vanished under it, and Beatrice is desperately holding onto a cleat, her legs hanging in the black water.

"Hold on!" I scream, but my leg is caught in the snarl and web of rigging.

Another eel lunges at the eagle and the drone, misses and swamps us with water. I tear free and grab Beatrice's hand, pulling her back on the trawler. She points to the fallen mast and the sinking fabric of sail. "Stutz!" she screams.

Stutz is floundering in the chaos of the sinking boat. His head goes under the black water, then appears again, disappears, then reemerges. He pulls himself toward us, but there is a sleek, black hump as the eel surfaces and plummets him under the water.

Beatrice screams; a yelp, a wail. She reaches into the air, her neck a chord of muscle and vein, face red and blotchy. "Stutz!" The water churns and foams, gray and violent. Stutz emerges with his machete clenched in his teeth. He holds the wreck of flotsam and jetsam hacking at the gaping mouth tearing at his legs. There is blood and gore and black foam and flesh scattering about him. Another eel surfaces, mouth open, ripping apart the decapitated monster. Stutz swims toward us, just as another eel surfaces, knocking him into the tangle of sail and rigging and sinking mast. He disappears under the surface, and does not appear again.

The trawler tips and takes on water as a leviathan splinters the wooden deck into a hundred pieces. The eagle is gone. The drone is gone. The Trawler, sail, mast and all that we thought safe is now under water, and as I swim for something to support me, a tangle of line snags my ankle, twists in my effort to get free and pulls me under and into the vortex shiver of colossal eels.

Chapter Twenty-nine

I have thought quite a lot about the Generation Tanks since my conversation that day with Beatrice on the trawler, and our similar and yet profoundly different existences. There is something to her wish for death, the complicated undercurrent to that. We both lived the same amount of time. Both were existing in the world of men and time and things. The difference is, I was cocooned, a harvested thing to be used eternally in the act of creation. I would learn much later how wrong I was about what a Generation Tank actually is, but suffice it to say I was the oblivious one...Beatrice was actually living. There was no weight and cost in my world, for I was unaware of my surroundings, and like a beast in captivity. I did not recognize the glass walls to be what they truly were. Beatrice knew pain, sorrow and suffering, the great cost of friendship, of terror, of hope, of hopelessness, a great desire to establish relationships with those of this world, knowing it would always end, forever and forever, a rending, and with each mending, the stitches looser, the gap widening, and to mend it exhausting. How many people had she grown to love, to lose? What was it like when she realized so many were merely clones and the enemy: mechanical beings designed to hunt her to extinction? That was not the case with Stutz and Caravaggio. They were equals. There would never be a mending, for there would never be a rending in the first place.

Four hundred years together and roots grow deep, deeper than what humans in the world of men and time and things can ever know. Four hundred years and the most heinous of offenses become, over such expanse of time, mere isolated family squabbles. Four hundred years and one knows the other, deeply, truly, at times madly. So, when the rending does come, an unexpected separation, surprising and final—when that happens, the weight and cost turns into madness or hardens you into something not human at all.

When Stutz goes under, Beatrice grows silent. When the trawler folds in on itself, splinters and explodes into pieces, she lets go of me and sinks. I pull her to a large piece of floating debris, shove her onto it, her eyes vacant. I search one more time for Stutz, but the shiver of eels is now unleashed into a feeding frenzy one upon the other, and no human could survive such a thing. I kick and paddle further and further away from the eels, Beatrice's lifeless eyes staring forward. I can feel the current picking us up. We seem to move with the waves, up and down, up and down, up and down. Soon, I can only hear the eels in the far distance, the sound of the waves and wind now picking up. I can't tell if its evening, morning or night, for the gray is always the same, the black water the same. At every moment I expect something terrible to snatch us both into oblivion.

Fortunately, they don't, and what I see is the horizon, the cityscape of Cogstin. I realize that the current is pushing us back to shore.

"I need your help," I say to Beatrice. She does not respond.

She lay on the slatted wood and fiberglass shard, loosely holding on, her mind still somewhere back in time and space.

"I need you to kick," I say again and shake her from her memories. "The coast. I see the coast. You need to kick with me." She does so, and for what seems like ages, a night and a day, we kick and paddle. With every stroke closer, Beatrice becomes more and more present, until she has returned to the land of the living, and is paddling with me, kicking with me, and we finally run aground on the sandy shoreline far to the West of where we initially launched.

I stand up, the grit and slime and feces from the water saturating my clothes, my hair, my skin. It is night, and it is hard to determine where we are, if the NRM waits for us or if they are expected or have already left. Beatrice walks to a rock formation and sits down next to it.

I begin a litany of questions. Where should we go? What should we eat? Should we stay on the beach? Do you think they can track us here?

Just like that, Beatrice is upon me, her forearm against my throat. "Shut up!" Her voice is a growl, a ferocious animal pushed to the breaking point. "I should have listened to him. He was right. You will kill us all!"

She is breathing hard, her hand trembling. She releases her grip, and I scramble to safety.

I once again think of the snail's shell and the hardened layers of suffering. I am alone in the wind, sand and stink of the lake. At first, I do not wander far for fear of the NRM, but the day's events have drained my energy. My muscles cramp and I am exhausted. I find an abandoned boat shed, two sides folded down from storms, and huddle in the adjacent corner. The roll of the waves, the blowing sand and the smell of decay are a constant interruption to my sleep.

It is Beatrice who shakes me awake, and it is several hours before sunrise. "Come with me," she says, her voice still harsh and void of feeling. "You need to get warm."

When we arrive at the campsite, there is an inviting blaze with almost no smoke, the wind shifting to the north west. This gives her the ability to stoke it, and warm us both from the night's chill while the shelter of the stone walls blocks the light. I want to crawl inside the orange flame, it feels so good. Beatrice has killed something...a dog perhaps. She has it roasting on a spit, the sinews and fat bubble and snap in the heat. We sit in silence as the warmth from the fire steams off the moisture of the night.

"I don't know what's real anymore," I say. "I lived a life I thought to be real, but it was manufactured, fake, imitations."

Beatrice says nothing, just checks the meat, a pool of blood rises to the surface and smolders and sizzles as it mingles with the juice. She sits back on her heels a bit and leans against the stone wall.

"Was there ever a time when you did?"

"Did what?"

"Know what was real?"

We are silent again for fifteen minutes, Beatrice humming something softly to herself. I almost think it a hymn to the dead Stutz. I say nothing...just listen.

"Even before The Event," Beatrice says, "what was real was just an illusion. Just because there are Generation Tanks makes it no less unreal or mimetic. You say everything is make believe. I say, when has it not been? It happens throughout all of time. The good, the beautiful, the sacrifice for the many—these are illusions. It takes a catastrophic event to show

147

everyone what was at stake, but even then, it is too late. It's always too late."

She cuts a piece of meat off the carcass and hands it to me. I eat it greedily, sucking on the juice, wiping my cheeks with my sleeve. "When the world was younger, we cut the throat of an animal so we could live. That was the bargain we made. The one for the many. With great weight and cost, that animal gave up its blood, its life, so others could live. Think about this act. With all of its life, from a small calf struggling through illness, worms and disease, to an adult fending off coyotes, with all of this life lived—it is brought to the wooden block for sacrifice. When that knife is pulled across the jugular vein, and the life force flows out, it is messy, terrible, and filled with a sadness for that once history that trails behind all living things. When we eat the meat, the weight, the costs are real, hard and real. With every bite we affirm the truth: The few must be killed so that the many can live." She is silent again and seems to be humming that same hymn. She stops abruptly. "That is real, Christopher Dante. A world with wrapped beef or chicken or lamb in Styrofoam, with plastic bags and napkins hanging above the meat aisle to wipe our hands; God forbid we get any blood on us...this pre Event world...this is the world of make-believe." Beatrice spits into the fire, then grinds her teeth. "There is a weight, Christopher Dante. There always is a cost—whether we choose to believe there is or not. The world of men and time and things will exact its penalty for life. The few will always be sacrificed, even if the many do not understand or care that they are. We may sand and polish and dull the edges, but this world has teeth, and its appetite is insatiable."

She stares at me, and I feel her eyes boring deep inside. I look away because of fear or shame or doubt. "You have awakened from your sleep to find the world you knew to be a lie. It is the first step." She looks into the fire and whispers. "Perhaps it will be your last." She stands up. "We need to put out the fire. Dawn will break soon, and we must head back to Cogstin.

"We're going back in?"

"Yes. He was right all along. Now it may be too late for all of us."

"Listen," I say. "Stutz just..."

Beatrice raises her hand to me, finger like a dagger. The veins at her temples raised, her teeth clenched.

"You have not earned the right to mention that name. Do you understand?"

She eases up, breathes in deeply. It was a storm of emotions suddenly, with great effort and practice, a resolved will, secured. "Now put out the fire. We haven't got much time, and we have a three-day journey ahead of us."

It is impossible to tell if the sun has risen or not, but the gray seems to be lighter, the air thick with dust. We have no filter masks, so we improvise. We tie torn shirts around our face and nose. We are two insignificant images disappearing into the haze of a ruined city. I think of what Beatrice said about the few and the many, the slaughtered calf. I wonder how dangerous will be the teeth that wait for us in this world of men and time and things.

Chapter Thirty

We walk most of the day, if you can call what we do walking. It's more like crouching, hiding and scurrying like rats in a flashlight beam. The NRM is everywhere, pocked, placed and positioned so nothing can get past. Every road, every major ruined building. They are not in the tunnels, and soon this is our way to bypass the check points. Even these are filled with dangers: sudden falling stone, old subway tunnels dead ending, consciously sealed up or inadvertently caved in. Each time we turn around, backtrack for miles on end, venture down the next tunnel, stop, turn around, backtrack. I have lost track of time, of space, day or night.

The tunnels are dark, and we have no food, water or light, save for a small piece of spark flint Beatrice scrapes with her machete blade. Every once in a while, I can hear—or think I hear—footsteps, a slight splash, a rumbling of disturbed stone, but I'm lost in the oppressive sightless world. Every now and again, a blink or flash—no more: two green dots somewhere far behind us, like eyes watching.

All the while Beatrice sings, under her breath, a whisper song, and I do not recognize it. It comforts me, gives me hope. The tunnels are filled with decay and dampness, a thick, oily scent of something long lived and hidden. The song expands in that black space before us, this whisper song, and like a bat with sonar, it paints images of that which surround us. We sidestep, bend low, crawl on our bellies. Always the song echoing out, bouncing off the cement tunnel, and back again.

Beatrice stops at a divided passage before us, the song painting a picture of every rock and puddle, protruding rebar, and fissured and crumbling obstacle. I can smell the decay and mold and ancient earth emanating from the tunnel to our right, so overwhelming that I turn my head and breathe through my mouth.

"My god," I say. "What is that smell?"

"That is our way forward."

She looks about her, turning, tuning into something unseen. At last, she hurries over to a wall. I cannot see her with my physical eyes, for we are in pitch blackness. I know what she is doing, her song strong inside my head. I see her bend down, scrape and pull at the wall, removing several cement blocks then taking cans and a clay jug from the hole. Soon we are sitting against the tunnel wall, gulping down the contents of pineapples, peaches, the thick syrup streaming down my stubbled face.

She gulps from the can and nods her head toward the terrible smell. "Sector 17, the building, the Cave Art," she pauses, "and everything else...is down that way."

"Why could we possibly want to go back there?"

Beatrice is humming again; then she stops. "We have no choice now. There is only this."

"I don't understand."

"The Event." I feel her move her arms in a gesture, but I cannot see anything. "They were digging the subway tunnels, and broke through to find a cavern, a network of caves. On their walls... What they didn't know, couldn't know was how ancient...from the very beginning. That was when the portal opened."

"To IMAGO," I whispered.

"Your father was the first to enter it. It would be known forever as twenty/twenty. Geoffrey Dante entered the portal for twenty minutes, before he returned. What he thought was twenty minutes was actually twenty years in the world of men and time and things. You were conceived in IMAGO, the first hybrid between Earth and the Multiverse. Elizabeth, your mother, was the last Fabulist. All the tests we have run confirm you are a genetic match. Now you are the last Fabulist; Elizabeth and Geoffrey's offspring."

I can hear the determination.

"We must go back."

"How?" I ask. "I thought the portal closed with The Event."

She stares at me in the darkness. I cannot see her face, but I know she is calculating something, questioning her decision. "It did."

"Then...why are we going?"

"How did you escape the generation tank?"

"I don't know."

"No human could have released you." We are silent. Beatrice tosses the can to the floor. "We still have two days to go. It will only get harder and more dangerous from here."

We enter the tunnel, and the oppressive smell is so great, I have a hard time concentrating on Beatrice and the song-whisper. I begin to sense something quite terrible is waiting for us, perhaps stalking us, lurking just out of reach, a horrible mouth gaping and pressing near, before pulling back. Like a floater in the eye, when I glance toward it, it is gone. I keep hearing the occasional splash or crumbling rock. I reach out blindly for Beatrice, grasping her coat.

"I can't see," I say. "We need to stop. Something's wrong."

Beatrice turns her head toward me. "It's strong," she whispers. "We must keep going."

I feel it like a wave of heat, but it is more internal than external. It is a growing sense of annihilation, a stripping away, particle by particle. With each step, into the darkness, I can feel the prying, pricking, hardened, yellow talons piercing, scraping, scratch upon scratch. We press on. Beatrice tries to sing her whisper song, but it disappears into the black void before us.

"It knows we're here. It knows." She stops. She is panting now as if we have risen thousands of feet, the oxygen spread thin. She is hunched over. "It knows. It always knows. I should not have come here. I should not have tried on my own." She stands and we press on, leaning forward, like two travelers in a sandstorm.

My mind is black now, like the surrounding tunnel. The smell is overwhelming, layered: decayed flesh, souped and leaky with bloat, and that mixed with ancient earth, dusty, molded, dry as bones. It is an oppressive blanket.

"We need to turn back," Beatrice says. "We should not have come." Immediately, I hear her say. "Run!" She is gone.

I reach blindly with both hands. All I feel is empty air or the smooth cement walls of the tunnel.

"Beatrice," I whisper. Even my words fall flat and fade into the oppressive surroundings. I hear something from behind, running, stopping, running again. "Beatrice!" I shout now and do not care, for not to shout is to be lost in the void. I can hear laughter...or is it the wind through the tunnels?

That is when Beatrice screams. It is loud, filled with terror and pain, and it is an impossible distance away. I understand her words and they settle on me like a cold fog. "Run! It is a trap! It knows...It knows...It knows!"

It is a scream unlike I have ever heard from her, but I am helpless to follow. I try to think of her, but it is now only darkness. I can hear the crackle and static of hundreds of NRM soldiers. I try to imagine the cave art, the lion, anything, but it is only black and pitiless shadows swirling, chortling.

I begin to run toward her, toward her sobbing. I am cut down by crumbled cement and rebar, scraping and gashing my shins. I tumble to the wet ground. The blood is flowing freely now from my legs. I know the wound is deep. I am lost, abandoned, and unable to move forward.

I hear something close behind, but when I turn, it disappears. I sense the Ghūl, and the image I now see as clear as the sun in my imagination, is the one I saw that day in Sector 17. I know it is lumbering, tooth and claw, coming for me. Its will is severe and determined. It does not know where I am, so it sniffs, bends and scratches at the dirt, then ever forward. I cannot call. I do not know which way to go. I stand, fumble and run into the night, away from the hunter. My mind filled with fear, a blind rage of panic; the wildebeest's flight from the croc. I am limping, dragging myself through the darkness. I see flashes of light, then tiny green dots that seem to bounce and dance in the air far away, then closer, closer, closer. I know I am hallucinating. Our collision nearly knocks me to the ground.

"We must bind your leg, or it will follow us," hisses a voice in my ear.

I know this voice. The sound and my present situation make it nonsensical.

"Give me your leg. Quickly!"

I feel the pressure on the wound as the bandage wraps tight, and I want to cry, to sob, to hold on to him forever. I see the small green eyes glow in the darkness, night vision goggles strapped to his forehead, and when he lifts me to my feet, I can feel the tenacious, wiry thin muscles of the man I saw taken by eels so many days ago.

He holds me tight, gentle but firm. "Can you walk?" I shake my head, still sobbing from the hope, doubt and fear that washes over me. "I will carry you," he says.

I am off the ground, like a rag doll. I feel the power in his body as he rushes quick and certain down the tunnel, fast, so fast I think it is a dream. All I can hear is that roaring wind, and the explosion of light as we surface into the land of the living.

Chapter Thirty-one

We are compartmentalizing beings by nature, our minds filled with tiny hermetically sealed chambers like cells of a honeycomb. Speak to the sufferers of this world, those who have seen the teeth of death; the 'jagged edges that tear the flesh', as one once told me. Speak to them, and you will understand that idea to be true. If our minds can absorb every memory, the eyes truly a portal as well as with the ears and sensory agents on the skin, every impression, every second of every minute, hour, day, weeks on end...the honeycomb walls filling, creating new walls, filling. Certainly, there must be a moment when the cells collapse, the memory too big, too dark, too traumatic it begins to press like a great fist on the next wall, breaking through, and the next and the next until it is a tsunami of pain and darkness, until it obliterates every cell...and a self is created, the self we understand to be the other.

What of me? What cells have I known in the Generation Tanks? What impressions have created myself? Three hundred and eighty years of nothing...and I am pushed into the world with Hal and Max and U-Salvage, working in Cogstin, dreaming dreams, wanting, eating, sleeping, waking, forming cells, filling them with the present, creating a thin film of self, when what is real, what is true, what I know to be self—all of these are actually an illusion, an image. Do we all have other selves? Are all of us from childhood to adolescence to middle age and beyond, nothing but constructed honeycomb selves, the Id, the Ego, the Super Ego, all of this a wall to keep the other selves from cascading and obliterating one another like a ruptured dam? All I know to be real has vanished. All I understand to be the world of men and time and things is no more, no anchor, no mooring. I am adrift in a universe of uncertainty, and my only reaction to it all: *fight or flight*. I choose the latter.

~ * ~

I wake up to Other Hal hovering over me, his sideways mouth stretched back as if with wires. He is tall, and his hair is scattered with large patches of baldness at the top. He wears overalls, but they are baggy and loose with gaps on either side of his hips that you could slide a dictionary in. He steps back as I fully enter the land of the living. Other Hal, with his sideways mouth and tiny arm, grunts at me and points. I look over to Stutz and Governor Max hunched over the small, metal table. They are arguing, Stutz stoic while Governor Max gesticulates. Other Hal grunts again. I feel myself closing down. All I want is old Hal and old Max, my old life at U-Storage, and the concrete. I drink from the plastic cup of water and thank him. He smiles a snaggle toothed grin and grunts.

"Ah, he's awake," Governor Max says.

His face flashes anger toward Stutz, then a polite smile back at me. "Perhaps you will have more time to rest later." He glances again at Stutz.

I am silent and can barely look at either of them. I sit down. A cup of coffee is poured and placed before me.

"You are safe," says Governor Max, interpreting my silence in a particular way. His small, half-closed eye blinks. "Ignorance is bliss...better for us all if you do not know where you are. Courage and sacrifice have kept this place safe. It is still here in Cogstin. In some more than others."

Stutz looks at Max, then over to me. His face is blackened from Cogstin's ash, goggles pulled down around his neck like a scarf, a clear demarcation line around his eyes where they once were. He is worn, weathered, same sharp nose and long forehead like Beatrice. I think they may be related somehow.

"I saw you go under," I say. "Nothing human could have survived those things."

Stutz smirks, "For that reason, it's a good thing I'm not."

"Stutz has a way of surviving," Governor Max says, "when others do not."

Governor Max sips his coffee, but his hand trembles. The two search each other's face, a jousting match with the eyes.

"For all their colossus, eels are half blind," Stutz says, calmly, emotionlessly. "I managed with what I had."

I think of our night in Cogstin where from the scattered, discarded material he made a garbage pile to hide from the NRM soldiers. I imagine him floating in the inky swells, the leviathans splashing about, calm and steady as a buoy, drifting to the wreckage, pulling what fragments he can from the splintered boat, sail, mast, the flotsam and jetsam, working it all into something of absolute disguise, a part of the debris, maybe the image of the very eels themselves.

"That I am dead, or thought to be," Stutz says, "can only help us."

"It's madness. Especially now," Governor Max says. "Complete and utter madness."

"Beatrice did the only thing she could," Stutz says directly to me. His voice still calm. "Believing me to be dead, she tried to take you to the Cave Art. When we all stand before it—so says your book, the book you wrote in captivity—when we are all present before the portal...it will open."

I look at my cup of coffee, the deep black swirling with the dollop of milk.

"That's right," Governor Max says. "Now the Ghūl took her and now she will pay dearly."

Stutz wipes his face in frustration, or in exhaustion, it is hard to tell. He looks right at me. "Is it true," he says. "Is it true the portal will open? Is this just another make-believe story, some mythology in your head?"

I sip my coffee. Other Hal has dropped a tin dish. It spins, shimmers and wobbles to its arduous conclusion.

"She thought I was dead," Stutz says. "The Painter...well, who knows what bargain he's made, and with you...she had to try. It is too strong for one of us. It may be too strong for all of us, but that is something we shall never know." He looks directly at Governor Max. "We must act with what we have."

"Perhaps we could stay here to plan, to think things through. Why do you insist on such secrecy?"

"There is nothing to think about. There are no more choices," Stutz says.

"They have Beatrice," Governor Max says.

"When the hen just waltzes into the fox's den..." Stutz says. "Beatrice believed if she could get you to the cave and see the forms, you could open the portal."

"Is any of this even possible?" I whisper.

"It's an irrelevant question. According to your book, in order to open the portal to IMAGO you must see the actual cave art. It is also a fact that a Ghūl waits for our return to the cave. A most certain trap. It is a fact we cannot defeat it, and even if we could get to the cave, gathering the four of us is now impossible. *To open the portal—everyone from IMAGO must be present*, these are your words. These are the facts, unvarnished." Stutz glances at Governor Max before he turns to stare at me.

"So, the young Dante should stay," Governor Max says. "Here he will be safe. You state the evidence better than any lawyer. What advantage could going to Sector 17 possibly gain?"

"None the likes of you could understand." Stutz's voice is nearly a hiss of anger.

"Therefore, it is settled."

Stutz looks at me long and hard. I look down at the dollop in my coffee, look up, and he is still staring at me.

"We leave at dawn tomorrow," he says and stands up abruptly. "To wait longer will be to wait too long." With that, he walks out of the room.

I find the silence and Governor Max so irritating; I decide it's time to leave.

"Stay inside the barrier," Governor Max says and smiles kindly. I see the half eye as a nightmare, and this dark warehouse and damp cold and humming and buzzing of low whispers and muffled laughs and humped and limping humanoids and shadows all as partial truths, disparate moments of dream logic that have ceased to make sense. I nod my head to Governor Max's words, and spend the next hour searching the grounds for escape.

By early evening I am stuffing whatever I can find into a military style canvas backpack scavenged from an adjacent supply room. It is dark in this corner of the room, and I lean into the shadows of the pantry door as another deformed imitation of what I know enters, grabs a can of condensed milk and exits. I slip out and hurry to the darkened room where I awoke this morning. I place the sack under my cot. When I turn, I see the tall, thin shadow of Stutz sitting in the corner observing everything I did. He motions me to sit. I do. In a low tone, quiet, almost a whisper, he begins to talk.

Chapter Thirty-two

How long are we willing to wait? This is a question that goes unanswered most all of our lives, and yet, it is at the core of our existence...the very core, from the moment we splash into the world of men and time and things...we cry because we cannot wait. We do not understand the concept of time and we fill our lungs and blow because not to is to die. We don't die, often times, we learn to wait for food, for comfort, and eventually those things we need or desire. We call it patience. We are told it is a virtue. Beatrice was right: it is time that causes the teeth of life.

So, we spend our early days waiting to get older...waiting to begin, to finally start a journey we have observed others start around us. The journey to begin is really only another level of waiting. We wait to be educated, we wait for employment, a partner, wait to have children, wait to get an apartment, a house, and when midlife overtakes us because we have waited for so long...we get bored or depressed and we wait for the next moment to make us feel better, a new opportunity, a letter from the NRM Board of Corrections, an official notice from Universal Salvage to go to Sector 17, something, oh God, something that will change the trajectory of our waiting, wait, wait, wait, wait, wait.

In the end we wait to die. All we do in this world of men and time and things is wait. How long are we willing to wait? Those trapped in time and space have a span of eighty years, and there is no more. This is an enormous question, with even more profound answers, with every human being weighing in subconsciously, unconsciously or even consciously. How long are humans willing to wait: twenty years, fifty years, eighty? Some can't wait that long and exit. Some exit because of a mistake, a bad choice, an accident, a bullet to the brain from war, from another, from one's

160

own hand. Some stop waiting with pills, with jumping from tall places, a slice of the wrist, a belt around the neck, carbon monoxide gas while you fall asleep in the car in the closed garage. Ah, to sleep, and end the heartaches of this world. A consummation devoutly to be wished. Right?

What if, like Stutz, you did not have a choice? What if there was no exit plan, and waiting for something specific was your only choice? After a year of trying all that you knew, three hundred and sixty-five days of trying, twenty-four hours, every sixty minutes, every sixty seconds...a year goes by with you desiring only this one thing—to go back home—after a year you realize it cannot happen. So, you wait. You plan. You hope. You build scenarios of hope, what if's, and another year goes by. Then five years, then ten. What does that look like? What happens to Stutz's internal self? Soon the time spent searching and making plans for that one thing, the escape. The only reason you believe that explains your existence in the world of men and time and things...one day while hunched in a corner staring at the Great Black Lake you realize that 'time has slipped by' and you have waited for—what they call in this place—an actual lifetime. The life you have spent was not your own, it was a life trying to find the way back to the life you once had, a life now faded at the edges, for the new life, this life of searching, waiting, hoping is all that you know, and it has become the only existence you understand.

This is depressing. So, melancholy, alone, and still waiting, you decide to stop waiting. You make the hard choice to quit. Ah, but there's the rub. You are Stutz, not like the men and women of this universe. You can't quit. There is no such thing as giving up, letting go, giving in. You ask: Is It physically, existentially impossible to leave this world you find yourself in? What a question! How will you know? Of course, after that, it is a tragic-comedy of errors, for to test that theory is to test the very capacity to quit. There are heights that surely must allow you to quit. No, it is a fact...there is not. A lot of pain, time to heal, but indeed—no exit. Surely to kill the body is to kill the soul, to end all things. So, after experimenting on this very concept, you learn the hard lesson: you are, indeed, immortal. One may chop a limb, limbs, any and every appendage—who would think without a head one could survive. There it is—and to even consider the time involved in decapitating one's self when there is no other to do it for you—these are Nobel Prize worthy inventions, but alas: white hot pain, sleep, and presto—magic man has returned, hunched in the ruined corner staring at the Great Black Lake in a place you are now calling hell. The second hundred-year span unfolds before you

So, if you cannot exit the world, at least you should know the world you can't exit from. This now becomes your obsession. You try to cross the Great Black Lake. You die and return into the land of the living. You walk as far as you can, through the ash city of Cogstin, the shadows of humans, the carbon shadows now forever in the dirt. You walk and walk and walk and die and return to that spot before the Great Black Lake. You come to the Great Sand Flats, and cross into that wasteland, die from dehydration and starvation and come back to face the Great Black Lake. Cogstin, always Cogstin. You are trapped in the world of men and time and things, no way out, no way to get back. One day, you discover, you are not alone. Oh, you knew you were not alone, the world you find yourself in has been filled with replicated humans. The same thousand or so over and over and over. You can kill them. They come back. You can maim them, they die. They come back. They are worker bees in a dead city, the city of ashes, mining, salvaging, collecting.

You watch them strip steel, pulverize cement into gravel, load their barges, trucks and trailers. You spend your hours, an unlikely anthropologist, studying them, how they work, what they believe, the component parts of their lives, what they know to be true and good and beautiful, their similar personalities, and you even become fond of them, naming them like a marine biologist names a pod of whales. One day you realize someone else is there with them, someone else observing them...observing *you*!

You have been in this world for over two hundred years, and suddenly there is another like you, from the same place, trapped in this universe, on this prison planet as you are trapped. His name is Caravaggio. He is a painter. He is verbose and zealous, moody. He, like you, has suffered in isolation, the same inward journey. The same outward journey. You compare notes. You talk about IMAGO. You laugh, and the sound of such a noise makes you weep, for you thought this would never happen again, this feeling...joy...and a tiny, the tiniest you can imagine, a tiny spark of hope returns. This man is annoying. He is commanding, demanding, raucous. In your past life, you would have called him insane, a drunken fool, probably lock him up somewhere, but in this world his gifts are god-like in their ability to create illusions. You have never seen anything like it. A hundred years goes by with this man. You love him, hate him, miss him when he is gone, loathe him when he hangs around drinking and painting. One day you hear the song.

It is a song like you have never heard, and yet you have heard it all of your life, your other life, the life now gone forever. It is music, organic, like the wind through trees, the buzzing of beetle wings, the rolling of a brook over rocks. It is the music of the spheres, the turning of the world on its axis, and you realize this song can only come from another like you. For a year you and the Painter try to find the source of the music. Every day, hour, minute, you search, wait and watch. She commands the insects, the living detritus around you, but when you try to trap her, she is gone...like the wind or rain, a whiff of wonder, then gone.

One night around the fire, she appears. Beatrice is young, thin and weathered and stained like you, like the Painter. She is somber and morose, driven. She has seen things you cannot imagine. She speaks of another. She speaks of the fabulist, one like you, but utterly unlike you as well. He is the link to their return. What? There is a way back? She speaks of this way, of a book she has discovered, a book the Fabulist has written. It speaks of ancient cave art. She has seen it, but it is watched by forces known only as nightmares in the world that was. She knows this terror, has battled it and nearly was lost forever. It is an evil that followed her through to this world, to the world of men and time and things. It zealously guards the only way back.

She speaks of a plan. She speaks of a return. She speaks of calling the boy who she believes has been released into Cogstin. She speaks of Generation Tanks and a diabolical world of enforcement called the NRM Bureau. So, you wait...all three of you wait...three hundred years you have been waiting, and you wait another hundred together, a team, a dysfunctional family—wait and test and wait and test and wait and test until the fabulist appears, hears the Singer's Song, responds...and the waiting is finally over.

Chapter Thirty-three

"You see," Stutz says. "There is nowhere for you to go." His voice is still a whisper, toneless, someone who has given up. "You believe you have a place to go, because you do not know anything else. It is all make-believe. What is real, what you must bend your will toward, is Sector 17. Whatever happens...no matter what happens. This is all that is before us."

He grows silent, his long thin body seated in the small chair, concealed behind a weather-stained coat, reminds me of a gnarled and ancient tree root.

"You see," I say to him, hunching forward with my elbows on my knees. "You have had the time to realize this...this path. What have I had? Last month I was stripping copper from the inside of a ruined building with my Uncle Hal. Less than three weeks ago, I was a prisoner on probation."

Stutz stares at me in silence.

"I'm Alice down the rabbit hole, and there is no bottom."

"It is real," Stutz says. "This reality is what you must base everything else upon."

I start to laugh and shake my head. "Reality? A slippery slope, you would have to agree."

"Slippery, yes, but still a slope."

"Let me discover that for myself," I say.

We are silent for a moment. I hear the rummaging of bodies, the clinking of glasses and running water. Someone laughs suddenly, and it evaporates in the empty spaces of the building. I see a small beam of light penetrating through the slat of wood that comprises the makeshift wall of our room.

"You have looked at your world like we are looking at that beam of light," I whisper. "You see the particles of dust, the beam, the spot on the floor that it illuminates. Stoop down and look along it. You see what I see. The shadows of people, the empty space, the wood and fire. They are two different ways of seeing, but both true, both just as real as the other."

I turn and face Stutz. "I just need time."

"There is no room in this world for time. Not anymore." His face is cold, distant. "The Ghūl has the book, your book. Without it... Well, Beatrice says you need that damn book to get us home." He stands up. "We leave at sunrise."

A week passes, and Stutz has vanished. Every day I mope about the compound bored, trying to remember. Every night I have the same dreams. They are dark, and I drift in and out of strange memories that have no anchor, no mooring. When I turn to truly see them, they shift in place and time. They are all unsettling, a deep-rooted fear that causes me to cry out, an excruciating pain that one realizes, but does not remember, like a patient coming out of anesthesia, the distant violent and intrusive act tied to the post traumatic present. I am in the white room with the white chaise lounge staring at the deep blue water beyond, and then it enters. The shadow that haunts my memories is the same, tooth and claw. At one point it hovers over me, pawing, stroking, caressing. I'm conscious but unable to move. I feel the talon stroke across my stomach like a surgeon's blade, a thin line of bright red trailing, spreading wider and wider. I see an erotic delight in the black eyes, and I know the being before me has been sexually aroused. I watch its mouth unhinging, the serrated dagger teeth too many for the biological framework to contain, watch as it stoops slowly toward the long gash...and feeds.

That is when I sit up, sweating, pale and shaking like one with a fever or pulled from ice water. I experience a deep penetrating coldness to the bone, a realization that so heinous a dream maybe...is...real. I sit in the darkness, a blanket wrapped around my shoulders as a barrier to the night when a disappointed Governor Max steps to the doorway.

"Stutz is waiting for you." He stands silently for several seconds, then shakes his head. "Against my advice, he has the ludicrous idea you need to see your Uncle Hal." He suddenly grabs me by the shoulders and holds me firm. "Do not trust him. Stutz's thoughts are about Stutz, and he will betray you when you least expect it. That's what he does." He releases me and walks away.

Stutz is hunched over a table, a worn, coffee-stained and weathered map unfolded before him. It has deep fold lines and would have long separated if not for the heavy woven cloth material. It is a map of Cogstin. it is a typical city map with long lines of streets paralleling the coast of the Black Lake, and those connected—like rungs of a ladder—by hundreds of smaller streets. I see the Cuyahoga from the furthest most southern edge, bisecting the city, snaking, turning, rambling and ending in the Great Black Lake.

"Since the fire, our safest avenues will have become too dangerous. We can't go through the city. We'll have to go around."

He points to where we are, and slides his long finger, blackened nail, scarred skin to the west and loops it around, then back along the Cuyahoga.

"I thought you said Sector 17 was our only goal."

Stutz does not look up. "It still is."

"What about Beatrice?"

"There is something more important."

"You can't just abandon her like this."

"She will be okay. There is something else we need to do."

"How do you know?"

"Know what?"

"That she will be okay?"

"It doesn't want her."

"It took her."

Stutz looks up. His eyes are small and dark to his large nose, the white lines from the goggles distinct. "It wants you."

He looks down to the map and traces the path again, tapping every now and again for emphasis or a potential problem or whatever the hell it is supposed to be for, but I am lost in his words.

"We are walking into a trap," he says, "and therefore we have time. The trap will be there...waiting for us no matter what we currently decide." He folds the map. "Now pack your things. Take only what is necessary. We can resupply when we get to Riverside and the salvage yard. It's a two-day, three-night journey. Meet me at the armory for weapons in ten minutes. Daybreak is in half an hour."

Chapter Thirty-four

Our lives are fickle things, mutable and illusive. I am told that the Pre-Event World was a soundbite world where everything was an elevator speech designed to encapsulate some idea with as little words as possible. A student, a teacher, a doctor, lawyer. She's good, he's bad, that one a betrayer. These are self-contained and meant to deflect, detour or delay, obfuscate from the true, the complex, the multilayered and uncomfortable. The Pre-Event world constructed themselves for themselves to protect themselves, and create those selves around them to make them forget the logs in their own eyes, but how could these surface selves withstand the true scrutiny of the inquisitor called Time. What soundbite stands up to four hundred years of scrutiny? The constant, persistent observer's lens annihilates anything before it, and replaces the feather-light soundbite with a terrible animal saddled with a chain so heavy and with such cost, that to dwell on it means our annihilation. Sometimes that annihilation begins with a single moment of confrontation, let's call it—a single stoppage of time and space where the constructed self and the true self meet in a reflected image while looking into a gas station mirror, a makeup compact, the cold smooth ice of a winter's pond, or, let us say for the sake of argument—in the eyes of one's own child. There you are, it comes sideways, and you see them both clearly. One with weight and cost and suffering, the other as light as a breath of air. You are left with a choice—choose the soundbite or wrestle with the ponderous chain. So, you choose the former. The debt owed shoved upward, and you live under the sword of Damocles once again. Until, perhaps four hundred years later, while on the border of what seems the very edge of the world, you come face to face with that heavy weight and cost. The rope breaks, and the terrible sword falls upon you.

~ * ~

The edge of Cogstin looks like the landscape of an uninhabitable planet. I cannot push from my mind the twenty or so years of complex as well as multi-layered deception. How many times had Hal and I watched the TV in absolute ignorance of the real world about us? What then were the broadcasts, the sitcoms, the news programs that so permeated our universe? Beatrice and Stutz called it make believe, and I am wondering if there is actually a *real* at all. Far to the East the sun emerges within the red clouds of blowing desert. I can sense the presence of the Great Sand Flats before I can see them. It is an oppressive heat, a hot wind that strips bone and turns organic objects into stone. We travel for hours, heading south, on the borders of the city, the shadows, short and stunted in the first light. We follow an abandoned train track, the iron rails splayed and humped, the ties splintered or missing like a grotesque mouth full of broken teeth.

Stutz and I huddle against the wind, every once in a while the mic in my ear crackles with a command: *Stop at the corner. Down! Head to that wall. Keep alert.* We clabber over ruined bricks and negotiate sink holes, always moving south, always avoiding the tunnels under the earth or the eastern parts of the city. Stutz comes to a clearing near another line of broken tracks, crouches down and studies the earth. When I arrive, I can barely make out what holds his attention. That is when I see it. A long line of oddly shaped footprints, elongated, taloned, like a wild cat or the claw of a bird. Stutz stares after the trail which heads into the city. He turns and looks behind him. He looks toward the red sun through the gray clouds of mid-day. "Well, it is what it is," he says.

"What made them?"

"Something I hoped to avoid."

"Whatever it is, it's gone to the city," I say noticing the single line, the long gait.

"*They*...not *it*. *They* are a hunting party. They are hiding their numbers." He looks back to the city once again then stands up. "We must quicken our pace. Let's go."

We hurry through the wasteland of the outer city. I notice the burned-out husks of houses, row upon row upon row of blackened and scorched shells. The roofs have collapsed, most of the walls rotted and disintegrated, leaving only the facade of bricks and the footprint of block foundations. Every once in a while I notice the familiar elongated footprint with the taloned toes, some solidified in dried mud, some small, some very large. We travel for four hours straight. Stutz finally stops at a large lagoon, or what was a lagoon. It is now empty of water, a smooth, concrete space.

"We can rest here for a moment," Stutz says. "It used to be a water treatment plant. Its elevation allows for a good view."

We climb the stone stairs to the cement building, and find ourselves in a small room with openings on every side, the glass long since gone, now brick-framed eyes to the surrounding world. The air is clear, and we remove our breathing masks. To our South is the Great Sand Flats, an endless stretch of red clay and clouds. To our North is the city of Cogstin, its upper most buildings hidden in haze. I can see the black expanse of the Great Lake beyond. Stutz hands me a can of fruit, the steel top jagged and bent to the side. I drink the juice, then use my knife to eat the peaches. Stutz takes a few bites of some dried meat, then begins to sharpen his long machete with a whetstone.

"This world," I say, looking out at the red clouds sweeping across the great plain of desert. "It is so harsh. It seems impossible for it to exist without us knowing."

Stutz smiles, a thin, sardonic smile. He keeps sharpening. "We see what we choose to see."

"This...this wasteland outside our doors, and nobody..."

"Of course not. Who does?" It is not until you are forced to face the world of men and time and things that you actually *see* it for what *it* is."

"What does that even mean?" I say and stare at Stutz. His face is gaunt, scarred and worn from his time in Cogstin. His nose is ever pronounced, the bone humped and bent from breaks. I wonder who he is, what his agenda might be, and how little I know him.

"How did you explain the red soot that settled upon your trucks and found its way into your house?"

"It was from the mineral mines."

"What mineral mines?"

"I see your point, but how could we not know?"

"Why would they lie? They're just like you? They think like you, want what you want. Your hopes and dreams are their hopes and dreams? You are good. They are good. You want what is best for your personal world, and they want what is best for their world, the whole world, all of mankind. The sun rises on a bright new day. You wake up eat your breakfast, brush your teeth and believe everyone is doing the same, thinking the same, wanting the same."

There is a venom in his voice now, one I have not heard. He spits on his whetstone and begins to glide the now razor-sharp blade across it again. "What if the world has teeth, young Dante? What if there are those whose only desire is to do you wrong? Ignorance has a weight and cost. There is always a cost. You wake up one day only to realize that annoying and persistent dust from the factory down the road is actually human ashes. What you thought was the pillar of the community's factory is nothing more than a death camp, a final solution, to exterminate an entire race of people."

"That's a bit of hyperbole, wouldn't you say?"

"Is it?"

"Listen, I know your world is harsh and without mercy. Mine was not. You keep forgetting that."

Stutz smiles, and it is almost malicious. "The red clay dust is from the mineral mines."

"Was it wrong of me to love, hope and dream?" I say in a furious exaltation of breath. "Is that my fault? You talk like I should have known, that I'm culpable. Your teachable moment overlooks that I was the one in the Generation Tank. I did not actually get to experience even the world of make believe. The time in the tanks...of that I have no recollection. Do not lecture me on what is real, Stutz. I follow you blindly through a city that is unreal to me. You lecture me about ignorance, weight, cost, and even before we leave, the Governor pleads with me not to trust you, the betrayer, tells me that you will deceive me. Yet I go because I so desperately want to see the only anchor, I know...my Uncle Hal. Tell me, Stutz, tell me why you are any different than the world you mock me for believing in? Why is the Governor so distrustful of you? Why does he dislike you with such passion?"

Stutz's facial features markedly changes. "People dislike what they don't understand."

I turn to look out at the city in frustration. "Whatever."

Stutz lifts the blade, checks the edge with his thumb, then spits on the stone and continues sharpening. It takes me a moment to realize he is talking.

"I knew this place for only a brief moment before The Event. I saw the great city, the deep blue of the lake, the harmony of hundreds of thousands of people living out their lives as single organisms serving a greater whole. I am a selfish man, young Dante, and sometimes it takes a great deal of sorrow to show us there is something besides self. To me, this place was a thing to be used...like a match stick. How wrong. How perilously wrong.

"I was the head of the security team for the IMAGO emissary, the Chief Intelligence Officer to Elizabeth, your mother, when she decided to unite our two dimensions. I had not trusted Geoffrey Dante, your father, when we first met, but after he spent time in IMAGO, I learned to trust him. In fact, I took an oath to protect him and Elizabeth with my life or death. The world of men and time and things was not like our world, nor their world to us. They seemed selfish, petty, limited in mind, body, and soul. What I perceived to be a weakness back then, I now see for what it was— a being trapped in time, and nothing more. When the portal closed, I was with Geoffrey in this world. Life is a complicated thing, young Dante, and I abandoned my post for...well, such reasons are empty words now. Whatever the reasons, Geoffrey died in The Event, and so did Elizabeth. It came down to me, and I failed, causing the death of your parents and the annihilation of the city. The echoes of this story have morphed, changed and resurrected over the centuries. It is my burden alone to carry. This is the reason the Governor does not trust me. He does not really know why, it is rooted deep in his conscience, a story told generation after generation for four hundred years, a label placed, the gray transformed into black and white. I do not blame him, and perhaps it is wise to heed his warning. For indeed, as you have said yourself, what appears to be an anchor is but the flowing river. It is, as it has always done, moving you and me toward an inevitable conclusion."

Stutz stands to his feet and stretches, his bones cracking and popping. "We have five hours of daylight left, and we must make it to our first camp before sundown."

We gather our belongings, strap and tie them up, pull on our breathing masks and head into the gray haze of midafternoon.

Chapter Thirty-five

The next four hours are brutal. Old gates and ruined walls, miles of abandoned cars locked together as makeshift barricades. I keep wondering, who were they keeping out? Themselves or something else? The wind has picked up, gathering with it the red sands from the Sand Flats, along with the grime and dust of the forgotten city. The filters in our breathing masks continually clog, and we find ourselves stopping and huddling against any wall that will provide a respite. Stutz hurries us toward our first campsite. Every now and then he bids me to stop and wait as he loops back and around to check for any attackers. By the time we arrive at the campsite, an obliterated town with a great stone church rising tall and high, and Stutz cooks what little food we have, I am nearly asleep.

"We will have to push very hard tomorrow. Very hard. We cannot be caught out there at sundown."

"What's out there?" I ask, but it comes out as a yawn. I eat the small crisp legs of a dog or a cat or a rodent. I'm too tired and hungry to care.

"Just one more consequence of The Event," Stutz says. "They call them the Clan. No one knows if they were always here or just emerged. A hundred years after The Event, they started attacking. First it was stray travelers from the eastern part of the city. Eventually, their territory expanded to the outer belt, always at night. Some said they crossed the Black Lake. Some said they came from the ground or trekked across the Great Sand Flats. I have my own theories. Suffice it to say, they came. They thrived in the new environment, no predators, and they're nocturnal. I've trapped and dissected my share. They are humanoid, strange familiarity, a consistency, but what their origins may be...I could not guess. Once we left the city, we entered their territory. I was hoping for as little interaction as possible."

Stutz peers over the stone ledge of the bell tower, then pulls his coat collar up around his ears, the light from the small fire illuminates only portions of his features, and he looks like a great brooding, alert bird of prey. He stirs the embers, and the fire ignites once again in the large metal bowl before us. It is dented and tarnished from weather and the change of seasons. Just before I fall asleep, I imagine Stutz huddled up here, alone, hundreds of years ago, searching for signs of anything else alive.

The yelps wake me up. They are cackles and growls. I realize I have heard these same sounds all my life. Max used to shoot at them in the fields beyond his house. Yapper hunting. Like every other illusion, I wonder if he knew what they were he was shooting at...or believed them to be the animal in the history books.

Stutz has already put the fire out, and I feel the cold damp settle upon my wool blanket wrapped around my shoulders. I peer with Stutz over the smooth stone ledge, the moonlight so bright it has cast the night world into a multitude of shadows. Again, the yelping, yapping, at times high pitched, then low growls. They are beyond the town, beyond the stacked car wall toward the west. I move to get a better look, and Stutz holds me back. He raises his hand, finger out and pressed to my lips. He slowly motions a silent code, pointing two fingers at his eyes, then to the street adjacent to the church. He now holds up three fingers.

I turn ever so slightly and see two shadows move silently down the street. They are hunched over, arms longer than a human's, legs shorter. They have a loping gait, and as the two enter the street, they separate; one headed north, one south down the lane. Stutz raises his hand to me again, points to his eyes, then to the alley. I see nothing but shades of darkness. He motions me to wait. At last, it steps partially into the moonlight. It is larger than the other two, a massive chested thing, one shoulder raised higher than the other, a hump on its back, tuft of hair or flesh or an illusion created by the shadows. This one wears the semblance of pants, tattered at the knees as if hastily cut or torn. Its hair is long, but sparse on its irregularly shaped head. It sniffs the air, then squats on its haunches, motionless.

We wait and wait and wait. My leg is numb, my back knotted and cramped from the awkward way that I sit. Still the thing below does not move. Every once in a while, it will sniff the air, growl, then silence. An hour passes, and the other two arrive, one holding what looks to be a dog, the other is empty handed. One yelps and yaps, then the other, and then the leader stands upright and growls and joins the cackling and yelping. He pulls the freshly killed dog from the other one and growls. It falls to the ground, and the leader tears into its chest, eviscerating it. The other two claw and snap. Like a pack of rabid dogs, they snarl, bite and swipe at one another until the leader wins out. The other two pace back and forth. Soon they are all at the dog carcass, pulling, tearing, faces and clawed hands covered with their feasting. The leader sniffs the air again, then growls. Each one moves into the alley. I lose them in the shadows.

Stutz leans his back against the stone wall of the bell tower. This is my cue to stretch and massage my thigh that has cramped and knotted. "A scouting party," he whispers. "It's a good guess they spotted us. The pack is too far away to call for assistance. We need to leave here at first light. They will be tracking us come dusk, and attack at nightfall. We must be through their territory by then."

Neither of us sleep, and as the light comes up from the East, we are already moving. The tracks from the Clan are obvious, and they no longer try to hide their numbers. Stutz guesses thirty and says they will attack this evening. I can't help think of that massive being crouched low and waiting, sniffing the air, knowing that we are watching. We clamber over abandoned cars and hurry through alleyways until we are on the outskirts of the town. The wind has picked up. The dust from the Great Sand Flats is now prominent and steady. It stings my exposed skin, the tiny particles like my Uncle Hal's sandblaster. We bend low against it, and our urgency is muted by the increasing ferocity. By the time we hit midday, the storm is so bad, the wind so strong, we are forced to take shelter in an empty root cellar, the doors long gone, the hinges pulled upward and rusted. It is dark, damp, and cool, a waft of decay from something discarded.

Stutz is impatient and walks back and forth, then steps up the stone stairs to check on the storm, but immediately comes down, defeated, pacing once again.

"Why did you abandon your post?" I say above the howl of storm and sand. Stutz keeps pacing, stops and looks at me.

"What?"

"Why did you leave my parents, if your job was to protect them with your life?"

I can see Stutz pondering something, a debate in his head about what is to come next. He squats down near me. "I had to leave my post. I had no choice. I thought I would have more time. When I was able to return, The Event had already happened. Geoffrey and Elizabeth were dead. I should have died with them...it would have been better...for all involved. So, now I live with the great debt to repay, and I live with the reputation that debt incurred."

"Did you know me back then?" I ask Stutz.

"Yes. You were very young. You played with my daughter in the Great House."

This takes me by surprise. "Was she killed in The Event?"

Stutz is silent; he has faded back to someplace secret, a time forgotten.

"I'm sorry," I say.

Stutz stares at me as if to say something. Finally, he shakes his head and stands up. He paces again, then heads up the stone stairs. The sandstorm has not really abated, but he says it has. Soon we are hurrying through the swirling, biting red clouds toward the southeast.

Chapter Thirty-six

Whatever tracks The Clan have made during the night have been blown away as the afternoon moves into evening. I cannot help but see the anxiousness in Stutz, the quickened pace, the constant scanning of the horizon with binoculars or the naked eye. The elevation has markedly changed, and there are more hills and ravines and dried creek beds that remind me of my childhood. South Brooklyn was the town next to the town I grew up in, Riverside. We are only twenty miles from it now, but twenty miles is the same as a million if the sun goes down and we are not out of The Clan's territory. There are enormous spaces of empty ground, surfaces that have been stripped clear by the initial explosion of The Event or by the corrosive power of the wind and sand and time. We wrap our necks with extra clothing, tighten the straps on our breathing masks. We hunch forward against the wind and blowing debris.

Just before sundown, I hear the yelps and cackles north of us. They are scattered and sinister, violent, each time greater in volume, in excitement. Stutz searches the area for defense, but we are vulnerable here, and we need to make it to the outskirts of the next populated area before the sun disappears. An hour later we come to an abandoned gas station, the front glass blown out centuries ago, the rusty metal and stone now all that remains. The foundation makes for a defensive barrier, and Stutz moves and rolls objects about so as to make a choke point. He has disguised the other exposed areas so well, that it appears to all observers to have only one-way in. He shows me the side exit, a thin opening toward the back that will be our escape plan. We hear The Clan's call and response, growls, cackles, and yelps—each time closer, each time a quicker response.

"We are three miles from Riverside, but there is no way to make it now. They will attack shortly," Stutz says, pulling the machete from its sheath. He sees my panic. "They are a pack mentality. They will come in waves, the most reckless first. Swing out from your body, broad strokes that will do the most damage. Wound enough of them, and they will disband."

"For good?" I say, but my throat is dry and it croaks out.

"No. There will be more waves after that, more strategic, cunning." He looks at me, and his features soften. "Just remember, watch our flanks. Never let them get behind us." He corrects my grip on the machete and demonstrates how to sweep the blade out and up. We can hear them growling and running toward our choke point, yelping, grinding their teeth with rage. Suddenly, they are upon us.

Stutz moves so fast I do not at first realize he has taken the post in front of me. With every swing, he is lopping heads and arms. I stand back amazed at his ferocity. The wave of Clan dissipates into howls and yelps. Some are dragging themselves away, some hobbling, crawling, some turning on their own wounded and devouring them. The next wave is stealthier, and several come from the sides, shoving and stuffing their fellow Clan into the choke point, before rolling away and looping around. One hits me on the side of the head, knocking me to the ground. It is not concerned with me, however, for it and another immediately race at Stutz who is now completely overwhelmed by the frontal assault and unaware of the animals from behind. I stumble to my feet, but the beasts are too far away. The howls and groans are too loud for me to scream a warning. I watch in horror as the animals leap upon a brick face and lunge from both sides at the exposed back of Stutz.

"No!" I scream and extend my hand.

There is a flash of light, and they hit Stutz's back. They crumple to the ground, their spines broken from the impact. Stutz turns in amazement, glances at the ground, sweeps and spins in large arcs at the oncoming second wave. Soon, they too are defeated and disband in chaos. Stutz leans against the brick wall exhausted.

"What happened?" he says between deep gulps of breath, but there is a glint in his eyes I don't understand.

"I don't know. They hit you and...just, just...fell."

He kicks them and rolls them with his feet, their necks limp. I can see their canine teeth, the strange shaped head, and stand aghast at my realization. There is a resemblance to... I pull out the flashlight and illuminate the corpses. Yes, it is there, in every one of them. A recognizable visage of Max, of Hal, of Mr. Tough; a vague and warped resemblance disguised by mutations and humps of flesh, tufts of hair, tooth and claw.

"They did not touch me," Stutz says, still with that strange look in his eyes. "I did not know they were there."

"They must have run into each other."

"Perhaps," Stutz says.

I know he is right, for as I reached out, just before the flash of light, I saw the object that was there, a great metal shield, like a wall of iron, a great slab swinging out crushing cartilage and snapping bone. A shield that was not there before I screamed, thought and imagined in an instant of creation.

"Prepare yourself," Stutz commands. "They are coming."

They come, thirty more, fifty maybe, and they overwhelm us and claw us and snap and fall and yelp and snarl, turning on one another, falling into piles of maimed and discarded hides with gaping wounds, a bath of blood.

Stutz screams and points to the exit slot, and I pull myself through. "Run!" He screams, rolling on his back and squeezing through. "We only have a few seconds until they realize our escape!"

We are running. Three miles away is the border to Riverside. Three miles away. We are tired. They are yelping and calling to one another, leaping and racing to catch us. We jump over a wooden fence, and splash across a small creek, clamber up a muddied ravine. Still they come howling and hooting, yapping. Stutz turns and cuts down a scout. I look back and see them in the moonlight lumbering, some with their uneven arms swinging with their gait, others waving, confident. The pack is larger than I thought, fifty, perhaps more, and I realize it is a trap. We have traveled two days into a planned, calculated, vulnerable moment where the Clan have organized and prepared. We will not make the dawn.

We come from a clearing and enter a large open space, an empty parking lot, tiles of asphalt here and there as a distant reminder of what it once was. "That wall! See that wall?" Stutz shouts. "That's the border. They will not cross it."

It is far away, and they are closing fast. This time there is no stopping them from flanking us. As I run I concentrate on the wall in front of us. I hear the mob behind gathering like a storm of violence and hatred, an unstoppable fury. At last it comes to me sideways—the cave paintings, the sketches of lions, the handprints with the curled pinky finger, the gazelles and the great lions as they readied to pounce. I see them clearly, crisp lines, crouching huge shapes, hunched and savage. I see them pounce. Stutz turns at the terrible roar, like a waterfall, a thunderclap, the savagery of the lions attacking the Clan, one from each side, the unmistakable sound of rending flesh and snapping bones. He slows down, jogs to a stop and stands before the apocalyptic scene behind. I see him smiling, broadly, a facial expression I have never yet seen from him, and I wonder if this is not something planned from the beginning.

I feel strange, a dark rage building inside me, a fire smoldering, catching the straw and deadwood around it, and it terrifies me. I don't know what to do, so I grab Stutz by the arm and pull. "Run! We must run!" He is soon bounding with me down the ravine, up the other side, over to the wall and through the gate and into civilization with farmland, street lamps and automobiles and picket fences and grass yards gray in the shadows of the night.

Chapter Thirty-seven

Hal told me, especially when I got angry or depressed—which was often—Hal told me, "It's not the destination, Stretch, it's the journey." I guess that means the events unfolding in time and space are what makes us, well, us...and the destination is always something quite illusive.

Most of our journeys are constructed things, limited in scope, and those guiding us understand such things. They watch us fail and succeed with a wink and a nod. A child does not understand the teeth of the world. The parents who have experienced those teeth know what is to come. They know too that the child's ignorance and innocence will evaporate one day under the intense heat of life's pain and suffering.

Institutions are all similar in nature: the school, the hospital, the employer, the church. All those who have lived long enough have 'seen' the path or the potential path, the highs and lows, the indicators of success and failures. The teacher understands the pupils new found revelations, the doctor watches as the cancer patient hopes and dreams of cures. The boss instructs and nods as the employee sulks over shrinking markets and higher goals. The priest hears the confession with a sigh, for the affair will continue to the bitter end, and the sins of the parents will storm upon the children like a rain of fire. Those new participants must journey down a road already trodden, believing the journey to be new, which it is for them, and not truly thinking how so many others, hordes really, generation after generation from the beginning—have come before them. Biology, chemistry, psychology, predictable patterns of life and death over time creating paths, deep ruts, that if viewed from a distant become quite clear. If only we could get the proper vantage point.

Stutz and I sleep in an old barn in the town near Riverside. The loft is filled with hay, and we fall into it, cover our cold and numb bodies, and sleep.

Stutz wakes me around three in the afternoon, and we head to my old house to see Hal. It is strange, this world outside the city, so self-contained, so unreal and isolated. I look to the north, toward the great black lake and the eels and the city of ashes, the terrible wind and dust, and all that I can see is the forbidding clouds, grey, indistinguishable from the sky above or the ground below, a perpetual chance of bad weather. I look to the south, and I see the reddened hues far, far away. How did I not know about these things? I think of Stutz's words to me during our journey here: *We see what we choose to see.* And suddenly, I feel the weight of all that actually is. The worlds taking shape without any care or concern from all the imitations working and dreaming, and eating and living their spans of life in a connected world within the world, like rotating spheres in an ancient belief system.

We stop outside the southern end of the walled off acres called *Universal Salvage Company.* I see the red dust covering the stone and wipe it with my finger, rubbing it to a stain on my thumb.

"We need to check the complete perimeter before we enter," Stutz says. "The NRM are never far away from this area."

So, we walk. Stutz heads further south. I move slowly, cautiously toward the north. I can hear the whine of the hydraulic lift as Hal stacks coils of wire or bails of metal sheeting. I hear the beeping alarm as it backs up and positions one after the other. The wind is calm. After we wait and watch, crawl and stoop, scan everywhere, everything for any signs of danger—after an hour, we just walk through the front gate like we are delivering the mail. The large outbuilding is closed off. We head toward the back where the lift is still maneuvering around the neatly stacked materials. Stutz stands in the gravel path, his weather-stained garments, the filthy scarf around his neck matted with dust and grime, his nose and cheeks blackened by our crossing, the distinctly, clean goggle marks around his eyes. I walk over to my small hut, see the metal art placed on the small shelf, a flower, a horse, and I think, how beautiful, how perfectly constructed, how out of place in the make-believe world of Riverside.

Hal has stopped the lift, and is speaking to Stutz. I hear that familiar voice, jolly and large and deep, hopeful, optimistic...and ultimately unreal. Stutz says something to Hal over the noise of the lift, then he repeats it. At last Hal shuts off the lift. He nearly tumbles off the seat when he hears my name and sees me walking toward him.

"My god, boy! It's really you! Where you been, Stretch? I mean, we've been searching high and low..." He does not finish, choked up and hugging me like a great bear, his enormous belly hidden behind the bibs of his overalls.

"Where did you go?" he asks, pushing me out but still holding firm to my shoulders. "I thought maybe back to Cogstin, but they assured me you had not passed there. I thought maybe to Max's, but he said you'd not been there. We looked everywhere!"

He wipes his eyes, and I want to buy back into the dream. I want to hug him, cry with him, hope and dream his dreams, somehow, like a derailed train, get back onto the same tracks Hal is traveling on. Stutz pats me on the back, and I pull away from Hal.

"I took Mr. Dante to the Mineral Mines," Stutz says. "It's part of his rehabilitation requirements for his eventual release."

Hal looks perplexed, rubs his large jowls, stares at Stutz, then at me. He slaps the top of his head. "This old rock up here. I'm tell'n you, Stretch. I'd forget my head if it wasn't attached! I'm work'n too hard, boy. I'm tell'n you what. So, you're gonna be released soon?"

"Yes," Stutz interrupts. "He has other requirements, but who can say?"

"I thought you were here for good..."

"They phoned me," I say, "Remember? Right before we went to Sector 17?" How easy it is to lie, how easy it is to interrupt the world of men and time and things, influence a thought into the imitation, phony world of constructed moments.

"Sure, right," Hal says. "I'm telling you, I'm get'n old. The noodle is gone, Stretch."

"I wanted to make sure the boy was back for your big day," Stutz says, and this new line of thinking takes me by surprise as well as Hal. "The mines can be quite inhibitive."

Hal looks at me, then at Stutz.

"Don't you think we should celebrate your birthday with a toast?"

I look at Stutz, that gleam in his eye, a savagery, mocking, what I saw that night running from the Clan. Some other plan is unfolding, and it is one that does not include me.

"My birthday? Good god! This rock up here," Hal says again and knocks his head again. "It is my birthday today, isn't it? With all the excitement..."

"I hope we didn't miss the barbecue," Stutz points to the black smoke rising from behind the out-building, and I can smell the savory tang of cooking meat. "Now let's toast the big day." Stutz grabs two tin cups near my old hut and the bottle of vodka Hal has behind the chair of the lift. He pours some for me as well as for himself and hands Hal the bottle. "Cheers," Stutz says with a wry smile. I stare at him, trying to gauge what is happening. We all take a drink. "Now," Stutz says, "I think it's high time we had some dinner. I'm famished." Hal gulps more from the bottle, looking at me, then at Stutz. I know that crinkled brow. "Now, who'd you say you were again? Sorry, but the name slipped right away."

"Inspector Anthony Stutz," Stutz says as cool as a cucumber. "I'm the Chief Corrections Officer for the NRM."

We walk past the large out-building, the corrugated sides cold from the evening chill. As we round the corner, I see a charcoal grill with an enormous figure cooking behind it. His arms and legs are thick as trees, and on his face a great, shaggy brown beard. Caravaggio is wearing a black apron with white letters across the front: *I'M A GRILL 'N KING*. There is a table set before us with four place settings, drinks poured, a large salad bowl in the center. On the table next to the bottles of wine and spirits is a large box wrapped in pink paper with a great, gaudy white ribbon gilded with gold.

"Happy Birthday, old man," Caravaggio says as he raises his martini glass. He gulps it down and proceeds to make another.

My stomach is nauseous. I feel clammy and cold.

"This is my friend, Sam," Hal says pointing at Caravaggio. "He's helped me look high and low for you. What a savior. Boy, Sam, the egg's on my face," Hal continues, "Stretch has been at the Mines with this fine officer here."

IMAGO

"Well, who'd of thought," Caravaggio says and pours the cold vodka from the shaker into two glasses, stabbing several olives and plopping them in. "Here," he says and gives one to Hal. "Let's celebrate your big day and the prodigal's return." He toasts the air and looks right at me. "He was lost, but now he's found." Caravaggio smiles a wan smile. He turns back to Hal and says, "I think it's time for you to open your present."

"Let's eat first," Stutz says. "I am starving, and we have had so little to eat."

"They don't feed you at the corrections facility, officer?" Hal says, rubbing his hands together in gluttonous delight as he sits at the table.

I pull Stutz aside. "What is going on? You knew about this?"

Stutz pulls away like he is offended by the question. "Why, it's your Uncle Hal's birthday, Mr. Dante, and we are celebrating with our true and only friends."

We sit together; a large slab of steak is before us with crisp baked potato. My mouth is salivating, for it has been for what seems a year since I have eaten anything so sumptuous. I cut the steak and the plate runs with juice, the meat melts in my mouth.

"They must not feed any of you too well," Hal says, eyeing us as we all tear into the food. "I'm glad you like it, Stretch."

Caravaggio toasts again, gulps his martini down again, makes two new martinis and places the new one next to Hal's plate.

"Drink up, my friend," Caravaggio says. "Today is the day of destiny! Your birthday! A great day! A day to be remembered! Let's open the present."

"Not yet," Stutz says. "Now please, eat. There will be plenty of time for that later."

"Time," Caravaggio says, "the eternal gangster. Isn't that right, pal?" He toasts me with his full glass, gulps it down and wipes his beard. He stands up, firm as a man mountain, and makes another, completely unaffected by the successive drinks.

"How did you meet...Sam?" I ask Hal.

"Oh well, Stretch, funny story. A week or so ago, Sam came looking for work. He said he knew you, and that you and him had some deal to complete. I told him I was not real sure where you went, but he assured me you would be back in time. Probably a big misunderstanding of some sort. Boy was he right, Stretch. Anyway, he said he had experience with salvage, and I hired him on. You know since you've been gone...well...so much work. Sam's a damn good worker, Stretch. You don't find people like him around, I'm tell'n you what. Quick as lightening."

Caravaggio sits back at the table, his grilling apron still on. "One of a kind, pal. One of a kind," and he toasts the air again and gulps his martini. "It's almost like we are living in two different worlds sometimes, eh Hal?"

"Well, I'd like to live in yours tonight, Sam. You seem to be draining those glasses down like you mean it."

Caravaggio laughs. "Oh, I do mean it, Hal. I most certainly mean everything I say and do. Ain't that right, pal? Why, look at your drink, Hal. You've hardly touched it! Shall I fix you another, birthday boy?"

Hal finishes his one and points to the full one next to it. "I'm fine, Sam." Hal lifts his glass and toasts my return, toasts to good friends.

"Trustworthy," Stutz says.

"Ones that come through, do what they say...a deal's a deal?" Caravaggio says. "Right, pal?"

We drink again. Hal places a martini before me. "Let's have a contest," Caravaggio says. "A birthday contest." Stutz is silently observing. "First, you must drink that martini, then we will see who can drink the most shots."

"Oh, ho!" Hal says. "I think you will be wasting your time, Sam." He pats him on the back. "Stretch here is a true light weight."

"Oh, that shouldn't stop him," Caravaggio says, slapping Hal on his back, nudging him to drink the other martini down. He turns to me. "Go ahead, pal, drink up," and he places the glass in my hand.

"I don't want it," I say.

"Sure, you do, pal. Take a drink."

"No," I say.

Caravaggio leans over to me. "Drink up, little man, or we open the birthday present right now." He has a glare in his eyes, a darkness, bordering on malevolent.

"What's in the box?" I say.

"Let's find out, shall we?" He turns to Stutz. "I feel like gift giving."

I grab him. "Okay. I'll drink."

"Good boy."

I gulp it down, the liquid burning my throat. I swallow several times to keep it down. I feel nothing. Caravaggio has cleared off the table now and has placed plastic cups in rows next to each of us. He pours from Hal's vodka bottle into each one, some fuller than others. Hal keeps saying, "Ho ho, look at that, Stretch!" The martinis are getting to him now, fogging his head, making him speak with cotton in his mouth. Caravaggio sits across from me and we take the first glass. He drinks. I drink. We flip over the cup. He picks the next one, as do I, gulping, flipping it over. I get it. I got it from the beginning. He's making a point. I am like him, like Stutz, not like Hal. The alcohol does not affect me. We drink and flip, drink and flip. Ten in a row, and Hal is smiling, but he is hammered. Stutz stops the game.

"We need to go."

"One more parlor trick on this special day," Caravaggio says with a big smile. "You like parlor tricks, right, birthday boy?"

Hal laughs and nods his head up and down, like it is on some great loose hinge.

"Now, watch," Caravaggio says. "Watch your pal over there."

Hal and I turn to him.

"Pick up the steak knife, pal."

"No," I say, understanding what is happening now.

"Pick it up, or our birthday boy gets a final present."

"I love magic tricks, Stretch," Hal slurs. "You going to perform a magic trick?"

"That's it," Caravaggio says. "Now watch this, birthday boy! Behold as your pal cuts himself."

"Oh, I love these kind of tricks," Hal says.

I see the blade in Caravaggio's hand that has seamlessly dropped from his sleeve. He holds it near Hal's shoulder.

I take the steak knife and draw it across my wrist, deep, through vein, sinew and flesh. The blood begins to pour from the wound.

"Oh, god!" Hal screams. "What...what...what are you doing?" He sits forward, Caravaggio smiling.

He shakes Hal by the shoulder and leans to his ear. There is sarcasm. anger and mocking behind every word. "Now watch the magic show."

As the blood flows and streams, drips onto the patio stones, my mind races instinctively to the ancient cave wall. I see the chanting shaman dancing around the fire, but I cannot understand what he is saying to me.

"Well," Caravaggio says.

"I need a bandage," I say. "Get me a bandage."

Hal sits up. Caravaggio pulls him back down. "Sit tight, birthday boy."

"I don't know what you want from me," I say. "Hal, I need a bandage."

Stutz looks on passively, the glint in his eyes, as though he is expectant but doubtful of an outcome.

"Come on, pal," Caravaggio says. "This is a pretty shitty magic trick. I expected more from you."

"I need the book," I suddenly say. "I don't have the book. I don't know what to do. I need the book."

"The book, the book, the book," mocks Caravaggio. He turns to Stutz. "Obviously, you got it wrong." Stutz shrugs.

Caravaggio reaches in his pocket and pulls out a scrap of paper. He hands it to me. "You know, the audience is never supposed to help the magician. Damn sorry magic trick, pal."

I stare at the page. It is scrambled images. It is the page from Mendel, worn and burnt and blackened, an amalgamation of stuck together phrases and equations. I stare and do nothing; impotent.

"Physician!" Caravaggio yells. "Heal thyself!"

I read it again, and this time I know it. I improvise and reorganize, and the shaman chants and I see him and hear him and understand him.

Before our eyes the deep gash closes, seals up seamless so that only a stain of blood remains. Hal's eyes are wide with wonder. He blinks, brow crinkling.

Caravaggio slaps him on the back. "Now, that's some sort of magic trick, hey birthday boy? How would you like to try it? Either now or later...Ha ha! Why not?"

"We need to go," Stutz says. Caravaggio looks up at him, then slaps

Hals' back once again.

"Leave? How can we leave? Birthday boy hasn't opened his present," Caravaggio says.

He brings over the pink wrapped box with the gaudy bow, and sits down next to Hal. "You and I are different, aren't we, Hal?" he says. "Couldn't be further from each other, right, birthday boy? Two worlds apart...two universes."

"Oh, I don't think so," Hal slurs. "I think you and I are exactly the same."

"*Au contraire, mon ami.* I think I am one of a kind, and you...well. Let's test this theory. What exactly is the red dust that covers your fences, your trucks, gets in your house...you know...the red dust?"

"Oh, it gets everywhere, Sam," Hal says and brushes his knees as if trying to get at the dust. "That damn dust."

"Exactly. Well put, birthday boy. That damn dust! Where does it come from?"

"Everyone knows that. The Mineral Mines."

"Okay," I say. "You've had your fun. Let's just go."

Caravaggio hunches forward. Stutz is silent, alert. Caravaggio holds Hal's knees and leans to him face to face. "You have seen these mineral mines?"

Hal scratches his cheek, his jowls jiggling. "I can't say I have."

"Don't you think that is a bit strange? You are fifty years old and red dust settles on everything you own, and you never once went out to discover where the hell the red dust came from?"

"I told you," Hal blinks, "The Mineral Mines."

"Yes, the mines, right." Caravaggio is still staring at Hal. "The great wasteland right outside your door...you've never seen it?"

"Okay," I say. "That's enough." I walk over to Caravaggio, he suddenly and with lightning speed has his arm around Hal's shoulders, and in his hand is that small, thin blade. Hal is too drunk now to notice it.

"I think the birthday boy and I are just having a little chat about what is real and what is make believe." He nudges Hal. "Ain't that right?"

"Yup. What is real and make believe."

"Like this salvage company, that's make believe. As well as the

Mineral Mines, make believe. The corrections officer Stutz and your good friend Sam...all make believe."

I step forward. Hal is blinking. He's drunk, but he is beginning to sense the ominous intentions of Caravaggio.

"I think you have had too much to drink, Sam. I think I'll make us some coffee." He begins to stand up, and Caravaggio pulls him quite hard back in his seat.

"Let's open our present, birthday boy. Time for a reality check."

"What's in the box?" I ask Caravaggio.

"It's a surprise."

"Hal, you don't have to open that box," I say.

"No, Hal most definitely has to open the box, pal."

Hal tries to sit up, but Caravaggio holds him in the seat with one hand, the knife clearly visible to all. Stutz just sits quietly.

"Happy birthday," Caravaggio says. "Here, let me cut the bow off." With one swipe the ribbon falls across Hal's knees. He is sweating and pale and blinking rapidly.

"What's in the box, Caravaggio?"

"Who?" Hal says.

"What's in the box? Hal, don't open that."

"Oh, it's the birthday of destiny for this little imitation."

"Hal, don't open it."

"Open it, birthday boy, or this will be your last birthday." The point of the blade goes to Hal's neck. "Open...the...box."

Hal begins to cry, tears streaming down his red and bloated cheeks. His thick fingers find the creases and the flaps separate and the box opens. Hal closes his eyes and is trembling. "I don't want to see it. I don't want to see it. I don't want to see it." He shakes his head back and forth.

Caravaggio is laughing maliciously now. He reaches in and pulls the object out by the hair. "Take a good look, birthday boy. See it? Open your eyes!" Caravaggio's voice is so commanding that it shakes even me.

Hal obeys and stares at the head, the shape identical to himself, the eyes open and staring back, the bottom of the box damp with blood. I move to intervene, but Stutz holds me firm.

"Please," Hal says.

"Look at it! There are no Mineral Mines. There are no forests, no rivers, no wildlife." I realize that Caravaggio is talking to me, not Hal. This was for me...this was all for me, planned from the very beginning.

Caravaggio points at Hal. "He is a copy of a copy of a copy, and his life is worthless, like empty air!" He smacks Hal's head. "Look at it! You are cattle, a herded animal headed to a slaughterhouse." Caravaggio has plopped the head of the other Hal onto Hal's lap and is nearly punching him in the chest.

He turns to me and points his finger. "There is no going back! There is nothing to go back to! You and I and Stutz...this is what is real! The Black Lake, the Great Sand Flats, the Clan, the Eels, the Ghūl who has captured Beatrice...these are real! This fat man is make believe, an illusion designed to hide the truth...from you!" He turns to Hal in such a rage I think he will break him in half. "I should kill you. I should put this damn, ignorant cow out of his misery!"

"That is enough!" Stutz stands now, and he walks over to Caravaggio. "Let him go. You've made your point..."

Caravaggio stares at Hal with such ferocity, Hal turns his head in fear, in shame, in humiliation...it is hard to say. Caravaggio breathes deep, exhales and smiles a big broad smile, teeth and all. "Well, hell, Hal. It's your birthday! Don't want to kill you on your birthday. You'll probably do that to yourself later tonight. If you don't, you really need to think about going through with it." He pats Hal on the shoulders with both hands, hard, jarring, and steps away.

Hal pushes from the chair, the head of the other Hal dropping to the floor with a thud. He runs into the house, sobbing, covering his eyes, saying, "Leave me alone. Leave me alone. Leave me alone."

Chapter Thirty-eight

"I don't want to see you."

"You must. You must see me. We must talk."

"I don't want to talk about you...about them."

"I did not know they would do that."

"I don't care what you knew. Please, leave. I don't want to talk about it."

I get up to leave.

"Does Max know? Does he know about you?"

I stop and turn around, standing at his bedroom door.

"No."

"Are Max and I the only ones?"

"No."

We sit in silence for what seems an eternity. We both stare at the handgun on the nightstand. Then, his head is in his hands.

"You can live your life just like normal, like none of this ever happened. I am going away for good."

He laughs. His head still buried in his hands.

"You don't have to do this."

"Says you...whoever *you* are."

Silence again. Eternal, brutal silence.

"Are there others of me?"

"Others. You don't have to do this. I will walk away from here...we will all walk away, and you can..."

"I can do what? Cut scrap? Sit and drink with Max? What? What is left for me?"

"You will forget. It will take time, but you will forget, move on."

"Toward what?"

"I'm sorry. This is not what I wanted."

"What *you* wanted?"

"You are still you."

"So, I live my life...or...take it...and what then? Another me shows up and lives the life I took?"

"Yes."

He laughs again, but it is empty, hollow, void, a crushed package of empty air.

"It's time for you to go."

I see he has a crumpled piece of paper in his hands. "What is that?"

"Nothing to concern you. Instructions."

"You have a choice. There is another life. You still have meaning."

He grabs the gun and places it in his lap. Gun in one hand, paper in the other.

"This is all that has meaning now. You need to go."

He pulls the hammer back.

I walk out of his room, out of the small house, walk through the salvage yard. I am as changed as he is, and what is before me is as terrifying as what is before him. The world I return to is as bleak, dark and hopeless as his.

Part Four

Sector 17

Chapter Thirty-nine

We are all the theater of the absurd, every one of us wearing masks, our separate selves, multi-layered personas brought out to varying audiences during various dramas. Who are we, when no one is watching? Of course, someone is always watching, even if it is only those other selves. The pious pastor and the lustful secret life. The lusty prostitute who goes to college for an English Degree. The famous rock star who reads Jane Austen in solitude, and on and on and on and on. Many selves good, bad, blended in a swirl of gray. Is it good that bad people sometime escape death? Is it bad that good people sometimes die tragically? Is there any such person who is good? As the Pre-Event Bard once said: if everyone got what they deserved, who'd escape whipping! Stand before the great burning sun of moral truth...do any of us not burn to ash? What is moral truth? What is the good, the true, the beautiful? Perhaps they are just moments in time, brief images caught on film. A blossoming tulip, a green and yellow hummingbird eating at a honeysuckle, a smile, a simple "I forgive you." The selfish sacrifice of one's life? Snap, good, beautiful, true. If one were to wait but an hour, a day, a month, the tulip curls into a shrivel of black, the hummingbird eaten by a cat. The forgiveness turns to anger and rage and doubt. The selfless act of giving a life is really selfish, motivated by fear, doubt and envy. Which self and in which moment in time is good or true? Placed against self and motivation...the act, like the tulip blossom, withers.

~ * ~

Stutz, Caravaggio, and I head east from Riverside to the Cuyahoga

197

River and toward Sector 17. Nobody speaks for an hour after leaving Hal. We stop several blocks from the river, and huddle together under a cement bridge, the river flowing dark and rapidly toward the Black Lake miles and miles away. I've been hearing Beatrice's song since we left Hal's, and I know the others hear it too. It is not really words, but images, tunnels under the ground. All of us understand she is singing us toward her. We eat dried goat meat and sip water, trying to save as much of the rations as possible.

"This Ghūl," Caravaggio says. "This *Agent Smiley* as you call it...it will try to separate us when we rescue Beatrice. The key is to get that damn book back from the Ghūl, concentrate on the cave art, get as close to it as possible...with all of us together."

"No," Stutz says, "the key is to get to Beatrice, then defeat the Ghūl, then to the cave art."

"He needs that book. He can't draw his power from the cave art," Caravaggio's voice is escalating now, and I understand I am in the presence of an ongoing argument that once again does not include me. They bicker like two children, each emphasizing a different sequence of events.

"We must rescue Beatrice," I say.

That is our first priority. They are both silent. Caravaggio rubs his beard with both hands in frustration.

"Look, Pal. The Ghūl is not to be trifled with. It is unlike anything you have seen before. That tunnel event...when Beatrice was taken...that was a taste, pal. A drop of evil on the tongue. You don't remember, but those things in our world were terrible, now it is magnified a hundred-fold in this place. You must get that book from him, then to the cave art. *We all* must get to the cave art. Then and only then will we have a chance. You know what I'm talking about, pal. You know deep inside what this thing is...what it can do. It is the devourer of the living...and when it kills you...it feasts on the dead flesh. The tales are long and many concerning this thing, in this world and the other."

I know he is right. I recall the dreams. The absolute darkness, the terror of a thing hovering over my chest and bowels, sniffing, smiling, erotically excited, the jaw opening beyond what it should be capable of doing, and...the massive teeth and black gums exposed as it feeds. "How can we kill such a thing?"

"We don't kill it," Stutz says. "Not in this world." He throws a rock into the water. "This is not our goal. Our goal is Beatrice. We must find her. You are right. We must find her, rescue her, then and only then will we deal with this creature."

"It ain't like walking in the park, pal. You've heard the song. You know where we are headed. Those tunnels will be filled with his...what the hell do you call them. I don't know...slaves?"

"What does that mean?"

"The Ghūl uses his own *song*—if you can call such evil that—to master others," Stutz says. "He can use his will in any living being: animals, The Clan, the NRM guards, anyone or anything. They may be waiting for us."

"'*May*'? They *may* be waiting...They *will* be waiting, pal. You can count on that."

"We shall see," Stutz says. "Let's go. We have at least a day to the subway tunnels, then...who knows from there."

We get up and pull the breathing masks over our faces, the copper rims dull and scratched, the lens the same, and as I look at the others, I think of our first encounter after the dungeons of the Black Gate. It was another life, another me, an eon of experience between now and then.

Cogstin is gray and clouded. The wind blows the grime and dust. We pass through the outer rim of the city without incident. I wonder where the Clan could be, if they are watching, stalking us. Every now and then I jerk my head around to see what is behind. The city seems empty, save for the workers who are stripping scrap. I wonder how many of them are Hal, Max and Mr. Tough, faces hidden behind welding masks, never connecting the man in the mirror. We duck under overpasses, hide behind broken and decaying walls, we scurry across large expanses of open space, always following the river, always hearing Beatrice's song as it shows us the way forward. Night comes to Cogstin. We are close now to the various sectors and the subway tunnel.

That night it is the Ghūl that is on everyone's mind. Stutz tells me of his encounter with the fiend. It was when IMAGO first made contact with the world of men and time and things. Elizabeth made the jump to this universe and brought back Geoffrey when she returned. Stutz was Chief security officer for Elizabeth. The intelligence agency heard whispers about coming attacks, but no one took them seriously. Animal attacks are animal attacks. It was all too late when they realized something was targeting the royal family of IMAGO and anyone remotely related. Every victim had the same characteristics: throats torn out, hearts and internal organs missing. When the last victim's head was posted on a stake outside on the Royal Family's estate, it was a declaration of war.

"No one discussed if it was wise to enter this other world," Stutz says. "No one debated the cost and weight of such interaction. Because it was there, because someone made contact... Because we could cross over...we did. At what cost?"

The others who lived in the secret places, the hidden moments between time and space...the Ghūls and things like them...became more and more aggressive. When we bridged this world with IMAGO, they started crossing over. When you were born, the first hybrid of the two dimensions, *that* is when the real slaughter began. You are the first of your kind. You are not of Earth and not of IMAGO...you are a being from both and neither."

Stutz throws another rock into the river. Caravaggio stands up. "That's a great story, but four hundred years makes it a bit dusty, don't you think? We'll meet the Ghūl soon enough. The tunnels are just beyond that ridge, and we can make them before morning."

We clear away any sign that we had passed this way. We head north toward the subway tunnels as the gray of day turns to the gray of night and into eventual blackness.

Chapter Forty

The subway system of Cogstin, like all transportation systems of the early 21st century, were models of efficiency and punctuality, a way to move enormous crowds of people to and from and through the city. At least that is how the text books described them. Stutz has another view, one much darker. After The Event, what humans survived were driven into the tunnels to escape the radiation and fallout. Groups formed, clashed, claimed tunnels for themselves. At first, these groups were defined by the subway stops: West Side Market, 4th street, Lakeshore, Forest City Park, Edgewater, and since the city itself was ground zero, all the downtown tunnels collapsed or so they thought. As the surviving humans created treaties, subdued other groups, created safe zones, established the rule of law—the Ghūl began to establish itself under the city, nesting, gathering others, feeding on stragglers.

At first there were only whispers of some terror, a superstition or old wives' tales to explain the unexplained, the boogie man, the demon, myths rooted deep from before The Event. Soon it was quite clear, something diabolical—human or other—was gathering forces below the ruined city.

The first hundred years after The Event became known as the War of the Tunnels. Stutz mainly observed, choosing to investigate what the sinister force was, where it came from, rather than taking sides. Soon there was no doubt: what had established territory was actually a Ghūl from IMAGO, and Stutz decided to hunt it down.

He does not speak of that encounter, but suffice it to say, that he was captured, tortured, and whatever the Ghūl did to him, forever changed his involvement in the war. One hundred and fifty years after The Event, the second great war occurred, the deciding factor happening at the Battle of Edgewater. The Ghūl was defeated, and the slaves it controlled slaughtered, and the survivors of the tunnels lived in peace for another fifty years.

The world of men and time and things cannot kill a Ghūl from IMAGO. The being disappeared, lived in the space between time and things, gathered its strength and waited. It could wait...wait longer than humans can wait...wait as their laws broke down, as their lifespans ended, as their civilization under the earth crumbled...it silently returned. As the humans evacuated to the surface, as the NRM established law and order and guidance and protection. As the world moved forward, the Ghūl ruled its kingdom under the ground, and Sector 17, the cave paintings, the ancient portal to IMAGO were...forgotten.

~ * ~

We come to where the East/West line once thrived. The brick and cement buildings above are gone, only piles of rubble identifying that anything existed at all. Stutz finds the manhole and pulls off the cover. Caravaggio lowers each of us, then glides down the rope with little effort. Stutz pulls out the map.

"We have three choke points on our way. Here the tunnels merge into one. Here, we cross beneath the river. Here, are the pits. We can use these," he says, handing me a pair of night vision goggles, but only until we get to our first point."

We put on our goggles, and disappear into the world of eternal night. It is wide, empty, surprisingly damp, and quiet, the sandblast of wind now a howl a whine somewhere far above.

Beatrice's song is strong now, she is guiding us through the collapsed ruins, the sudden turns, or manmade drifts coming from the right or left. The voice is light and strong and beautiful. It is such a contrast to the ruined stone and cement tomb we wander through. Long gone are any signs of human habitation. Two hundred years of abandonment, scavenging, isolation. With every step toward Sector 17, I can feel the presence of the Ghūl grow stronger. At first it is something in the peripheral vision, a simple noise, a sideways moment of panic, a whiff of death that turns the head.

We travel about a mile, and the oppressive tunnels begin to work on me again, like it did when Beatrice was taken. We stop.

"There is no need for the goggles," Stutz says. "The Song is all we can trust. Even this technology cannot penetrate what the Ghūl wishes to place in shadows."

"The tunnel turns north just ahead," Caravaggio says, "and it parallels the North/South Line, then joins it. It will come from there, if it is coming."

Stutz pulls out the map, unfolds it and shines a flashlight upon it, cupping the light in his hand. "We are here. We just passed this line which will join the other two after the bend. There is only one way to the Cave Art from here."

We walk slowly, intentionally, single file and with our blades out. Caravaggio is behind, Stutz in front. The song in our imaginations is that familiar sonar, painting pictures of every object, every fallen stone, the walls, and cracks and ledges, and with each step the atmosphere becomes a heavy weight making us pant for breath. We come to The Merger and lean against the wall.

Stutz points to his right and we follow him. There is no wind, no air, only blackness, and the strange juxtaposition of the beautiful song swirling and creating in my head. I reach out to touch a spot on the wall, then pull back as I realize it is wet, but I cannot tell from what. It is too dark to be water, and I notice how it pools, then smears down the cement wall. Soon we merge again to our left and join another tunnel coming from the west. Stutz stops and pushes us against the wall. We listen, try to penetrate the great darkness, but the song only bids us forward: *Next step, next step, next step. Follow the song. Follow the song. This way.*

A hunting party of Clan emerge from the tunnel, and we see them clearly in our heads. They are hunched forward, arms long, ragged clothes. They snarl at one another and snap at each other, then yelp and howl. One stops, turns, sniffs the air and glares down the tunnel at us. The leader grunts, growls low, and the straggler joins the pack. They lope down the tunnel into the darkness.

"They saw us," I say.

"We keep moving," Stutz says.

"They will be waiting for us," I say.

"Let's go," and Stutz is moving across the vast expanse of tunnel and to the right. Soon all the tunnels merge into one great tunnel, four tracks wide, but there are no tracks, the ties long since burned and the steel ripped up for scrap metal. There is a great humming sound coming from far away, it makes my flesh tremble, shudder. The song increases in my head, calming me down—*Come. Come. Come. Follow my voice. This way. This way.*

We walk carefully, slowly, at times squeezing through fissures in the collapsed rubble, climbing over enormous pieces of cement broken off from the ceiling above, rebar stabbing out like ancient claws. It is hard work, climbing, crawling. Soon we come to a massive open space. I can feel the air, a cold blast; deep, biting cold that chills the marrow.

"We are close to the river pass," Stutz says.

Caravaggio shimmies off his pack and pulls out can after can of spray paint. "Stand very still," he says. He begins that sweeping motion, hands alive with multiple cans, one after the other, as he paints our clothing, our faces, chests, backs, and arms. He quickly does the same to himself, then holds out the can to me. "One sweep right across the bridge of my nose," he says. "Just one. Across the nose, pal."

I take the can—seeing his face in great detail because of the song in my head. I press the nozzle and spray.

"No!" Caravaggio hisses. "Give me that. Now, you've done it." Caravaggio sprays his own face.

"Painters," Stutz says annoyed, "Can't live with'm...can't shoot'm."

We squat down and survey the expanse. Stutz taps me on the chest. "Look sharp. We are not alone."

I understand the low buzz now, and as the song increases in its power in my head, I see the origin of that sound. The great horde before us. What they are is unclear, but they are misshaped bodies, gathering in enormous pools, before slowly dispersing. A pungent smell hovers in the cold air, rancid, a sweet, overripe tang of rotting flesh.

"The minion of the Ghūl," Stutz says. They are no longer alive, and not dead—in stasis, under its control. Clones, some Clan, animals, anything that it chooses to consume. They feed it, they protect it, they kill for it."

"What are we going to do?" I whisper.

Caravaggio stands up. "We walk right through them, pal. Let's go." To my complete horror, I watch the mountain of a man stride right up to the first group of wrecked flesh and push them aside. They part. He keeps walking, and disappears...really truly disappears, the camouflage of paint a perfect blend of shadow. He is absolute night incarnate, a ghost among the dying. Stutz prods me to follow, he close behind.

The journey is a collage of varying nightmares. Just as one group parts, another group blocks our way. They are so many, the putrefying gashes, the missing limbs, broken limbs, half eaten torsos, the mashed skull, missing mandibles, and yet everyone a uniform mark; empty eye sockets, the soft melons brutally torn out, the savagery apparent on every skull. Caravaggio makes his way, then is enclosed by an ocean of the dying. I don't know where to go and stop. I am overwhelmed by the stink and horror. Something brushes my face, and I see it is a man with a half-eaten shoulder, another gaping wound where the throat has been torn away, the head tilted on an angle, exposed vertebrae. I realize I recognize the face. It is Hal, a form of Hal, the bib overalls, the belly now black and purple and bloated with decay. It moves into me, the empty eyes, the ancient smell of earth and dying, of great sorrow and suffering. My legs start to tremble with the humming and buzzing. I realize it is the wheezing and thrumming of the half dead as they breathe, bones cracking, chests heaving, lungs spitting blood and air, bubbling, black foam.

"Step forward, push forward," a familiar voice whispers in my ear. "Listen to the song, hear the voice, the beautiful, the good, concentrate on the voice." Stutz pushes me forward, brushing past minion Hal and the Maxes and the Mr. Toughs and the half eaten and decayed Clan, women, children, past rabid and blackened dogs, broken and dragging limbs. We are only halfway through the enormous space, Stutz guiding me with his hand on my shoulder, pushing me to my left, pulling me toward an open space. I try to focus on the song, but the great darkness is beginning to overwhelm me, and my pace slows.

"You must keep moving," Stutz whispers. "They are gathering from behind. You must move or we are lost."

His voice is far away, even though it is screaming in my ear. I realize the minion, the horde of the dying have suddenly awakened in some way. They are moving now from behind us, the great buzzing and thrumming louder, pushing us forward. My arms are thick and my legs are thick and my head is fogged with a darkness, a blanket of terror I felt when Beatrice was taken. Stutz is screaming into my ear, but the words in the sentences are separating, random, swirling like windblown leaves. I concentrate on the words, pin them down, organize them. They flit and roll about unintelligible. There is something else in my head, something on the border. That is when I remember Beatrice's song, the beautiful background noise, the cadence, the soothing sound that has been there all along. I see the music flowing above us, around us, moving effortlessly through the world of men and time and things, not hindered by the dying or dead, by time or space.

Stutz crouches down, pulling me with him. He shoves the torn and folded page in my hand. It is the notes from Mendel, the bastard, nonsensical imitations of the book. "Read the damn thing," Stutz hisses in my ear. "Do something or we'll all die!"

I glance at the phrases, the fragmented equations. I hear Beatrice's song flowing around us. I concentrate on it, allowing it to envelop me, envelop Stutz, the stranded Caravaggio pressed against the wall. The cave art images sputter and disappear, then reappear, fading in and out of my imagination like specters. That is when I see the pattern in Beatrice's song, the speed of its movement, the grace and peaceful flow of the song river, how it combines with the equations on the paper. I step into it and allow it to carry me.

"What the hell happened?" Caravaggio says, his deep voice hoarse with panic. "What the hell did you do, pal?"

We are beyond the great space, past it now. We still hear the thrumming and buzzing of the minion, but it is far, far behind us.

"I was ready to just...just...start swinging," Caravaggio says. "Now I'm here." He is not talking to me but to Stutz who is once again studying the map.

"Next time," Stutz says, "We stick together."

Caravaggio stands up with a humph and walks a few steps from us.

"No magic is going to get us past the Black Gate and the dungeons."

I think of the last time, Agent Smiley grabbing me and dragging me down the ancient stone stairs, deep underground, the terror of the dungeon cell, the ferocity and savagery of the event. Stutz lights the flashlight and cups it in his hand.

"There is only one way through the tunnel," Caravaggio says. "It is highly guarded. We'll have to use a diversion."

"That's not your worry," Stutz says. "Let's move."

He taps the map, clicks off the light, and we are once again in complete darkness. The song stronger and stronger. The images before us clearer and brighter as we get closer to Sector 17 and Beatrice.

We travel quickly down the abandoned subway tunnel, a narrow passage now, the dampness revealed in the cold misty air, the beading on the stone walls, the sound of dripping, and trickling and steaming water as the great Cuyahoga searches and fingers its way deep into the earth.

Chapter Forty-one

The Black Gate was not created by the Ghūl, it was created by the world of men and time and things, by the NRM hundreds of years after The Event. It was a way to protect Sector 17 and Cogstin from the outside world. What about the dungeons below? Well, that is a different animal altogether. They were not built by the NRM, they were built by the Ghūl and its slaves.

The NRM abandoned the world below, calculating that such malicious evil, such a diabolical place could only help protect Sector 17. Let the mythology of the monster pervade, expand, develop into something truly prohibitive. Did it matter if some were snatched away in the dark of night? Did it matter if the thing below was gathering its horde? Let him feed and gather, thought the NRM. The terror of the guard dog benefits everyone.

The Black Dungeons of the Ghūl are a labyrinth of ancillary tunnels and stone chambers, and the only way through them is a restrictive double iron door that closed off the east and west subway tunnel. And these twin, impenetrable barriers are directly below the Black Gate and the River. The wall that separates the two sides is fifty feet thick of crushed and pulverized stone, enormous slabs of discarded cement and rebar and debris, settled and mortared over hundreds of years so that not even a mouse could pass through. The great metal doors, guarded by minions on both sides, specialized killers taken from the elite military of the NRM. Mr. Toughs dressed in black suits armed with automatic weapons. It is a place for the dead not the living.

~ * ~

Something is wrong, and I can sense it. The song in my head is struggling with the great darkness, an oily and oppressive suffocation, like someone extracting all the air from the room, making us labor for breath. Caravaggio leans over to me and whispers in my ear, "Remember, pal, no matter what happens. A deal's a deal."

Stutz is already many paces ahead of us, the landscape, even with the song in our heads, now dim and filled with impenetrable shadows. I hurry to catch up, and when I arrive, Stutz crouched just behind a fallen boulder, I can see the great metal doors separating us from the other side. They are gaping wide like a mouth, and there is absolutely no one around.

"Wait," Stutz says to Caravaggio.

"Wait for what?"

"There maybe..."

"It's empty."

"I thought you said it was highly guarded," I say.

"It is."

"Let's go," Caravaggio says. "We may not be so lucky next time."

"Luck?" I say.

Caravaggio is already scurrying along the wall, his breath from the cold and mist evident in every pant. I follow after. We make it unnoticed to the fallen wall, crouch, then move quickly to the open doors. Caravaggio peers around the corner, then moves through the opening, each door massive, black, irregular beads of welded metal snaking this way and that. When we pass through, it is sudden, such a darkness, such an overwhelming sense of dread and death and suffering, that the song in my head is nearly extinguished, and I fall to the ground groping like some helpless thing.

"We must keep moving," Stutz hisses.

"This is not right," Caravaggio says. "I can barely think. Something is wrong, some witchcraft at work."

"Keep moving," Stutz repeats. "There is a stairwell past the pits."

I can sense it rather than see, the song's power rapidly fading. I know the tunnel narrows ahead. It is like trying to head face first into a blast furnace. Such pain making the body instantly resist, but it is not heat, no, it is something else, maybe freezing cold, maybe, maybe purely psychological, like a blindfolded patient blistering with the touch of a piece of ice. I imagine standing above us looking down, and I understand that what we feel and what is actually happening is nonsensical. Our heads are screaming with agony and pain, our bodies struggling against the oppressive darkness like one walking against a riptide...but from above...I see only the deep of night, and a band of three blundering buffoons, exaggerating every motion, like children in an elementary play.

I hear the grinding of hinges.

"This way," Stutz screams. "Keep moving."

"They're closing the doors," Caravaggio says. "They're closing them!"

"The stairs. We must get to the stairs!" Stutz shouts.

"We're locked in! It's a trap," I scream. I hear the great doors seal behind us.

We come to a tunnel, the intensity of the darkness, so great, so oppressive, a terrible hand smashing down upon us, we are crawling on all fours. Stutz stands against it, and we follow, hunched over, now stepping forward, then leaning against the stone wall, now moving forward again. The tunnel disappears, and we are back in a vast open space. There is another presence now inside my mind, a willful darkness that delights in showing us our surroundings, delights in snuffing out the song, and though it is still pitch black, our minds see the vast decay, blood and gore of the Death Pits. Something is feeding below.

It is a place unlike any I can imagine. It is a place of torment, a place that captures the moment of absolute terror just as the murder victims understand their fate. It is the feeling that overwhelms the soul, deep and profound as a horrific realization settles. The GI's discovering Auschwitz, the great smoking ovens, the mountains of collected clothing, jewelry and luggage. The photographer witnessing the twisted and strewn bodies on the plains of Gettysburg. The shadows of humans glassed upon the dirt of Cogstin, or the ashen carbon remains a week after The Event. It is the absolute feeling of despair, absent of hope, an extinguished light, the definition of apocalypse.

I crawl with Stutz and Caravaggio. I recognize the sound I hear is of us, our sobbing at the suffering. The absence of everything good, and this empathy allows us to hear the song again, a whisper now, a dimly lit candle in the night of eternal space. We drag ourselves down the stone pathway that bisects the pits of death. We crawl, slide and pull our way to the stone stairway. With each step up, our burden is lighter, the darkness less oppressive, the night of mist, cold and terror, manageable. The song of Beatrice stronger and stronger, beckoning us to *come, follow the song, this way, this way, come.* Soon we are through a doorway, and Stutz closes it behind us. We climb a set of stone stairs before we collapse upon the first landing.

Chapter Forty-two

We huddle like wounded things, leaning against the wall, the sunlight from above dimly lighting some opening far, far, far above us.

"My god," I say, "What was that?"

"It does not matter now," Stutz says. "We must get to Beatrice. We must climb, climb to Beatrice."

I see that he is still in anguish, his eyes wet with emotion, the horror of what we just witnessed.

"Above us," Caravaggio says, "are the dungeons. Above that, the Cave Art. Above that, Sector 17 and Cogstin. Each stratum is connected by a stone staircase."

Stutz pulls himself to his knees, then stands. He begins to lumber up the stairway. Caravaggio hoists me up by my jacket and whispers in my ear. "Remember, no matter what happens up there. A deal's a deal, pal. You promised to get me back. You promised." He shoves me quite hard with an anger I cannot decipher.

We climb, every step like a step toward the summit of a great mountain, the air thin, the environment cold, harsh and forbidding. There are hundreds of stairs. We stop and sit to catch our breath. Something is not right.

"How could we just walk right through them," I say.

"It doesn't matter now. We did," Stutz says.

"I'd rather be lucky than good any day, pal," says Caravaggio. "Why question it?"

"It doesn't make sense. This is the same thing that came to my house, the same thing that my Uncle Hal was working with. It tried to get us then, but it couldn't."

Caravaggio laughs. "If it wanted to get you, it would have."

"One way or the other," Stutz says, it gets what it wants." He is pensive, withdrawn.

"Okay, pal, listen close. This is like nothing you have seen before. Whatever you saw above, well, it's what it wanted you to see. It takes a form, pal. Plain and simple. What we see up there can kill us. No magic tricks. No sudden healing. It's from IMAGO, and what's from there can kill us all. That thing," he motions with his hand..."is hidden, it slips in between space and time, a reflection of sorts." He pulls out several cases from his bag and hands one to me. "You'll see it in the corner of your eye, peripheral vision, a shape, a movement. When you see that, use the mirror I gave you. Hold it up. You'll at least know where it is." He turned to Stutz. "Okay," he says, as if settling an argument between them. "Okay, we'll do it your way—Beatrice then the Ghūl, then we go home. I've always thought your plan was stupid from the beginning, but there it is... What can you expect from a...hell, what are you?"

"Let's go," Stutz says, face stern, a weight upon his brow like he too has decided on something.

We climb the stairs, slowly, plodding with every step, the song of Beatrice dimming, then strengthening, then dimming again, like a radio signal interrupted. We don't need it to see, for the light from above, the gray light of Cogstin has filtered through exposed windows and secret cracks above. We come to another metal door.

Stutz hesitates. "This is it. We must do what we must do." He sighs and turns to me. "Come on, it's time."

Suddenly and with great force, before I know what is happening, he pulls me through the door and into absolute night.

It takes me a moment for my eyes to adjust. I see shades of doors, and realize it is a cellblock, the dungeons of the Black Gate. I feel the great and terrible weight of something cloaked, something akin to what we felt near the pits below. Beatrice's song is snuffed out. Stutz grabs me hard by the arm and pulls me forward into the middle of the stone hall. Caravaggio has closed the door and vanished.

"I did what you asked!" Stutz shouts. "I brought the boy!"

I try to turn towards him. "What? What are you doing?"

"Shut up!" he hisses in my ear. He turns around. "Show yourself!"

Nothing happens.

"Show yourself, damn you!" After a moment he continues, "Show me my daughter!"

My mind is swirling, half from what Stutz is saying, half from the sudden presence of such darkness that I have to catch my breath.

From the corner of my eye, I feel a sense of dread, a disturbance just out of view. Beatrice appears, her face barely visible in the shadows. "You should not have come," she says.

"Let her go," Stutz says.

"It's a trap," Beatrice says. She is held back by some invisible force, and I know it's the Ghūl behind her.

"I know."

I hear a voice, it is soothing, silky, smooth and sharp like a razor blade's edge, the damage done much after the blade has passed. It seems like it is only talking to me, but I know that it is the Ghūl. "Give me the boy," the oily, smooth, voice says, but it is not in words, not physical words, mouthed. It is more like images, feelings appearing and vanishing in seconds.

"My daughter first, then take what you want."

"You know this is wrong," Beatrice suddenly shouts. Her words are harsh compared to the Ghūl's; violent, unwarranted.

"He should not have been released," Stutz says.

"It is not your decision to make."

"You should not have called him," Stutz says.

I feel distant from the scene, someone outside looking at a stage. I hear the arguments back and forth, Stutz's words reasonable, heavy with weight, Beatrice's like nails on a chalk board, angular, empty of power. I find myself agreeing with Stutz. Of course, I should be given back to the Ghūl. That is reasonable. Why would someone release me in the first place? Stupid, stupid, petty and presumptuous girl.

"I don't care what happens. I gave you that damn book. That's what you wanted. Now take the boy and release my daughter."

"Release the boy to me," the Ghūl says in his image voice, cool, articulate, reasonable. "Come to me, Son of Dante."

All I want to do at that point is obey. I shake off Stutz's hand. He grabs me again.

I hear myself talking, some other self, deep inside. "This was the plan all along," I say. "You tricked me, all of you."

"Yes," says the Ghūl in his image voice. "They are liars, tricksters, all of them. Come to me. Walk to me. Walk away from these liars."

"You sang to me," I say to Beatrice. "You sang to me from the beginning to put me back in the generation tanks." The realization is falling upon me like heavy bricks now. "You called me to you, so you could...capture me."

"Yes," says the Ghūl, "She betrayed you. All of them betrayed you. Walk to me." Its voice is so reasonable, empathetic, the only one in the stone hallway that understands how alone I am.

I hear my voice again, "Your song was a lie?"

"No," Beatrice says. "Christopher, listen to me. It was your mother who set you free. She rescued you. She was the one who placed you with your Uncle Hal, the one before! He was killed by...this thing!"

"My mother?"

The words are harsh to my ears, unreasonable. How could such an empathetic creature have anything to do with murder.

"Release my daughter," Stutz says. "I have done what you asked." Now his voice is harsh and grating to my ears.

"Where is the other one?" the Ghūl asks.

I am once again separated from the conversation, a child asked to sit in the corner. "Our bargain was for both."

"He is here," Stutz says.

I feel the doubt, a vague uncertainty from the Ghūl.

"Sculptors," whispers Caravaggio into my ear, "Always plotting something, right, pal."

The Ghūl's spell over me is broken for a moment, my mind clears, and I break free from Stutz. Caravaggio vanishes into the darkness. I hear the hiss of spray cans from the corner of the hallway, then a rumbling from the other side. At the same moment, Beatrice shouts a pulse of song into our heads. The hallway explodes with light, every crevice, every rat, every smooth imperfection of stone wall. The Ghūl is behind her, it's eye sockets empty and hollow. It's mouth huge and filled with teeth. Fingers like long daggers ending in talons, and I think: tooth and claw. Caravaggio is leaping into the air, his great machete cocked back to strike. I push Stutz to the ground, and run at the Ghūl.

"Enough!" booms a thunderclap of image and sound. Something filled with victory, overwhelming and final.

The Ghūl throws out its hands, and Beatrice's song is silenced. Caravaggio and I are cast to the floor as if smacked by a great hand. Stutz alone stands before it. "The boy. Give me the boy."

I can feel the presence now, the power behind the cloak, more visible, but still hidden. It is the same feeling we had at the pits, unfathomable hate, evil unrelenting.

"He deserves to be free, father." Beatrice says, her head pressed to the ground. "You cannot put him back. He was freed for a reason."

"She had no right to free him," Stutz says. "It was not her choice. Some things should not be free." He turns to the Ghūl. "We had a bargain. Will you fulfill it or not?"

"*You* had a bargain," says the word pictures sarcastically. "I had a plan."

In an instant, Stutz, Beatrice and Caravaggio are all swept against the wall. They hang in suspended animation, dangling, heads limp to their chests, silent. I alone stand before the Ghūl.

Chapter Forty-three

I am once again a spectator, outside myself watching, listening, a spell like heavy liquid cast upon my thoughts. The Ghūl, hidden in darkness now, speaks, and its voice is reasonable, pleasurable, empathetic.

"I will not go back to the generation tanks," I say. "You will never take me back there."

"You are already here," says the word pictures, calmly, sensibly.

"Why?" my voice sounds like a whiny child, an annoying cat call.

"Because of who you are," the word pictures say. "You need this. It is for your own good. For the good of humanity."

This settles upon me, a terrible weight, a horror, something so oppressive but known, pushed away, forgotten—*je accuse*!

"What?"

"Oh, poor boy," says the Ghūl in the word pictures, empathetic, comforting. Like a priest or social worker who understands and needs to explain things clearly. "You do not realize." The voice pauses and continues, "The NRM did not create The Event. No, poor child. *You* were The Event. You did this. Cogstin is of your doing, only you. You created the city of ashes."

I am silent before the accusation.

"You were born of both worlds," says the Ghūl in image words, smoothly, calmly, a lawyer stating a case. "IMAGO and this world of men and time and things. Two parents, Geoffrey from Earth... Elizabeth from IMAGO. This should never have been. A bastard of both worlds has no rights to either."

This sounds reasonable to me. Yes, yes indeed. Who would have created such a monster? How could they?

"Don't listen to it," cries Beatrice, and her voice hurts my ears.

"You have a darkness in you," says the social worker Ghūl, the lawyer Ghūl, the empathetic parent Ghūl. "It is a terrible darkness that you have understood all your life. It is of the world of men and time and things. It is corrupt and corrupting, uncontrollable, violent, destructive."

Images of The Event spool through my imagination like a black and white movie. I see towers of glass, steel and cement blast away in a shock wave of unimaginable power, humans turned to ash, their shadows imprinted on the soil, melted into the macadam, human, animal, insect obliterated. "We tried to stop you, but we could not," the lawyer Ghūl says. "So, after the fact, we did the humanitarian thing. We confined you, put you in the Generation Tank."

"Don't listen to it!" Screams Beatrice. "It is a liar!"

"Liar?" says the lawyer Ghūl. "Am I not telling the truth, father of the girl?"

Stutz's says "Yes," like a judge and jury convicting a criminal.

I see it now, this Generation Tank, a clean white room with clean and comfortable chaise lounge while I stare out at the peaceful, endless, blue horizon, food and clothing and peace, sealed off from the world I destroyed. Sealed off from ever creating such destruction again. I understand the wickedness inside me. Have I not felt it all my life? Wasn't my Uncle Hal protecting me from this hate, this anger. I am a bomb. I cannot control the destructive power.

"You must come back to the Generation Tank," says the social worker Ghūl. "It is for your own good."

"Yes," I whisper. "Yes. I must be stopped."

I think of the dark dreams, the inferno of hate, the raging furnace within. Think of the great lions tearing into the Blood Clan, and I think of the flaming compound, the helpless Doctor Mendel, his chard remains. "I must die."

"It lies!" Screams Beatrice. She is sobbing now. "That is not what happened."

Prosecutor Ghūl exclaims, "Lie? Has he not been put in prison, watched? Is this not a world in which he must be guarded, controlled? Is this not a world of theater, a prison planet so he is contained? Is it a fact, father of the girl, the boy caused The Event?"

"Yes," Stutz says.

"Is it a fact he was confined so as to protect the many...the poor, poor helpless souls?"

Stutz is compelled to answer. He hangs his head. "Yes."

"I must die," I say again. "You must kill me."

"Oh ho ho," chuckles the priest Ghūl. "No, we will never do that. You must come to the Generation Tank. It is the best for everyone."

"I have such an evil in me. I know it is there. I have known it all my life. I killed them. I killed my parents."

"Yes," says Mother Ghūl. "Yes, I know, but we will extract it, and when we are finished, we will make a new one of you, one that will grow and be and become...whatever you desire."

I walk to the Ghūl, the kind empathetic father, the priest, the social worker who desires only to help me, to restore me.

"Come, my child," says the word images. "This way. Through this door, and all will be well."

As I walk, I hear Beatrice sobbing. She is suspended in the air, head down as if dead. That is when I hear a subtle song, a whisper, something beautiful, a song of a bird in the morning, the rustle of leaves on an autumn day, the laughter of a child and her mother. Each step the song grows. It is a song of empathy or forgiveness, the song of reconciliation. I know the Ghūl has spoken truth, and I understand the guilt upon my head. The Generation Tank is what I must have. The blood of the world demands it. The one for the many. I think of the hut in Sector 17, the blood on the door posts, the smoldering sacrifice upon the alter, and I understand now...it is I who must be punished, for it is I who have caused such pain and sorrow. The pits below are from me. The dust and ashes of the city are from me. The warped and deformed Hal's, Max's and Mr. Toughs are from me. I am the cause, and I alone must pay the price for such reckless use of power.

The song is stronger now, the Ghūl once again uncertain. I resist the song, step up to the Ghūl, look into the eyeless sockets, the gaping mouth with huge serrated teeth. I step into the cell of stone and iron. To my mind it is clean, white and cushioned, smelling of lavender and vanilla. A place protecting me from the world of men and time and things, and most importantly, them from me.

Beatrice's song will not relent, it is there like background music, like a grain of sand trapped between toes, relentlessly chaffing, a finger of hope sliding between the open spaces of the conscience. It too, is showing me something in her song, something subtle, with weight and cost, and I understand it is true. The song tells a story, before The Event, a woman kneeling over her dead husband, the Ghūl about to strike her down, and a young boy racing toward her, helpless, hopeless, caught in the world of men and time and things, afraid and alone. Such a rage, such an anger, such sorrow and loss that when he screams for the condemned woman it becomes a force unimaginable. The song continues... A prisoner, shackled wrist and ankles to the dungeons below the black gate, shows the door of the cell open. A monster with tooth and claw enters in, shimmers like a shadow, and hovers, then slowly, meticulously, a glutton enjoying a sumptuous dinner, strokes the naked abdomen, kneels with mouth gaping...and feeds until it is satiated, feeds while the chained victim screams in agony, feeds until the stone cell puddles and pools with blood. It is then that I understand the Pit of Death, the fear and loathing, the terror. It is from me. I am in the pit. Four hundred years of me, like Prometheus, forever. The evil eaten away by the lusty Ghūl. What remains, the good, regenerated and cloned for Christopher Dante to live in the world of men and time and things with his Uncle Hal. Salvaging the steel and rubble and glass from the city of ashes.

The iron door of the cell closes: Clank! The bolt thrust through, and even though I understand my mistake, I am helpless behind impenetrable walls of iron and stone.

Chapter Forty-four

I have read there were moments in the world of men and time and things, sometime in the forgotten past, that songs and sculptures and paintings and the magic of words—art before The Event—acts of creation so artfully arranged, they could stop time: Billy Holiday, Mozart, Beethoven, Michelangelo, Rodin, Botero, Monet, Caravaggio, Cervantes, Dostoevsky, Joyce, Whitman, Kundera...a list longer than I can record where something percolated up, emerged from the slick and shiny world without weight or cost...to rebel, revolt, become a witness, penetrate and proclaim the truth.

As I hang in the cell below the Black Gate, I hear the beauty of Beatrice's song. I understand how powerful that act was to call out the very source of one's destruction, the faith involved, the power of forgiveness. I am back to the land of the living, the Ghūl's spell shattered. I am fully conscious of the darkness that takes the shape of light. I see Caravaggio and Stutz and Beatrice hanging in the air, their latent power suppressed by the witchcraft of the Ghūl. I think of the Cave Art, the lions the ancient magic of the storyteller and the hunters gathered around the fire. The more I try, the more they fade. They are shadows of what was permanent.

"Go ahead," says the Ghūl in a sarcastic and thin voice. "Try to escape the power of the Black Gate and the Pit. I have the book. You are useless without the book. Besides, where will you go? Cogstin was built for you, to contain you. This world was built to contain you. What will you do? You are for me...flesh and bone...just for me."

Beatrice's song is stronger now. I realize it is no longer a song, but the equations from the book of caver art, the thaumaturgic power of living and inanimate things trapped in the world of men and time. She is chanting

221

from memory, but her memory is fragmented. The equations scrambled and fading. I use what I can and imagine a hammer to smash the door. One thunderous blow, but the hammer fades. I imagine it again, this time sustained blows: poof! It is gone.

The Ghūl laughs, Beatrice's song fades.

I am helpless, mind disorganized. I imagine the hammer, but then combine it with an elephant's head, an iron and steel thunderclap of power, an unstoppable ramrod, blowing through the iron cell door, flinging it to the stone floor. I hear the equations from the song. It is a power unleashed, a tidal wave of energy and magic shakes the foundation of the Black Gate and fragments the stone floor in front of me.

I step out, a fire, at first smoldering, now radiating stronger and stronger. I am a prisoner unleashed. I am the fire as it hit the accelerant. I am the rage and witness for Cogstin. The ash city, the guilt and sorrow that I caused. I look up and see Beatrice and Stutz and Caravaggio hanging limp in suspended animation.

"Show yourself!" I scream. "Face me!" I take out the small mirror and turn to get a glimpse. A slash appears across my cheek, chin to ear.

"Oh, I will," says the word images, cold, hard. "But first..." The Ghūl appears. He is holding the book of cave art in his hands. "Such a simpleton," he hisses. "So dependent. Behold!" I hear him hiss, a chant, something dark, long forgotten, a thaumaturgic structure from centuries of hiding. The book of cave art erupts into flame, a blue and yellow and red conflagration of light. It burns, and the blackened wings, the velum of ash, drift and crumble. The book is gone.

Another slash appears across my chest, tearing my shirt, blood trickling to my waist. "... Let's play a game..." it hisses in my ear. I turn, but am too slow and cannot see it. There is a flash of movement. I hear Stutz, Beatrice and Caravaggio scream. They are gone and I know the Ghūl has taken them down below. I am alone in the dark. I sense laughter, if such a sound can be interpreted that way.

My mind calms, and all that has transpired, the layers of lies and half-truths, the deceptions, all of it begins to solidify in my head. I know if I do not follow them immediately, they will be destroyed by the Ghūl. I know what Beatrice told me in her song was true, and that I was the one who destroyed the city, destroyed all those living. I was the one to hang in a stone cell and be eaten alive for eternity as a punishment for my great sin. It was my mother who released me, and Beatrice who called me. Stutz was her father, and I was the bargaining chip. Whatever comes after, I know what I must do now. "A deal's a deal," I whisper. My will is solidified into stone.

There is no book. There is no song. I have no access to my thaumaturgy, and I understand the rules of the game now. The Ghūl is testing me, forcing me to choose. There are three captives, and three places: the great hall with the horde, the black gate below the river, and the pit. What I did not know then, what Stutz knew, and Caravaggio was guessing at the time—each place should have been certain death to all that entered, but we passed through unnoticed. The Ghūl allowed it. Now, it was a certain trap. I have no way to help any of them.

I hear the screams from Caravaggio, Beatrice and Stutz. They are screams of torment. I know I am already too late. I feel the anger building in me, that uncontrollable rage toward the Ghūl, toward Stutz' betrayal, toward Beatrice and the testing, and it builds. My mind flashes to the black and white movie reel the Ghūl showed me, the massive destruction, the glassing of an entire city, humans, instant shadows on the ground...and I hear the Ghūl laughing at me, taunting me, my impossible decision. All I can do is melt the world. I am an uncontrolled destroyer. I see clearly now the image of me, hunched over the book, writing the equations, hurrying before the next encounter with the Ghūl, scribbling in the white room with the wall-to-wall glass. This was my way out. This was my singular goal once I escaped, my mechanism to control...me. There is no book. I am a supernatural bomb.

It comes to me sideways, the human shadows on the ground! Yes, yes, of course. I smile. I think, and I am moving instantly downward, through rock, soil, metal and stone, down, down, my electromagnetic wavelength tight, unstoppable, a blast of X-ray, and I am in the great empty space of the abandoned subway. Beatrice is gagged and hanging just out of reach of the horde that is pawing and gnashing their teeth, pulling off her boot, her hands and feet bound. I see in my imagination the rope breaking, and Beatrice falls. I imagine the spear of the hunter on the cave wall and throw it piercing, penetrating, slashing through head and shoulder and neck until it hits the target, pinning Beatrice to the wall, her bound arms above her, the spear propping her up like a picture hanging on the wall just inches above the clawing writhing horde.

It takes only a moment for Beatrice to free her hands on the razor-sharp spear head. She swings with grace, like an acrobat, pulling the tape from her mouth, and the space immediately fills with her song.

I hear it, and allow it to envelope me, her, and we are moving in sound, through space, through the masses of decayed flesh and cracked bone. Swirling in rhythm and meter beyond their reach and out into the subway tunnel before the Black Gate. We crouch down in the shadows, and we can hear the Ghūl laughing, can hear the horde released from behind, running to attack us.

The guards are mounted around the black gate, the doors closed. I understand now, they are not made of iron, but of lead. Lead has been strewn through the stone walls on either side. We are trapped. The men have their ears stopped up, so Beatrice is ineffectual. Caravaggio is pounding and screaming somewhere within the cement and lead walls. Beatrice begins to sing, softly, a chant. *To me to me to me. Come to me to me to me. Under rock, root and tree, come, come, come to me to me to me.*

The horde is a hundred yards behind us and coming fast. I imagine the fire from the cave art campsite, and I fill the tunnel behind us with a blaze twenty feet high as a barrier. Beatrice stares in disbelief at the fire behind us. "The book," she says.

"There never was *just a book*," I say.

Beatrice's look is one of terror, anger and doubt. She turns toward the gate and sings louder, a focused, singular will.

The guards start to shoot at us, our figures distinguished in the bright light behind. Something remarkable happens: the guards, one by one begin to claw at themselves; slapping and pulling, swiping, throwing down their guns and tearing off their vests at the millions of tiny stinging ants that have now covered the walls and doors and stones around them. We run to the huge black doors, Beatrice singing a song, the ants entering the key holes and moving tumblers and releasing levers and the doors swinging free. Caravaggio shoves the iron door of his cell open, his face swollen and gashed from the interrogators. He is a man mountain of anger.

"Time to kill a Ghūl." he says, and his fists are great hammers of violence.

We hear the horde storming toward the gate, many on fire, smoking, burning flesh and bone. The Guards begin to shoot and are overwhelmed as the first wave begins to feast. Caravaggio, Beatrice and I run through the last tunnel. Stutz' voice is clear. He is screaming, in agony. There is something logical and intentional. We feel the horror and weight, the full force of the Ghūl. It nearly knocks us to the ground. We see the pits, and understand Stutz's words. "Leave me. Leave me to die. Get to the Cave Art." He screams again.

The rage has kindled again, and this time it is focused only on the Ghūl, a pointed arrow head of anger. The world around us is night eternal. The pit large and empty space. Beatrice sings loud, a song of light and hope. The Ghūl's spell is too great, and it is immediately snuffed out.

"This is my world, son of Dante," says the Ghūl in word pictures again. "Four hundred years. Do you smell the sweet tang of your flesh and bones?" Suddenly I am seeing Hal and me in Sector 17, me walking to the stone hut, the blood upon the doorpost the smoldering parts of me in various stages of my generation, baby, young adult, middle aged, old and worn— parts of me on the altar. There is the Ghūl, tooth and claw, feeding on my bones. "Yes," it says.

The memories of Hal and me in Sector 17 are not fading from my imagination. I know I am terrified, but I cannot get Hal out of my mind. It is not the Hal from my memory. It is not the Hal with the 9mm on his lap. No, this is someone else, thinner now, determined, grime and dirt on his forehead and under his nails, copper rimmed goggles on his face, a bandana tied around his nose and mouth. He wears a great necklace of shrunken...the image fades, and I am back to the terror of the Pit. Stutz is screaming for us to go, leave him, save ourselves.

"I cannot find him" Beatrice yells.

"We must stick together," I say.

"Yes," says the oily voice of the Ghūl. "Yes, stick together."

There is a sudden movement in my peripheral vision, and once again it slices my chest and arm.

"Two can play at that game," Caravaggio says.

I hear the bag open and the cans of paint rattling in his hands. I see the movement in my peripheral vision, and hear the spray paint, as the Ghūl makes another pass, slashing Beatrice on the face and neck.

"You cannot hide yourself from it," I say to Caravaggio.

"That may be, but now it cannot hide either. Not with barium paint on it."

I understand, and imagine an electromagnetic pulse, the equation in my head, a frequency of 7.77×10^{14} s-1, and I send out a sudden explosive wavelength that fills the huge space. There it is. This time we need no mirror to track it, for it shimmers and glows as the particles in the barium are magnetized and activated. The Ghūl spins and moves, dashing toward the stairwell.

Beatrice sings loud, and the room fills with a beautiful song of hope and peace. Like fingers, it searches the great open pit through decayed flesh and aged bone. It seeks out Stutz, and I imagine us all into the song, wrapping it around us, all three, and we are back into the hallway dungeon of the Black Gate. Stutz is deeply wounded, enormous chunks bitten out of his leg and shoulder. His neck is bleeding. Caravaggio holds him up.

"Go. You must leave me," Stutz says. "It is all too late."

"Too late?" Beatrice says. "Too late for what?"

"I'll carry you." Caravaggio cradles Stutz in his massive arms. "We will make it home together." He shakes his head. "Sculptors, always giving up too early."

We climb the stone stairs and see the traces of barium, a claw print here, a footprint there. We stumble and climb, breathless, exhausted, the oppressive witchcraft of the Ghūl like a suffocating blanket. We stand in the great cave, the stalagmites hanging down like teeth, the dry air and sand from hundreds of thousands of years ago, and there with its arms out is the Ghūl.

Chapter Forty-five

The thaumaturgic power of the Ghūl is matched by the geothaumaturgic power coming from the ancient paintings on the cave wall. It is flowing around us, through us. The Singer, the Painter, the Sculptor, and now the Fabulist, together, and this triggers something beyond our dimension.

"It's working!" yells Caravaggio. "You did it!"

The Ghūl is quick, a blur. Caravaggio is determined, and he smashes it with his fists. It vanishes, returns, and tears at Beatrice as she is singing, her throat is torn open, a great mouth of red flesh and blood below her chin, and she falls to the ground. The cave art moves and shifts, the portal expanding then contracting.

"No!" screams Caravaggio. "No!" He races toward the stone that is now swirling like a pool of liquid rock. "Why is it closing? It's closing! It's closing!"

I hear an explosion above, sand filters down from the stone ceiling. Then another and another, some distant, some just above.

"What is happening?" Caravaggio says.

The Ghūl shimmers, and moves to strike down Caravaggio, but I pin it to the wall with a great spear from the Cave Art. It writhes and hisses as if on fire. Caravaggio jumps at the portal and in a flash...vanishes. Again, an explosion. Again, the walls shimmer, more sand, gravel and larger pieces of the ceiling above begin to fall. The Ghūl pulls the spear from its body and laughs.

"Fool! All from IMAGO must be present."

"It must not open," Beatrice says, desperately gasping for air, her hand useless against the flow of blood and life running through her fingers.

IMAGO

"It knew all along!" I yell. "We could never open the portal. It knew this."

Beatrice cries. "Elizabeth is alive!"

I turn to the Ghūl and raise my hand to the lions on the wall.

"How soon you forget," it says in its word pictures. "What happened the last time you released your little flowered pet."

"This time, I can promise you tooth and claw."

There they are, two enormous beasts with enormous teeth and taloned paws. They are hunched and ready, then launching toward the Ghūl. The explosions above again, like timed detonations bringing down a building, the cave wall rumbles, more pieces, large now, fall to the ground. I race over to Beatrice, tearing off my shirt sleeve and pressing it on her neck to stop the bleeding. Stutz is delirious, whispering over and over, "It's too late. It's all too late."

"What did you do?" I yell at him and shake his nearly extinguished body. "Tell me. What did you do?"

Stutz is smiling, blood coming from his ears and mouth, the great wound in his neck and shoulder and thigh. He reaches out suddenly and grabs my arm, pulling me to him with great force. "You cannot go back. You cannot stay. You know this."

I pull away just as an explosion rocks the earth above us, and the ceiling collapses. The great stones kill the lions, that writhe, yelp and go silent. The Ghūl takes on the shape of Agent Smiley, as the gray sun of day casts itself upon the world of night. The ground trembles below, and I realize the Black Gate has crumbled and the Cuyahoga River is filling up the dungeons, drowning, washing away the centuries of horror created below.

"It is over," mouths Agent Smiley in his strange and wheezing voice, the syllables all wrong, the cadence off. He is holding Beatrice by the neck, the blood from her wounds soaking her shirt and pants. "Your friends are dead, and you cannot kill me. Not in this world." He stands tall, pale, his head and body completely without hair, seven-foot-tall, enormous mouth, pointed ears. "You know you cannot leave here. This is a prison. This world is your prison. It was designed and created to contain you. You are my sweet gift, and I your personal guard. You know you have only one choice." The voice is squeaky and grating to the ears, hissing at times, lisping or silent at others. "I will take you to the cell. I will place you in comfort in your mind, and you will no longer harm anyone. There is nothing else you can do." Agent Smiley's grin explodes with the enormous teeth.

I see Beatrice dying in his hand. I know what he says is true. I know that what I have done, the great suffering I have caused, I must pay for with my life, and I remember the words of the ancient poem, the poem I penned to myself when I was first imprisoned in the cells below the Black Gate.

Sing to me, oh muse
Of the Man full of sorrows
Who wanders the plains of ashes...

"Yes," hisses and whines Agent Smiley. "Yes, you are that man. Yes. There is nothing else you can do. Your life for hers."

I stare at the ruined cave paintings, the wrecked lions and fissured storyteller, the great lineage of the Fabulist...now all but disappeared. It is then I finally understand what is asked of me, the sacrifice I must choose, and I understand for the very first time all of the tales that were told, of Stutz and Caravaggio and Beatrice, and how I fit into this, and what I was created from my mother to do. "Yes, yes," I say.

"You cannot kill me," he wheezes and hisses. "You know you cannot kill me."

I walk into the black cell, the gate closing behind me, Agent Smiley glowering and slobbering for the feast to come. I enter the white room and the white chaise lounge and the great blue water behind the wall-to-wall glass, and I think of Beatrice and I think of Caravaggio and Stutz and Hal and Max and all the Hals and Maxs—"My life for theirs," I whisper. "It is finished."

I see the Ghūl as he enters the cell, his mouth wide, eyes gluttonous. He drifts over to my now shackled and stretched body. "Yes," he says in his priest Ghūl voice, "she will live because of you." As he feeds, I think of Beatrice, remember her song, the power of her words, and I know that they are magic with a deep power from beyond IMAGO. I think of the ancient storyteller around the fire, telling the story of the hunt to the wearied and fearful hunters. I understand now the true power of this story, and I understand the roots that go deep into the beginning of all things. The Ghūl is a symbol, a tiny letter in the great story. I concentrate with all of my mind on that very fact. I stare at the ruined cave paintings, the wrecked lions and fissured storyteller, the great lineage of the Fabulist...now all but disappeared.

"No." I whisper. "It does not have to be this way." I raise my hand to Agent Smiley, his face full of my gore, and I see his smile fade, eyes widen.

"What are you doing?" he wheezes and hisses. "It is finished. You said this. You said. You cannot kill me."

"I don't have to," I say and think of a simple thaumaturgic equation. So, so, simple. Foundational. With a nod of my head, Agent Smiley is gone, poof. The white room and the white chaise lounge and the wall-to-wall glass with the deep blue horizon vanishes. I see dust and rubble and destruction from the collapse of the cave. I look to the cave painting and see by the cracked lions and the headless Gazelles and the all but obliterated campsite...a small black smear, a symbol, really, an ancient rune from an ancient time symbolizing something that lives in the darkness, something that hunts the straggler, the helpless, the one lost in the woods. The Ghūl is a symbol now on the wall, a letter in my alphabet, newly formed.

Beatrice stirs, and I am back to the world of men and time and things, my world, the world that I destroyed. The chains that bind me are from this world, and they have no power over me. I hurry to Beatrice and bind up the wound on her throat and I carry her out of the rubble and the chaos of the caves, up though the ruined shack and crushed altar of burning bones and flesh and into the gray light of Cogstin, the wind and dust and sand pecking at our faces as we make our way to shelter.

Chapter Forty-six

A year has come and gone since the banishing of the Ghūl, and Beatrice and I have wandered through Cogstin and the surrounding land, searching. A skinned and gutted dog burns on a makeshift spit. A man is hunched over the fire, poking it, blowing on the embers.

"There is plenty. Help yourself," he says.

We sit down near the flames, the warmth radiating over our chilled bodies. Beatrice huddles close to it.

"So, you are here," I say.

"I am here."

We are silent for a time. The man carves pieces of meat with an enormous blade of his own fashioning. He stabs it, then points the blade at Beatrice who takes it greedily in her hands, blows on it and chews.

"You made a choice," I say, and I see that the great necklace he wears is ringed with small shriveled heads. It makes sense now. "You blew up the gate." This is the image I had seen in my mind so many months ago.

"It's not real. This is real, Stretch. You all proved that to me." He chews the meat, and sips from a vodka bottle, then passes it to me. I see his once fleshy features are withered, leathered and worn from his new Spartan life.

"How did you know?"

Hal pulls out a note, creased and stained with blood and dirt and gun powder:

If you are reading this, you have made a choice. He cannot make it to IMAGO. He cannot make it out of here alive. Blow up the Black Gate. Flood the tunnels and the caves. Blow up Sector 17. Save your world.

I fold up the paper and hand it back to Hal. He cuts another piece of meat from the dog and passes it to me.

"There are two of us," Beatrice whispers, her throat still healing. "You can't win."

Hal laughs. "That's what these jokers thought." He takes a large swig from his vodka bottle and passes it to Beatrice. "I took that gun and put it in my mouth and wanted to pull the trigger. You see I knew I was one of many. I'm no snowflake! Hell, I'm more like a lemming. But every lemming can make a choice. It just takes one. We make choices, Stretch. We wake up every morning and make a choice: hope or despair. I'm not sure which I have chosen just yet, but I'm willing to give it a little more time." He stabs the ground with his great blade and shifts around the sand. Then he throws another piece of wood on the fire. "You really do all of this?"

I don't answer, and I can feel the tension mounting, Hal deciding something heavy. I am tired, and lonely, and filled with a deep sadness. "Yes," I say. "I guess I did."

"That's a hell of a burden, Stretch. With no way out." He drinks from the bottle again, hands it to me, but I decline. "Like the mark of Cain, or something," he says and drinks again.

"A man of sorrows," I whisper.

"Someone's still running the show, Stretch. There's no such thing as the NRM. As much as I can figure, it's a local thing. Maybe it actually meant something, or like all of this, maybe it never did. Somebody, somewhere is pulling the strings. It can't all be theater." Hal stabs the ground again with his great knife and then rubs his face in frustration, like he's debating with himself, trying to come to a difficult decision. He fingers one of the heads. "The first time I saw another me, well you were there.... That was tough. It gets easier, though. Didn't think it would. You know I found a whole group of me and Max and other freaks." He fingers the heads again, one after the other, like a rosary. "This one here was the first, the one in the box. It has special meaning. This one...well, he called himself a governor. Imagine that. A freak for a governor. Now it's a kingdom without freaks and a freak king without a head." He swigs from the bottle again.

Beatrice is sitting bolt upright. I place my hand upon her arm to calm her. Hal grabs his giant blade again and stands up. "I've got to piss,

Stretch." He starts to leave, then turns suddenly around pointing the great knife at me. "The next time we meet, we'll have to have words, Stretch. You understand that. I just can't leave it like this. Not this time. We all make choices. God knows I've tried to make good ones. But the world has changed, Stretch. It turned out differently than people thought." He tosses a piece of metal at my feet. "Found this when I blew everything to hell." He swigs from the vodka bottle again and walks into the night, the shriveled heads of cloned Hal's rattling against each other.

I hold the piece of metal up to the light. Imprinted on it is a single word followed by an image of a butterfly, like the one Caravaggio had painted on the walls throughout the city of Cogstin. The plate reads:

CONSTANTINOPLE

It has a butterfly with long magenta tails off each wing.

I cover up the last half then take my hand away, and do it again.

CONSTANTINOPLE

CONSTAN

COGSTIN

"It was to be the city of hope," Beatrice says.

"And now it is the city of ashes," I say and toss the metal plate of faith and hope and dreams of the future onto the fire. "We'll travel into the Great Sand Flats tomorrow."

"What about Hal?" Beatrice says. "He'll come back."

"We'll see him again, I'm sure, and there will be hell to pay, but not tonight."

We are silent for a long time, the fire burning down, the sun a brighter gray coming up in the east.

"They say this is a prison," Beatrice says. "This is a prison planet. The whole thing."

"We need to find her," I say. "My mother. We need to find her."

"How will you find her?" she asks.

"You heard Hal. Someone or something is pulling the strings. It's time we find out who."

We are quiet for a while.

"The Ghūl was right, you know," Beatrice says. "What if this happens again? What if it's destiny? Like Oedipus. Nothing has really changed. You are who you are."

We watch the dawn break, the great clouds of ash and gray swirling and sweeping the ghost city. We pull on our breathing masks, the copper rims, the scratched lenses that Hal has left for us along with several days' rations. We strike out north to the Great Sand Flats and the unknown world beyond. I see a huge sprawling sign painted across a ruined building: *Awake oh Sleeper.* This is followed by an enormous and beautifully painted butterfly, and I think of Caravaggio and Stutz and their great struggle now over. I think of Beatrice and our uncertain future. Then I think of the poem that I wrote so many centuries ago when I was trapped in the white room with the white chaise lounge and the blue water beyond. And I understand it now. I understand the power in the last line, and what I am tasked to do...no matter what is to come. And this time I savor the last lines because I now understand the context, tucking it away, believing the words and the hope, however fleeting and tenuous:

Sing to me, oh Muse
Of the man full of sorrows
Who wanders the Plains of Ashes....
...To set the Prisoners Free

About the Author

Greg Belliveau's most recent book is the Science Fiction novel *IMAGO*. He is the author of the novel *Go Down To Silence* (Multnomah Publishing) which was a Christy Award Finalist for Best First Novel; and a collection of creative nonfiction entitled *Seeds: Mediations on Grace in a World with Teeth* (Crosslink Publishing, 2017). His short stories have been published in *Fathom Magazine, The Atticus Review*, *The Cleveland Review*, and *Vine Leaves*, where his vignette "LG Don't Want To Fly" was selected for their *2012 Best Of Anthology*, published by eMergent Publishing. He is a Christopher Isherwood grant recipient and teaches Creative Writing at Antioch University, Midwest, and has taught at The Antioch Writer's Workshop, Yellow Springs, OH. He teaches writing at Capital University and lives in Ohio with his wife and two daughters.

CPSIA information can be obtained
at www.ICGtesting.com
Printed in the USA
LVHW011730160921
697981LV00010B/1409

9 781624 204609